# IF I CAN'T HAVE YOU

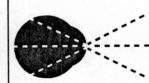

# IF I CAN'T HAVE YOU

## MARY B. MORRISON

**THORNDIKE PRESS**
*A part of Gale, Cengage Learning*

GALE
CENGAGE Learning

Detroit • New York • San Francisco • New Haven, Conn • Waterville, Maine • London

## GALE
### CENGAGE Learning®

**LIBRARY OF CONGRESS CATALOGING-IN-PUBLICATION DATA**

Morrison, Mary B.
  If I can't have you / by Mary B. Morrison. — Large print ed.
    p. cm. — (Thorndike Press large print African-American)
  ISBN-13: 978-1-4104-5274-0 (hardcover)
  ISBN-10: 1-4104-5274-3 (hardcover)
   1. African American women—Fiction. 2. African American
businesspeople—Fiction. 3. Large type books. I. Title. II. Title: If I cannot
have you.
  PS3563.O87477I3 2012
  813'.54—dc23                                    2012030646

Published in 2012 by arrangement with Dafina Books, an imprint of Kensington Publishing Corp.

Printed in Mexico
1 2 3 4 5 6 7 16 15 14 13 12

*Breast Cancer Survivors*
*Margie Rickerson, my sister*
*Myrenia Harris, my friend*

*Breast Cancer Warriors*
*Marion Bean, my sister's best friend*
*Lucille Baloney, my grandmother, and*
*Mary Ann Henry-Barnes, my aunt*

Your greatest fear shall come upon you.

# ACKNOWLEDGMENTS

Life is an awesome journey through the unknown, a priceless adventure of countless experiences. We are the pilots of our passion. We never control the outcome of our choices, but with each step we navigate the road ahead. What you do with your life is up to you and nobody else. It's impossible to be everything to everybody. Please don't die before you decide to live to the fullest. Release your sexual inhibitions. Dance naked in the rain. Love and make love to yourself; you'll be happier.

Remember, no man acquires success independent of another. For my achievements I'm thankful to the Creator, my publishers, editors, family, friends, and to each of you. I acknowledge and appreciate your emotional and financial support. You are a blessing to me and I pray somehow, even in a small way, that I, too, have or will positively influence you.

Darrin Gipson (Grand Lux Cafe) of Houston, Texas; Jay Fountain, Battalion Chief, Port Arthur Fire Station No. 1; Officer Mark Temple, Clemetric Thomas-Frazier, Ron Lockett, LaToya Fontenot, Mrs. Kathleen Fontenot, Rick Smith, and the Honorable Vanessa Gilmore, I thank you for welcoming me to your wonderful cities of Houston and Port Arthur. The information each of you provided is priceless.

The main reason I smile is because of my son, Jesse Bernard Byrd Jr. Honey, you're the best. I'm proud to be your mom and I love you unconditionally. Another reason is my guardian angels — my mother, Elester Noel; my father, Joseph Henry Morrison; my great aunt, Ella Beatrice Turner; and my great uncle, Willie Frinkle — always lift me up when I need them. Wayne, Andrea, Derrick, and Regina Morrison, Margie Rickerson, and Debra Noel are my siblings. Thanks, guys, for always believing in me. A special thanks to Richard C. Montgomery and Barbara Cooper for your continued support and unconditional love.

I genuinely appreciate all my Facebook friends and fans, my Twitter followers, MySpace crew, and my McDonogh 35 Senior High alumni. Happy thirtieth reunion to my class of 1982!

10

Thanks to my editor and friend, Selena James, at Kensington Publishing Corporation. To Steven Zacharius, Adam Zacharius, Laurie Parkin, Karen Auerbach, Adeola Saul, Lesleigh Irish-Underwood, and everyone else at Kensington for growing my literary career.

In loving memory of Walter Zacharius. I miss you. It is my honor to be a part of your undying legacy to the world of literature. Your spirit will dwell within me forever.

Well, what's an author without brilliant agents? I'm fortunate to have two of the best agents in the literary business, Andrew Stuart and Claudia Menza. You are appreciated.

I thank everyone that is making the *Soulmates Dissipate* seven-film project possible — director/producer Leslie Small; Jeff Clanagan, CEO of Codeblack Entertainment; and producers, Dawn Mallory and Jesse Byrd Jr.

Wishing each of you peace and prosperity in abundance. Visit me online at www.MaryMorrison.com and sign up for my HoneyBuzz newsletter. Join my fan page on Facebook at Mary HoneyB Morrison, and follow me on Twitter @marybmorrison.

11

# PROLOGUE:
## GRANVILLE

"I came to tell you something," she said softly.

Loretta sat across the table from me at our favorite restaurant, Grand Lux Cafe, on Westheimer Road. Her naturally chocolate lips were perfectly painted with that sweet raspberry gloss I'd tasted twenty-three times. I wanted to lean over the table, suck it all off, up my count to twenty-four.

"You look ravishing," I growled, then snapped my teeth. I complimented her all the time because I never wanted my Loretta to think I'd ever take her for granted.

Finishing my third beer, I'd been anxiously waiting for her for almost an hour. I had arrived thirty minutes early. She was equally as late. She'd texted me earlier that she had to wait for her mom to get to her house so her mother could watch her little girl. She wanted to postpone our date until tomorrow, after her daughter's father picked up their child for the weekend, but I insisted on seeing her today. I couldn't wait another twenty-four hours to gaze into her large brown eyes. Plus, I wasn't good at keeping surprises a secret.

"I ordered you your favorite martini, but it's warm now. I'll get you another one. . . . Excuse me, Darrin, a fresh lemon drop for my baby, please," I said, handing him the glass. I'd been there long enough to know a few things about the waiter, like he was twenty-three, had a deep voice, which made me slightly envious, and we were both Houston Texans' fans.

Darrin nodded at Loretta. "Glad you made it. I'll be right back with that —"

She shook her head. "No, but thanks. I'm not drinking today."

"Then I'll get you some water," Darrin said, then asked me, "Sir, another beer?"

I nodded. I was feeling good and wanted to keep my buzz going.

Loretta's big brown eyes connected with mine. When her thick lips parted, my dick got hard, making me reminisce about the first and last time she'd given me fellatio. Loretta had said, "I'm never sucking your dick again," because I came too fast. Hopefully, she'd change her mind; but if not, that was okay with me as long as she kissed me

14

somewhere.

Today was special. I'd requested a booth for us. Sliding close to the window, I said, "Come sit next to me."

She shook her head. "I'm good."

The space between the high red velvet cushion behind my back and the edge of the table grazing my stomach was a little snug for my wide midsection, but the smooth vinyl seating comforted my rock-hard rear end. My muscular body was still fit from when I wrestled in high school, and I earned my money doing construction work for the past twenty-five.

As I stared outside, there wasn't much of a view, except rows of cars and the stores' signage for Sport Clips, Nothing Bundt Cakes, and Stride Rite on the other side of the parking lot.

I looked at my girl and moved back to the middle of the booth so I could sit directly across from her. Her wide pink tongue peeped at me, commanding my attention. The scent of fresh bubble gum traveled from her mouth to my nose when she sighed. Loretta's mouth was always inviting. I winked at her, then smiled.

"You know what you just did to me, right? You gave me another woody," I whispered.

"You gave me a woody." Then I started grinning.

Sighing heavily, she said, "Your dick is always hard."

I lifted my brows twice, narrowed my eyes, and kept smiling at her. She made me feel sexy; she had done things to me no other woman had. She'd once tied me to my bed — naked, except for my cowboy boots — then rode me like she was a cowgirl and I was her bucking bull. My bald head banged against the headboard as I screamed, "Loretta!"

My woman exhaled and rolled her eyes to the corners; then she returned her gaze to me. Her stare was dreamy. Or maybe it was my reflection that I saw. It didn't matter. Either way, I was in love.

If she said she was pregnant, she'd make me the happiest man in the world. I swear, I'd jump on the table, wave my big Texas hat, and shout to everyone in hearing range, "We're pregnant!"

Yelling too loud would hurt my throat. But the announcement of my very first kid would be worth the joy and pain. Twenty years ago, when I was twenty-five, I was shot in the shoulder and the bullet grazed my vocal cord. The damage was permanent; my voice was still deep, but since that day it's

16

been scratchy. When I first met Loretta, she thought I was hoarse. The louder I tried to speak, the more it hurt, but I loved to talk. I was brilliant and enjoyed sharing my wisdom with anyone who'd listen. Some women actually thought my voice was sexy. But not Loretta. When I talked too much, I annoyed her.

My baby rubbed the side of her nose. "I don't want to go out with you anymore. You're nice and all, but I can't do this again. I met you here to let you know that this is our last date."

*Not another "let's just kiss and say good-bye" bitch.*

Usually, I'd want to ram my tongue down her throat and give her one of my juicy kisses, letting the saliva drain from my mouth to hers. Now all I wanted to shove in her mouth was my huge fist. Rip away that yellow blouse with the dangling collar, bite her breasts. Raise up her short skirt, spread her legs with my thigh, give her this woody throbbing against my zipper. Making her cum would make her stay with me.

The restaurant was packed on this blazing hot afternoon. Lucky for her, we were not alone. That, and I didn't hit ladies for no reason — even when I felt they deserved a slap or two.

An affectionate pat on the back from me had sent a few grown men stumbling. "Watch it," Loretta would scold when I touched her face. Then she'd ask, "When was the last time you washed your hands?"

Most of the time I had no idea. I was a manly man, operated heavy machinery, and used my hands to haul bricks and dig ditches. There was no way I was going to run to a restroom every time I felt like touching her.

It was my turn to exhale. "I don't understand. I thought things between us were getting better."

"For you," she said.

Frowning, I said, "For me? I've done everything you've asked me to do. I even went to that sex therapist you recommended, Numbiya Aziz. I can't lie. She taught me some things. Especially how to take my time when making love to you. Now that I know how to make you cum really hard, you can't deny the sex between us is the best you've ever had. Right?"

"For you," she said again.

*Bitch, if you say that shit one more time!*

I wiggled my brows, pressed my lips together, then smiled. The heel of my custom-made boot lifted, then thumped to the floor. Again and again. Suddenly my jeans felt too tight. I shook my left leg sideways, rubbed my thigh.

Darrin placed Loretta's water and my beer on the table.

"What about the lingerie I just bought you? You trying to use me? You gon' put my shit on for some other nigga?"

Darrin quietly walked away.

Loretta opened her oversized blue Coach purse, handed me a red plastic Frederick's bag. "I thought you'd bring that up. I never wore them. Everything is there, including the receipt."

She placed the bag on the table. I left it there. I didn't want no fucking refund. I wanted her!

"Tell me what your problem is. Give me a chance to fix it," I pleaded. This woman was close to making me act irate, like a guest on an old episode of *The Jerry Springer Show*. What was I supposed to do with the $15,000 ring in my damn pocket? She was the one who'd told me that a man had to spend at least two months of his salary on an engagement ring. That was her way of asking me to marry her.

Her eyes turned red as she said, "I'm not the problem. You are. I'm tired of telling you that you talk too much. Your voice is irritating. You don't listen to what I have to

19

say. Your shoving your tongue down my throat, draining your bodily fluids into my mouth, is horrible, but you think each kiss is 'the best kiss ever.' You think we're in a relationship, when I keep telling you . . . we're not!"

"We are in a relationship!"

"I'm not your woman."

Staring her down, I had to break her. Make her see things my way. I told her, "You are my woman. We talk on the phone every day. We go out every other day. And we've had great sex. Any decent woman would expect me to be her man. What's wrong with you?"

"You. I've only known you for three weeks and my stress level has gone from calm to calamity." Loretta slid to the edge of the booth. "As nice as you appear to be, you are not the man for me. You're not the guy for any woman, Granville. You need help. Medication. Something. I barely know you. You're too possessive. I could go on and on, but . . . ," she said, standing in front of me. "Take care of yourself."

*Bitch, you're the one who gave it up and sucked my dick on the first date.*

There was someone for everyone, and Loretta was mine. I couldn't let the love of my life walk away from me. I grabbed her wrist.

"But we haven't eaten. Look, I'm sorry. I apologize. I love you, Loretta. If you think I need meds, I'll make us an appointment to see my doctor. Sit down. Let's have lunch. You talk. I'll listen. You're right."

"And you're desperate. Let go of me." She jerked her arm.

I wanted to release her, but I couldn't let go. What if she was serious? What if I never saw her again? My fingers tightened. Worse, what if she was trying to leave me for another man? I felt sweat beading on my head, then streaming down my forehead. I wiped my nose.

Darrin rushed over to our table. "You okay?" he asked Loretta.

Loretta picked up her glass of water and tossed it in my face. Darrin took off. This was one of those few moments when Loretta made me want to hit her. The first time had to be an open-hand slap. Second time, backhand. Third, fist to the face if the bitch disrespected me. But abusing her in public would land me behind bars.

Maybe I was overreacting. She was probably trying to cool me off. Maybe. I rattled my head to shake off the excess water. She jerked her arm again.

Why was Loretta treating me this way? All I tried to do was take good care of her. Treat her with respect. Buy her nice things. The first time I bought her daughter a gift, she gave it back saying, "The only men who are allowed to give my princess gifts are her dad and her grandfathers. That's it."

I respected that, because I had to, but what woman wouldn't let her man take care of her child? We were a family. I was willing to help her work out her issues if she'd give me the chance.

I dug deep into my pocket. I pulled out two 20-dollar bills and placed them on the table. Then I reached into my other pocket, pulled out the ring, held the box in my palm, flipped it open with my thumb, and knelt on one knee. Still holding on, I stared up at her.

"Marry me, Loretta." The shine from the bling made me smile.

"For real? You expect that will make me say 'yes.' " I squeezed her wrist as tight as I could, until she screamed, "Ow! Let me go!"

The people staring at me were supposed to be cheering for me, for us. I dumped the ring in my palm, snapped the box closed, jammed the box in my pocket, staggered to my feet. The baby I wanted us to have wasn't growing inside her? The woman I loved had to have a reason to love me too. Anger festered inside me as she broke my heart and my grip, then slapped my face.

"Yeah!" I grunted. "You know you love me."

Loretta marched out of the restaurant.

I snatched my hat off the window's ledge and put it on as I chased her past Carter's, down to Marshalls, and to her car. "Wait, give me one more chance."

"Ugh!" Loretta stopped, waved her hands in front of my face. "What is wrong with you?"

"What's wrong with you, skank-ass bitch? You'd better get your hands out my face. Hit me again and you gon' need medical attention. I told you I'd put you on my health insurance. You'd rather be a hometown ho, spreading your pussy around Houston like pollen, than to let me take care of you?"

Calmly she said, "Yes."

"You trifling bitch! You're not going nowhere," I said, blocking her driver's-side door.

"You need to get your fucked-up, crooked yellow teeth, nasty-ass crusty feet, 'slobbering like a dog in heat' self away from me and my brand-new BMW."

*Fuck her 700 Series. I should kick a dent in it. Now, all of a sudden, she's trying to say I'm ugly. She wasn't complaining when I was giving her this big, hard dick. My shit was long,* wide, circumcised, and worth worshiping every day.

My mother's voice echoed in my ears, *"You can catch more bees with honey, honey."*

I calmed down. This wasn't about me. It was about Loretta. I told my lady, "You're right. I apologize. Please forgive me. This won't happen again. Marry me." I fought to put my ring on her finger. She yanked her hand away.

"Officer!" Loretta shouted. "Help me!"

I hadn't noticed the cop getting out of his car until now. Wondered if that Darrin dude called PD on me. Regardless, I wasn't looking for trouble. I stepped aside, hoping Loretta would get into her car and go home. That way we could continue our conversation in private.

"Is there a problem, sir?" the officer asked me. His hand was on his gun.

"No problem. Just a little lovers' quarrel with my girlfriend."

Spectators were gathering alongside the walkway in front of Marshalls. Loretta cried like she was auditioning for the role of Tina Turner in *What's Love Got to Do with It*. Made me want to take off my boot and beat her ass like I was Ike.

"I'm not his damn girlfriend. He's harass-

24

ing me. I'm trying to leave, but he won't let me."

"Sir, let me see your identification."

"What did I do?" I asked. My eyes narrowed toward Loretta. "She'll calm down shortly. Women always exaggerate. Soon as you leave, she'll be begging me to come over to her house and you know what, man." I hoisted my big Texas belt buckle.

After all this shit was over, I needed to go kick it at Grooves Restaurant and Lounge tonight. Meet me a down-to-earth woman who knew how to enjoy herself minus all the drama. Buy her a few drinks. Toss back some more brews. Get wasted. Get my dick sucked and forget about Loretta until tomorrow.

"I'm not going to ask you again, sir."

*Fuck!*

I eased my wallet out of my back pocket and handed my license to the officer.

"Wait right here," he said. "Better yet, you come with me. Ma'am, you wait here."

I had to follow that nigga all the way over to Old Navy. Stood beside his car. Women could fuck things up in a heartbeat. When shit didn't go their way, they wanted the police to rescue their ass. Just like that, Loretta was about to know what I didn't want her to ever find out.

The policeman opened his door, got into his car. Ten minutes later he got out. "Put your hands behind your back and turn around."

"Why? What did I do?"

"I'm not going to ask you again . . . sir." The officer unfastened the latch securing his stun gun and pulled it out.

I faced the fuckin' patrol car, did as I was told. I knew the routine. The officer removed my hat, tossed it on the backseat, placed his hand on top of my head, shoved me into the car, and left the door open.

I sat there, feeling like an idiot. Watched him motion for Loretta to come over to his patrol car. She stared like I was in a lineup and she needed to ID me. I stared back at that ho. After all I'd done for her, that bitch didn't have an ounce of empathy for me. Just like the rest, she'd get hers.

"Let me see your license," the officer told Loretta.

She opened her purse and handed the ID to the cop.

"I don't know your relationship to this man, but there's something you should know," the officer said. "Granville Washington has three protective orders against him filed in Harris County by three different women. If he's harassing you, I suggest you do the same, Ms. Lovelace. This man is a ticking time bomb waiting to explode."

He didn't know me. If I was such a threat, why was I forty-five years old and making ninety Gs a year busting my ass building offices? What the cop failed to mention to *Ms. Lovelace* was that all three POs were unwarranted. And even if they were legit, Harris County had nearly 4.5 million residents, and Houston was the fourth largest city in the United States, with over 2 million people. It was hot as hell. Every heat record was broken this year. Folks in Houston were understandably agitated sometimes and the prisons were already overcrowded. So having a few POs was no reason to lock a brothah up.

"Arrest him! He's insane. I want to press charges."

"Wish I could, ma'am, but I don't have cause to arrest this man. He hasn't violated the law."

Watching Loretta walk away, I smiled on the inside. It would be in her best interest to take the officer's advice. I'd never violated a protective order. Better to get another woman than go to jail and become someone else's woman.

I wasn't finished with Loretta Lovelace

yet. If she were wise, she'd wear my ring, and she'd never turn her back on me again.

# CHAPTER 1
## MADISON

" 'You can't see it. . . . It's electric!' "

The music moved through me like lightning. Happiness filled the room with smiles and laughter. My hips swung to the beat and my feet moved along the hardwood floor as though my Louboutin red-bottom stilettos had wheels.

I was glad my girlfriend had let me sponsor her post-wedding reception at Black Swan and the Nest at Black Swan. My gift to her cost me twenty grand to rent out the entire space on their most popular night, Saturday. Food, alcohol, the champagne fountain, decorations, party favors, and all the trimmings were an additional thirty thousand, but Tisha was worth every penny.

We'd been friends since kindergarten, joined at the hip with Loretta. The stories we shared over the years from losing our virginity to pledging different sororities were beyond entertaining. What I loved most was, we weren't three of a kind. Each of us had unique looks and styles, and we'd taken separate career paths. At times our friendship was tested, but our bond was never broken for long. When things fell apart, Tisha was our glue.

As I spun around, the split in my green-and-gold spaghetti-strap dress exposed my left leg from my ankle to the space adjacent to my vagina. "Daring," "diva," and "delicious" best described my infectious personality. Every day I opened my eyes, I was ready to see the world and all the rich men in it. A broke man couldn't do anything to or for me.

I spun again, almost tripping over my man as he got down on one knee. I gyrated in his face. Feeling the heat of his hand against my inner thigh, I moved with an "uh, yeah, take that, and this" motion.

*Damn, if the place were empty, I'd shake out of my thong and let him taste me.*

My man strived to be the best at *e-v-e-r-y-t-h-i-n-g*. I did too. Our individual success made us a dynamic power couple.

"I love you, Madison Tyler. Will you marry me?"

In the midst of grooving, with over fifty people surrounding us and doing the electric slide, I stopped dancing. The moment

I'd been waiting for had arrived in style. I couldn't hold back the tears. What girl didn't want a husband to love and adore her for the rest of her life? I was positive I wanted to get married.

"Yes! Yes, I will marry you, Roosevelt!" I wasn't sure if he was the one, but he'd do for now. I was attracted to one of his assistant coaches, Blue Waters, but he wasn't the head coach or close to being hired as executive vice president/general manager like my man. Sorry, Blue. Any girl who knew her self-worth understood that status mattered.

Roosevelt didn't like his first name, but I appreciated it more than what everyone else called him, Chicago. I found Southerners strange in many ways. Being the fairest of Creoles from Port Arthur, Texas, I had a bundle of eccentric ways, but I wasn't crazier than some of my relatives who still lived there.

A teardrop clung to Roosevelt's eyelid. He had no middle name, so his family gave him a nickname when he was a toddler. They weren't from Chicago, and he hadn't visited the Windy City until he was in college playing football. The only rationale for his nickname was the Bears were his father's favorite team. Since he was firstborn, the name stuck, but his brother, Chaz, was always called by his real name.

The ice cube he was sliding on my ring finger blinded me. *Damn!* My heart pounded like a drumbeat. I held my hand in front of my face and cheesed the widest grin ever. I pulled Roosevelt to his feet by his lapel, leapt into his arms, smashed my lips against his, and held them there.

The "Electric Boogie" faded from blasting to silence.

"Did Chicago just propose to Madison?" DJ Chip asked. He was the DJ for our football team and mixed up the beat every Saturday at the Black Swan.

My arm shot up in the air. "He sure did!" I flashed my ring to all the bitches at my girl's wedding reception. All the single females' eyes melted in my shine. It didn't matter who caught the bouquet; I was the envy of them all.

The desperate ladies dying to get a man were not my problem. And if they believed catching a bundle of flowers was the way to change their status from single, all I could say to them was "good luck." I gave Tisha a big hug, because she had to be feeling really small right now. Wasn't my fault she divorced a cheating millionaire and married her broke-ass high school sweetheart in the name of love. What a joke.

Tisha trotted upstairs and into the Nest, the private room I reserved for her immediate family and her closest friends. Stealing the spotlight from Tisha wasn't planned. How was I to know my engagement ring would be a bigger solitaire than all the chips in her wedding band and engagement ring combined?

I'd turned to kiss Roosevelt again, when someone snatched my biceps. The grip was that of a blood pressure machine about to burst. My fingers automatically curled into a tight fist. As cute as I was, I wouldn't hesitate to knock a trick on her ass.

I didn't want to fight, but I swore if I turned around and saw one of those bold bitches who wanted my man was trying to ruin my moment, I was going to put my rock to work and lay her ass out, then glide over her as though I was on the red carpet.

These bitches were beneath me. All women were beneath me, including my best friends, Loretta and Tisha. When I saw it was Loretta, I uncurled my fist.

Loretta didn't have a date at the wedding because she'd wasted her time dating that loser construction worker, Granville Washington. She should've brought him, anyway. It was unladylike for a real woman to escort herself to a function. He worked for me. I'd heard of him, but I had never met him. I had too many employees to meet them all.

From what she'd told me, I told her not to do him. Told her just because that misfit allegedly had a big dick — "big" was relative to the woman — and since Loretta and I didn't travel in the same circle of men, I had no idea what he was working with. I said that she should leave him alone. He had nothing to lose. Outside of work, from what my girl said, he had no real interests other than taking her out, gazing into her eyes, drooling in her mouth, eating her pussy, and boning her.

From all the details she'd given me, Granville was a forty-five-year-old clumsy brute — six feet six inches, 285 pounds of muscle. The worst combination for a blue-collar man was to be good-looking, decent in bed, and to think he knew everything when what he truly was, was ignorant. Loretta should've taken my advice: took the dick and kept him moving. But no. Loretta always had to find the good in every man, until he treated her bad.

"Girl, let me —"

Before I finished protesting, I was being dragged off the dance floor, up the stairs, out the door, and onto the elevator.

"What the hell are you doing?" Loretta asked.

I flashed my ring in her face. "Duh. Trying to enjoy the moment. What's wrong with you?"

She pulled me through the lobby, then outside by the swimming pool. "You can't accept Chicago's ring. You're going to ruin another good man. You've already got what, six engagement rings collecting dust. It's women like you who mess it up for women like me."

"Correction. It's eight. This makes nine. And see, that's where you're wrong. It's women like you who allow men to dictate to you, instead of you training them like I've taught you. That's how you end up with fucked-up men like Granville. You give up the pussy, then find out they're crazy. By the way, have you filed that protective order, like you said you were going to do?"

"Have you fired him, like I've asked you?"

"He's not my problem, but I did inquire about him. According to his supervisor, Granville is an excellent worker and does the work of ten men. I'd be stupid to fire him, especially without cause."

"Forget Granville. I don't want you to marry Chicago. What are his parents going to say about this? If he marries you, our

35

entire football team is going to hell."

"Not my problem."

*So what if his parents hate me? I'm not doing them. Hell, they probably aren't doing one another. If they were, they wouldn't be all up in my business.*

Roosevelt appealed to me because he managed our professional football team. He was unquestionably a man of power: hiring athletes, chartering planes, making sure hotels, equipment, and food for the players and staff were taken care of. The scouts and video techs reported to him. He dealt with salaries, trades, and contract terminations. Made sure if any of his starters were hurt, he had talented backup. As the general manager, Roosevelt was in charge of everyone around him, except me.

No man could tame me. I had plans for Roosevelt. My first order of business was to make sure I married him right before he inherited the $20 million his grandfather was giving him and his brother, Chaz. Ten was for Roosevelt and me, and the other ten was for Chaz.

"Look at it like this, Loretta. The second the pastor says, 'You may kiss the bride,' I'm going to be on a first-name basis with the owners, all sixty-one ballers, the assistant coaches, and the head coach. You should be nicer to me. I might hook you up with a millionaire like Blue Waters, girlfriend. Stop hating on me because you can't find the right man."

"Fine, if you want to ruin Chicago's life, go right ahead," Loretta said, flinging my arm toward me. "But don't overshadow Tisha's wedding day."

"Not my problem. Tisha shouldn't have divorced her first husband and she damn sure nuff should've married a man with more money than Darryl. That way he could've paid for her ring and their reception."

Loretta shook her head. "Damn, Madison. She married her high-school sweetheart. Girl, you're lucky you're my friend, or else."

Marrying a high-school sweetheart when you're thirty-five was backtracking to the tenth power. That was a huge mistake for Tisha. Fortunately, her ex-husband paid her a solid $20,000 a month for alimony and child support, but that was about to decrease once the ink dried on her license. Why any woman would marry a liability was beyond my comprehension.

"You've got that one twisted. The soon-to-be Madison DuBois is going back inside to celebrate her engagement. I suggest you stay your ass out here until you cool down. Trust me, you don't want me to bust your business in front of Tisha's guests."

"Okay, Ms. Thang. Wait a minute," Loretta said. "Since you're so great at training men, I bet you that you can't train Granville Washington."

I stared at my girl. She must've been insane to give me a dare. She knew me better than that. Nobody challenges Madison Tyler and wins. I'd show her how good I was at getting my way with men.

"This'll give me something to do while Roosevelt is on the road. But before I agree, what's in it for me?"

Boldly she said, "Whatever you want."

That wasn't specific enough, but it was to my advantage. I could become Loretta's worst enemy by the time I won this bet. I threw up my hands. Why was I entertaining her?

"Look, I'm not sure you have enough to lose for me to charm that loser."

"Just what I thought. You're all talk. Just because you have a banging body, booty, you're gorgeous, and have a bubbly personality, you're not all that, Madison. Men want women with integrity," Loretta said, walking away from me.

*"Integrity"? Is she serious?*

I had all the assets men died to acquire. She also left out "scintillating." If a man could get a beautiful woman whom all his boys wanted to fuck, he wouldn't give a damn about her morals.

"Fine, I'll prove it. But I'm not having sex with him."

"That's the only way you can win."

I was so good that I could open an obedience school for men, but sexing Granville would go against my principles of giving charitable fucks. Not sexing him would give Loretta bragging rights . . . never. I'd show her ass. I was going to break this Granville guy in one weekend.

"Fine," I said, walking away.

"One more thing," Loretta said.

"What? Girl, what! You are ruining my moment."

"Better for me to ruin yours than for me to stand by and let you do the same to Tisha. You never asked me what I wanted."

I put my hand on my hip and placed my left foot forward. The split draped both sides of my leg.

Loretta said, "If I win, you'll call off your wedding with Chicago."

Whipping my dress like a bullfighter, I laughed, then shook my head. "Fine, bitch.

Because we both know I'm not going to lose. You are."

# Chapter 2
## Loretta

I stood naked in front of the bathroom mirror.

My once-size-six body wasn't perfect anymore, but my heart was in the right place. Below my navel, I looked at the stretch marks on my stomach and upper thighs. I turned sideways to see more broken skin on my buttocks.

"Loretta, you are absolutely lovely," I told myself. I smiled, but it wasn't from the inside out. If I didn't believe I was beautiful, it would show. Boosting my own self-esteem was harder than my friends and family thought.

Why hadn't I attracted a good man to put a ring on my finger? A man who appreciated my size twelve and all the love I had to offer. Millions of men in Harris County and I end up with Granville.

What was it about him that constantly irritated me? That dumb look that was supposed to be sexy? Or his voice? It wasn't his fault that he'd gotten shot. Well, actually it was. He'd told me that he wouldn't stop pursuing another man's wife after she'd slept with him. But when he told me that incident had happened twenty years ago, I figured he'd changed.

Should've listened to Tisha. She said people never changed. I believed people learned from their mistakes. And Madison didn't care if they did or didn't, as long as she got her way. Maybe this dare to have Madison sex and tame Granville was a bad idea.

I danced in the mirror, fighting back tears. My struggle for happiness was a tug-of-war. One minute I was cool; the next moment I was depressed.

If I were considerably lighter and could almost pass for white like my friend Madison, the scars that tore my flesh apart when I gained fifty pounds during my pregnancy wouldn't be as visible. Thankfully, my gingersnap-colored breasts remained firm. My cinnamon areolas had grown wider during breast-feeding and stayed the width of my favorite cookies, Oreos. Fortunately, my nipples survived five months of gnawing; but at first I swore they were going to fall off from all the sucking, cracking, and bleeding.

I stopped dancing. I tucked my hair behind my ears, then stared into my eyes.

The physical pain during delivery and nursing didn't last nearly as long as my heartache. I hated that I loved a man who didn't feel the same way about me. It didn't matter how many meals, pairs of underwear, gifts, or the engagement ring that Granville bought, he'd never be Raynard. No man had measured up to Raynard since our breakup six years ago.

Trusting a man who had lied to me so many times that I'd lost count made me part of the 70th percentile of African-American women who were single parents. I believed Raynard when he whispered in my ear, "We don't need to use condoms anymore, Loretta. I'm your man. I'll never leave you. You are the complete package. Beautiful. Intelligent. You own your house. You're a pharmacist. Have a job earning over six figures a year. Have my baby and you can retire whenever you want."

Madison warned me, "Don't do it. If you give a man everything he wants before you get the ring, he has no incentive."

She had her way of handling men and I had mine. I didn't get pregnant right away;

but two months after I did, Raynard started picking arguments. He blamed it on me, saying, "You've changed. Everything is about the baby, and the baby isn't even here. Plus, you're irritable all the time."

I'd admit I was more sensitive, especially during my first trimester, but I hardly considered that irritable. Throwing up every morning for three months made me miserable. If my enthusiasm for sex and Raynard had faded, he'd made me that way when he began coming over late at night. By the time he got to my house, we had sex and went to sleep. He stopped having dinner and watching movies with me. Then some nights he wouldn't come to my house at all.

Lying in the fetal position alone, hugging my stomach while crying myself to sleep, was not what I'd envisioned. After I started showing, my nose got wider, my face grew fuller, and my neck got darker. Raynard stopped being with me in public. When he did come by, his phone was ringing more than usual, even in the middle of the night. If it weren't for my mom and my girls, Tisha and Madison, emotionally supporting me, I probably would've gone crazy.

It took a year for me to stop chasing Raynard. On our baby's first birthday, I sobered up when he showed up late to the party, showing off his new girlfriend. She was nine months pregnant, and that was the first time I'd known he was dating someone. She clung to my daughter's father damn near the entire hour they were there. Her other hand was constantly on her hip, thrusting her naked, stretch mark–free belly in front of my family, friends, and Raynell's play-mates.

Guess he'd told her the same thing he'd told me, except he must've meant whatever he'd said to her. Gloria was her name. Gloria Fountain. She looked like she'd swal-lowed a basketball. Maybe he was cool with her because she actually looked sexy carry-ing their unborn son.

A tear rolled down my cheek. I let another one chase the first one, until I found myself sobbing like a baby.

"Mommy, you okay?" Raynell asked, entering the bathroom. Her lips quivered.

"No, baby. Don't cry. You know how I get when I think about your dad."

Was it okay for me to let her see me come undone? What was I teaching my daughter? That it was okay for her to cry over a man who didn't want her?

"Daddy loves you, too, Mommy," she said. "I know he does. One day, when he's done teaching my brother how to become a man, he'll come live with us."

Kissing her lips, I realized how naïve we both were. I even named our daughter with the belief that would make her dad come back. I still hadn't given up hope that one day I'd have the family I always prayed for.

Raynard was the best man I'd met. He willingly paid child support. Went to court before I could file. He gave Raynell everything her six-year-old heart desired and more.

Every penny he'd given to us could be his, if he just stopped looking through me. I know Madison disagreed with me, but having the man was more important than having his money. Didn't he notice how my eyes lit up whenever I saw him? I guess not. But I still loved him.

"Your daddy has another family, baby. Mommy will be fine. Go put your shoes on. Your dad will be here to pick you up soon."

Raynell's cheeks rose up toward her innocent brown eyes. The gap where we were waiting for her two front teeth to grow into was exposed up to her gums. "I love my daddy."

"I know, baby. Now go. You know he doesn't like waiting."

I wanted to add "in his car," but I didn't. Whenever Raynell wasn't ready on time,

Raynard would sit in front of my house in his Lexus LX SUV with Raynard Jr. and his wife, Gloria.

Their son was now five years old. However, after he was born, Gloria didn't like Raynard coming into my house. What made him stay with that . . . controlling bitch?

Maybe Madison was right. I was too nice, too honest, too trusting with men. The next man I met, I'd speak my mind instead of saying what I thought he wanted to hear. He'd be my bitch.

I slipped into my purple satin robe, dropped my cell phone into the pocket. I shook my head. I didn't even feel right thinking I could talk down to a man I liked. Wasn't it counterproductive for a woman to take on the role of the man? Or degrade a man she expected to uplift her?

Being at Tisha's wedding last weekend gave me faith that one day I, too, would walk down the aisle in a striking white gown with a veil over my face. Tisha had two boys from her previous marriage, ages three and four. Her husband loved those boys like they had his DNA. Loved Tisha like she'd never been loved before. I wasn't sure if Tisha divorced her multi-millionaire husband because he was cheating or because she never stopped loving Darryl.

47

Eventually my husband-to-be would un-
cover my face and gaze into my eyes. When
the pastor said, "You may kiss the bride,"
our eyes would close in unison and the
touch of our lips would fill our bodies from
head to toe with love.

*Buzzz. Buzzz.*

Quickly I covered my breasts, then tied
my sash in a bow. Raynell was at the door,
with her hand on the knob.

"You'd better not open that door, little
girl," I said, moving her hand.

"But —"

"No 'but.' You know the rules."

"Yes, Mommy," she said, lowering her
head.

I opened the door. Raynell jumped into
her father's arms. Raynard handed me a
shopping bag from Neiman Marcus. An
envelope was on top. I took the bag and
stared at him. No hellos or good-byes were
exchanged.

He'd said that Gloria had told him there
was no reason for him to speak to me:
Greetings led to hugs. Hugs led to kisses.
Kisses led to sex. Sex led to exes getting
back together.

She sat in the passenger seat and watched
us, as though she was a hawk and I was her
prey. She had the man I once had. I turned

48

away in defeat and gently closed my front door.

Opening the envelope, I discovered there was a check for $5,000. I tossed it on the coffee table. I guess I'd done something right. I wasn't a groupie, but I'd managed to have a baby for my wealthy gynecologist. Five Gs was a fraction of what he earned for delivering one baby. And considering he brought babies into the world almost every day, Gloria had retired her crown before she walked down the aisle with him.

I fell in love with Raynard because he didn't have a huge ego. He was educated. Caring. A gentleman. Knew how to wine and dine me. Sure, he'd seen countless vaginas, but I thought mine was the crème de la crème. Guess Gloria Fountain, the former Miss Houston, had a pussy that was more intriguing than mine. What was it about men dying to have a beauty queen trophy girlfriend to showcase?

As usual, the bag had pretty dresses for Raynell. Matching ribbons, barrettes, and bows were scattered in the bottom. I'd let our daughter keep the dress she liked most. The rest of the outfits would be taken to Second Baptist on Sunday and given to little girls less fortunate.

My attention was redirected when I heard

my cell phone chiming, signaling I had a text message: loretta my love are you hungry? lunch is on me baby. raynell should be gone by now. what time should I pick you up?

Was he spying on me?

I texted back: Not today.

I wanted to leave our communication open long enough for me to set him up with Madison.

I went to my sanctuary — my prayer room — and knelt at the altar. It was six feet wide and three feet high. Thirteen white candles were scattered across the top. Some were three inches high. The others were either four or five. I lit the tea light candle beneath the fragrance-burning lamp, which sat in the center of the altar. Eucalyptus oil mixed with water floated in the dish above the flame. The backdrop was a waterfall from Z Gallerie.

Forest green leather cushioned my knees; a black padded armrest supported my elbows. I opened my New King James Version of the Scriptures to page 790. The *Woman Thou Art Loosed* edition by T. D. Jakes was my favorite Bible. I'd grown a lot from reading his inspirational messages.

I read T.D. Jakes' message, "Letting Go." I'd read this before, but today felt I needed this word again.

Would I take my love for Raynard to my grave? As much as I'd read the scriptures, I knew what I needed to do but, as long as I was alive, I couldn't bury the emotions I had for —

*Buzzz. Buzzz.*

Raynard never came back. I blew out the candle, left my altar, went to the foyer, and peeped through the hole. I stared in disbelief, then slowly opened the door.

"Why are you here?" I asked.

"I need to talk to you, Loretta. Please, may I come in?"

# CHAPTER 3
## CHICAGO

Knocking on Loretta's door unannounced was inappropriate, but I had some questions that needed answers. In the midst of my feeling like the best man, I didn't understand why she'd dragged Madison off the dance floor right after I'd proposed. Madison had come back, smiling, like everything was all good; but Loretta walked in with an attitude and avoided Madison the rest of the evening.

When I had asked Madison, "What's up with your girl Loretta?" my fiancée of less than an hour said, "She's jealous of me, but she's also happy for us. Maybe one day we'll be the ones excited for her. But I'm sure that won't be anytime soon."

"Sure, Chicago. Come in. Is everything okay? Is Madison all right?" Loretta asked, closing the door.

"Yeah, she's fine. And I apologize for dropping in on you like this, but I didn't have your number."

"Just because I live next door to Madison, I'm not going to say this is acceptable, because it's not, but you're here now. Have a seat on the sofa. Can I get you something to drink?" she asked, wrapping her robe closer to her body.

The soft leather couch looked too intimate. I opted, instead, for the purple chair, with the seven-foot-high back, which was next to the antique mirrored coffee table, with silver trim. I sat facing the front door. Placing my arms on the amber wooden rests, I interlocked my fingers, then said, "Whatever you have that's cold. Cranberry, orange juice, and a shot of vodka would be cool, but I'm okay with straight whiskey, too, if you don't mind."

"Sure, no problem. Does Madison know you're here?"

"No, and I'd appreciate it if you kept this between us."

Loretta stopped and stared at me.

"I saw you at church the day after the reception, but I didn't feel comfortable approaching you."

Loretta's smile was amazing. Her entire face glowed. "You're a member at Second Baptist?"

I nodded. "During the season I don't get

there as often as I'd like and when I do I sit in the back."

She walked away without responding.

I glanced around. Nothing in the room matched. The area rug was red, sofa mustard, the armless Victorian chair had a white oval background with a portrait of her and a little girl in the center. I might have to borrow that concept as an anniversary present for my parents' upcoming thirty-fifth.

"It's nothing inappropriate. I'm not that kind of guy," I said loud enough for her to hear.

Every wall was meticulously covered with exotic paintings. I immediately recognized the 36-by-60–inch *Moon Beam* print by Alvin Roy from his gallery, Royal Grafix Fine Art.

*Ah, now I get it.*

Every color in Loretta's living room was a spin-off from the array of hues in the portrait. Nice touch.

I busied myself trying to find one color in the picture that wasn't in the room. I had a print of his *Court N Tha Queen*, which reminded me of how regal my mother is.

*Hmm, that's different.*

Loretta had indeed matched all the colors, down to the cobalt and gold life-size statue of Obama standing in her foyer.

*What's taking her so long?*

I called out, "Don't call, text, or e-mail Madison."

"Don't you think she might see your car in my driveway? Or did you walk over?"

"I'm not in my car." I wasn't that careless, and Madison isn't the type of insecure woman who would sit in the window watching her neighbors all day.

My heart raced, praying I was doing the right thing. Loretta returned with two cocktails and handed me one. She'd traded her robe for a pair of black leggings and a T-shirt.

"You know, Chicago, it's not okay for you to drop in on me. I mean, I'm glad my daughter is with her dad, but don't do this again." She sat in the center of the sofa, on the edge of the cushion.

"I'm sorry, and I promise you I won't." I sipped from my glass. "Whoa." I sniffed my way-too-adult beverage. "This vodka with a splash of cranberry was supposed to be the other way around." I wrapped my hands around the old-fashioned crystal glass, then leaned forward. I didn't see any coasters, so I held on to my drink.

"Well," Loretta said, tasting her cocktail, "what are you talking about? I know you're

55

not a lightweight. This is good."

"It is indeed," I agreed, stirring with my finger. "Nice print. I have one of his too."

Her eyes widened. "Really? Isn't Alvin the best? I so love that he teaches kids with special needs how to paint. I have *Court N Tha Queen* over my bed. Thought that was the appropriate place for it, but men these days don't get it."

Sounded like she knew the artist on a personal level. If so, we'd have a mutual acquaintance. Our conversation about art was a good icebreaker. Sliding back on the sofa, Loretta crossed her legs at the ankles. Her thighs appeared firm and shapely, like a track star's. Her stomach stuck out a little, not much. Her breasts were large, nipples hard. She wasn't wearing a bra.

I sipped my drink. "Some of us do get it," I told her. "I have the queen portrait too."

Her eyes widened again, along with a smile this time. She whispered, "Madison, Madison. Always gets the good ones."

"I guess this is a good time for me to talk about her, too, but first what did you mean by that?"

Loretta shook her head, raising her drink toward me. "To Madison," she said, then swallowed. "That's my girl."

*I'm here now. Almost wish I weren't. There's*

*something sexy about Loretta.*

Turning off the male sex gene in my brain, I silenced my cell phone. Then I asked, "Loretta, I know Madison loves me, but do you think she's marrying me for my money? I mean, if I weren't the VP and GM for our football team, earning an eight-figure salary, would she feel the same?"

Loretta hesitated. Her thick lips disappeared inside her mouth. She exhaled. "Chicago, those are questions you have to ask Madison, not me."

"But you're the one that dragged her off the dance floor last weekend, like you were upset that I'd proposed. Did I do the wrong thing?"

She bit her bottom lip; then she shifted her drink to her other hand.

"I'm asking you because I'm not sure Madison would be completely honest with me. I don't have a problem with her wanting to marry a man like myself who's well-off, but I don't want to be that guy who ends up getting used by an older woman. Did she tell you about the twenty million my grandfather is giving me and my brother, Chaz?"

"She mentioned it."

"See, that's what I'm talking about. How did she mention it?"

Loretta sighed heavily. "What's the real concern here, Chicago? It's not like Madison is broke. She has her own money. She runs her family business. We both know they're building that huge mixed-use development off of San Felipe and Post Oak. Since you're asking my opinion, I think what you guys should do is get a prenup."

Her defensiveness indicated I'd struck a nerve. Her leg started shaking. Sips grew into gulps.

"That's just it. I don't want a prenup, and I definitely don't want a marriage that will end in divorce. I want Madison to have our babies, and I want complete trust between us. She's already told me we have to have a nanny, and our baby has to have new clothes every week, just like Raynell. Madison has a lot of respect for you. I'm okay with what she wants, and I'm going to make sure she has a full-time live-in housekeeper."

Loretta shrugged her neck back an inch. "Oh no! That's what you can't do. I know my girlfriend, and she will not have another woman living under her roof, no matter how big it is."

I laughed. "You're right. Is Madison a one-man kind of woman?" I asked, taking a huge swig from my glass.

Loretta's beverage almost escaped her lips.

She covered her mouth.

I wasn't sure if she was covering for her girlfriend or not, but I wanted to believe her silence was confirmation that Madison would be faithful.

"Look, I don't want to worry when I'm on the road working. She's your girl. You've known her since elementary school, so you've got a head start on me. Please tell me the truth. I promise I won't tell Madison what you say."

"I can't give you her truth," Loretta said, shaking her leg. "What you need to do is make a list of all your questions, take Madison to dinner, and ask her. Now I have a question for you, if you don't mind."

Ready to let the conversation about Madison go, I said, "It's the least I can do."

"Thanks," Loretta said, moving closer to me. "I'm a good woman. I love hard. I try to give men the benefit that they're good, when I meet them. Like my daughter's father, Raynard. It breaks me down to know I still love him, and he left me for another woman. We haven't been together for six years, and he still hasn't given me a reason for ending the relationship. All he said was 'It's not you. It's me.' I wanted to marry Raynard, but he married someone else. Do you guys pick women like Madison because they're light-skinned, gorgeous, look like supermodels, and they're fun?"

Not so much the light-skinned part mattered to me, but I wanted to say, "Uh, yes. Men love strikingly exotic-looking women."

"Do I need to change to get my child's father to divorce her and marry me?"

"She's the former Miss Houston." I knew that because Madison had told me. "Gloria is used to competing, winning, and she has his son."

Loretta's eyes narrowed. "I had his child first. Am I not worthy because I'm not some damn desperate beauty pageant queen?"

Wow, I couldn't lie to Loretta. She was beautiful, but she wasn't Gloria or Madison. They had the kind of attractiveness and femininity that made men want to hand them their wallet. The first time I saw Madison, I paid the tab for her and her two friends by putting up my credit card without caring what the bill was. I later learned the two friends with her were Loretta and Tisha.

"You are worthy," I said, hoping to ease Loretta's tension.

"Then what made him leave me?" she asked. Her large brown eyes filled with tears.

I almost felt responsible for her pain. Loretta made me think of the woman I'd left to be with Madison. My mother loved my ex, and it wasn't that Mom didn't like Madison. But my mother did say, "That there girl is one of them light-complexion Creoles with parents closer to kin than kind."

What Mama had meant by that was down South, especially in the Golden Triangle — Beaumont, Orange, and Port Arthur, Texas — family married family to keep the white French masters' blood as pure as possible. Light would propose to light, including first cousins, before they'd marry dark like Loretta and darker like Tisha. I wasn't Creole, but I was fair-skinned; and I loved me some Madison and was blessed that she loved me too.

I wasn't sure why Raynard had left Loretta, but I was certain just like she didn't have answers for me, I didn't have any for her.

"Do you like that construction worker guy who works for Madison?" I asked, trying to take the conversation in a different direction.

Loretta hesitated again.

"What's wrong?"

"Have you seen him?"

"No. Madison mentioned you were going out with him."

"Besides your knowing way too much of

61

my business . . . that's just it. I liked him at first, but after a few dates — and please let's not talk about sex — he's history. But he's from Port Arthur."

"Light-skinned?"

"No, he's dark, but crazy as hell."

"Grew up near the tracks?"

"How'd you know?" she asked.

We both laughed.

"They're crazy too," I said. "All those refineries down there — and not to mention, one of them is expanding their plant — the pollution is killing folks. The people who live right across those tracks got it the worst. They probably have mental disorders, cancer, and only God knows what from inhaling fumes twenty-four/seven. So basically what I'm saying is even if he's not Creole, he's probably messed up in the head."

Loretta finished her drink. "Perhaps that's his problem, but I just think he's a compulsive pleaser who needs to be constantly praised. Maybe you can set me up on a blind date with your brother," Loretta said, then laughed.

Wondering how many other African-American single moms were in search of the man of their dreams, I understood where Loretta was coming from.

"I can't make any promises, but I'll see what I can do."

I wasn't sure I wanted to be responsible if things didn't work out. Then she might hate me. But Chaz was single, and he was a good man.

"Thanks for hearing me out. Can I ask one last favor?" I questioned.

"Only if you promise to hook me up."

"Consider it done," I said, then knelt in front of Loretta. "Since we're members of the same church, would you pray with and for me, and I'll do the same for you?"

Loretta knelt in front of me; we held hands. I knew Madison was Loretta's best friend, but Madison didn't pray. That didn't mean she wasn't spiritual. Her heart was in the right place. Right now, though, I needed a prayer partner.

"Lord, I ask that You guide us in the direction that will continuously serve you. If there is anything that should be revealed to us, we ask that You show us. Please protect Loretta's heart and in Your time, Lord, send her a man deserving of all she is ready to offer and receive. In Jesus' name, amen."

Loretta whispered, "Amen."

I stood. "I hope you don't mind if I call you from time to time to pray with me." My heart spoke to Loretta. She was a good woman. Unlike Madison, Loretta seemed transparent. But I wasn't confused. I was in love with Madison Tyler.

"I'd like that," Loretta said. "May I do the same?"

Of course I couldn't say no. We exchanged cell numbers. Before escorting me to the door, Loretta led me through her dining area and kitchen to a room at the back of her house.

"Wow!" My eyes lit up.

"This is my prayer room. I wanted you to see it."

"This is magnificent. I might have to do this."

Loretta escorted me to the door. I hurried to my brother's car parked in front of Loretta's house. He drove in the opposite direction of Madison's home on West Oak Drive North.

"How'd it go?" Chaz asked.

"I still love her, man. I'm going for it."

"Marriage isn't something you go for, like an onside kick or a first down on fourth, with one to go. You need to be a hundred percent sure about Madison. Mom has reservations and I do too. I was hoping your conversation with Loretta would have opened your eyes to the truth. Madison is in it for your money."

Chaz was a year younger than me. I was supposed to give him advice. After leaving Loretta's house I wasn't apprehensive about marrying Madison.

"You know Mom *isn't* the type that believes no woman is good enough for us."

I told Chaz, "Mom will learn to love Madison and so will you."

"Chicago, you have to pay attention to what Madison isn't saying. You do that shit all day in business. Do that shit with her."

My fiancée wasn't my client. She was the best woman for me, I was sure of that. She was incredibly gorgeous, blond, and smart.

"Changing the subject, I want you and Loretta to double-date with Madison and me."

Chaz tapped on the brakes. "Females of a feather, man . . . Forget that, no way." Pressing the accelerator, he smiled. "Maybe that's not a bad idea. I might be able to get Loretta to tell me what she wouldn't tell you."

# Chapter 4
# Granville

My lovely Loretta was the only woman I wanted. I couldn't let her go. Hadn't seen her in over a week since our date at the Grand Lux Cafe. I wondered if she caught the bouquet at her friend's wedding. That would prove to her that she should be wearing my ring. I prayed she missed me the same way I tossed and turned at night over her. Not communicating with my woman for the past twenty-four hours was driving me crazy.

Looking at the picture of Loretta on my nightstand, next to her engagement ring, I wished she were here in my bed when I opened my eyes this morning. Yesterday she'd texted "not today" to me, but today was a different day. I sat in my spacious one-bedroom apartment on Potomac, off San Felipe, texting her: baby give me 1 more chance . . . baby baby give me 1 more chance.

I laughed aloud at my great sense of

humor and timing to think of that song by Notorious B.I.G.

My two-story triplex had one unit up and two down. Mine was at the top. I didn't have a five-bedroom, six-bathroom double-decker, like Loretta had. Didn't understand why she had to have all that space for two people. My penthouse suited me fine. Had just enough space for Loretta and me; but with Raynell and when Loretta had our kid, I'd have to upgrade us to two bedrooms. Not right away. Raynell could sleep on my fold-out couch and share the living room with the baby, or the baby's crib could be in our bedroom. But first I had to marry Loretta. I respected her too much to move in with her. And I'd never treat her like a whore — the way Raynard had done by knocking her up and never giving her his last name.

Two minutes later she hadn't replied, so I sent her a second text: let me pick you up from work for lunch. please loretta.

I wanted to add, damn bitch, I'm trying to be nice to you, but I didn't.

Another two minutes had gone by and she hadn't replied, so I started typing, i'll be in the park . . .

"Damn!"

I answered the ringing phone, but hung

67

up on my brother's call without saying hello. I had to start my text all over. What I really had to do was get rid of this cheap old-ass cell phone. After lunch with Loretta I was going to stop at AT&T on Westheimer, near my house, and get one of those new iPhones.

Retyping, i'll be in the parking . . .

"Damn! What the fuck!" I shouted, then answered, "What's up, bro? What's up?"

"Hey, man, chill. Mom called. She's not feeling too good. We need to go to Port Arthur right now and check on her. I'll pick you up."

Today was my only day off this week. If I didn't see Loretta, I'd have to wait until the weekend. When she had her daughter, she didn't come over or let me visit them. I'd met Raynell once, by accident, when I'd shown up at Loretta's house an hour early. She'd warned me not to do that again. Something about not wanting a man around her little girl unless she was sure he was going to be a permanent part of their lives. I had to make certain I was that man.

"I'm on my way," my brother said.

Mom always claimed she wasn't doing well when she got lonely and wanted us to come by. Normally, I wouldn't mind and I'd pick up ribs, chicken, fish, shrimp, oysters, corn on the cob, and crawfish to grill, fry, and boil for Moms.

"Hey, I've got lunch plans with Loretta. I'll come down later and bring a spread."

"I thought you said she dumped you," Beaux said.

Growing up, his name was easier to pronounce than it was to spell. Moms could've just put "Bow" on his birth certificate, like the ribbon on a package, but she had to outdo her friends when it came to naming us.

"She wants me back, baby." I prayed that was true.

My phone buzzed with a text in the middle of our conversation: I'll meet you, but I only have a few minutes.

"Ha-ha, bro. I told you! I told you, man! That's her right there!"

"Calm your country ass down. You can take her out anytime. Mom needs us. I'm picking you up now. Stay put." Beaux ended the call.

I tossed my phone on the bed, ran from my living room to my bathroom. Showered. Shaved. Put on cologne, jeans, and my favorite black ostrich cowboy boots. Those were the ones I had on when Loretta rode me like she couldn't get enough. I felt the dreaminess in my eyes. I was the luckiest man in the world to have the most amazing woman.

Putting on my black shirt, I'd button it up later. I grabbed my hat, keys, wallet, cell, and ran outside to my black four-door Super Duty pickup truck. Usually, I'd do a walk-around and inspect everything from my chrome grille to the tailgate. But if Beaux got here before I left, we'd end up brawling.

Tearing out of the driveway, the back of the truck fishtailed. I sped toward San Felipe, hooked a right before the yellow light turned red, and drove off.

Sitting at the light at Post Oak Lane, I was a few blocks from Loretta's house, but she wasn't at home. I had to make it to St. Joseph's Pharmacy before her lunch break.

I parked and texted Loretta: i'm outside whenever you're ready baby.

Waiting for her was my pleasure. I'd stay out here until sunset, if I had to, just to see her again. I wished Loretta could take the rest of the day off, let her daughter stay with her mom or Raynard tonight, and then drive down to Port Arthur with me.

*Hot damn! Here she comes!* I almost peed in my jeans. Blinking my eyes, I turned on my sexy look that Loretta loved. I hopped out, ran around to the passenger side, and opened the door for her.

I stood with open arms. "Can I get a hug?"

She got inside and closed the door. That was okay. At least I was having lunch with her.

"Anywhere you want to go," I said, starting my engine.

"Somewhere close. I don't have time for lunch. Coffee is better," she said.

Deepening my scratchy voice, I said, "Okay, baby." I wanted to take her someplace nice and dine outside. The sun was shining to a romantic eighty degrees, but the service would take too long for her.

"Granville, I'm not your baby."

"Okay, dear."

"Let me make myself clear. I'm not interested in being with you, but if you're open to it," she said, handing me a business card, "my friend is interested in you. And wipe the sweat from over your upper lip."

I kept both hands on the wheel. Too pissed off to look at her, or give a damn about my lip, I stared ahead.

She dropped the card in the cup holder. "Keep an open mind. She's from Port Arthur and she's not exactly a stranger to you."

I had an admirer. Wow, that made me feel good, but I was no fool. Loretta was testing me to see if I was faithful to her. *Damn!* I should've gotten her engagement ring. She'd get it later.

"I only have eyes for you, dear," I said, driving toward the freeway.

"Where are we going?" Loretta asked.

I blasted one of my favorite country songs by Brad Paisley, then entered onto I-45N. I sang along with him. I had to give Loretta all my love. Didn't know what I'd do if she left me. Was she cheating on me? The thought of Loretta giving my stuff to another man angered me.

"Are you fucking crazy? Take me back to work!" Loretta yelled.

Ignoring her, I merged onto I-10E, driving seventy miles an hour.

"Let me out of here!" Loretta screamed. *"Stooooooop!"*

Checking my rearview mirror — the car behind me was a safe distance — I slammed on my brakes. Her body hit the seat, then flung forward. Almost hitting her head on the dashboard, she grabbed the door handle. I plunged the accelerator and watched the back of her head hit the headrest. The buckle snapped into place, pinning her to the seat. She was lucky that her air bag hadn't exploded.

She pulled out her cell phone, pressed a few buttons, then yelled, "Tisha! Help me!

I've been kidnapped! Granville —"

The face of a dark-skinned woman, with a spiky-looking Afro, appeared on Loretta's phone. Her teeth were nice and white. I wondered if that was the woman who had the hots for me.

"Hi, Tisha. You want to go out with me?" I asked, staring at Loretta's phone.

"You fucking idiot! I'd date a dog first! Take my girl back to —"

"Is that what you think I am? A dog?" I stomped the brakes and plunged the accelerator again. Loretta's body jerked once more. "We can do this until I run out of gas, and I'm on full," I said. "Fuck that bitch! Hang up the damn phone, Loretta. Better yet, turn it off!"

Loretta was more precious when she was vulnerable. I hated yelling at her. "I'm sorry, baby. It's just that you make me this way. If you'd do things my way, let me be the man, we wouldn't have to go through this. Tisha is pretty, but I don't want her. You're mine. To make this up to you, I'm taking you to visit my mom. You have to address her as 'Mrs. Washington,' or she'll go off on you. And be nice to my mom. . . . Oh, you can call your job and let them know you won't be back in."

Loretta was speechless. Tears streamed

73

down her chocolate cheeks, rolled over her raspberry lip gloss. She had clamped her phone between her thighs; she pulled it out and tucked it in her bra.

I laughed. "Lighten up. I'll have you home tonight, but you should have Raynard pick up Raynell."

An hour and a half later, we were on Highway 69, passing Target, Sears, Dillard's, Mall 10 Theatre, and JCPenney in Port Arthur. They'd put all the fancy stores and built the new residential neighborhoods as far away as possible from the refineries. The upscale part of town was populated with mostly white families and a few blacks.

We passed by Port Arthur Fire Station No. 1, where my man Jay Fountain was the battalion chief and headed down Gulfway Drive toward the black side of town. There wasn't a café or restaurant or any establishment where a person could sit his ass in a seat and be served a hot meal in my hood. Growing up, we had a few businesses on Memorial Boulevard. Not anymore. Some people in the hood without transportation paid twelve dollars for a loaf of bread off trucks and vans from Mexicans because the nearest grocery store was too far away.

"Loretta, all those boarded-up buildings on both sides of the street used to make lots of money. This is all abandoned now, except for Lamar State College. I almost went to college there. Oh, and City Limits. We'll drive by there in a minute."

"You're sick" was all she said.

"Yes, dear." I drove to the end of Memorial to Procter Street. "I love you."

Loretta unfastened her seat belt, opened the door, and got out. She ran across the street to the Port Arthur Transit Terminal. I was nice enough to give her a head start before following her.

I laughed, watching her tug on the doors. That transit station was closed. But I was still a gentleman and opened her car door.

"You might as well get in. Do you see any cars or buses back here?"

Reluctantly she got in and turned on her cell. I didn't care if she called Tisha again, because she was too far away to get rescued. She should thank me for letting her get back in my truck. I was her hero.

"Loretta, we're going to be okay. Let's go visit Mom and then I'll take you home." I looked in my lap; then I told her, "Baby, I got a woody. Hard wood. Hard enough to hammer you right now." I flicked my eyebrows.

Loretta held the phone to her ear. "Tisha, get Raynell, then come get me. This fool brought me all the way to Port Arthur. Call the police and tell them I've been kid—"

I snatched her phone and stared at her girlfriend. *I've got to get one of these. This is so cool.*

"You don't want to do that, Tisha," I said, then ended the call. "I'll hold on to this for you. . . . Now, where was I? Oh yeah. This is New St. John Missionary Baptist Church. My mom goes there sometimes, when she doesn't feel like going to church across town. You hungry? Did I tell you that we don't have a single restaurant, café, or a decent place to eat or shop for clothes on the black side? What we do have," I said, driving down Gulfway, across Terminal Road, to the other side of the tracks, "is we have refineries galore!" I lowered the windows, placed her phone in the cup holder, and then inhaled deeply. "Ah!"

Loretta started choking. "Put the windows back up!" She covered her nose and mouth.

"It smells great. I grew up on these fumes. You get used to it after a while."

"Please," she pleaded, acting like she was going to die if I didn't.

"All right," I said, raising the windows. "Let's go see Moms."

Beaux's car was in the driveway. I parked on the lawn in front of my mom's white

76

wooden-plank house, with the white porch and matching wood rails.

"Behave," I told Loretta as I opened her door.

She rushed into my mom's house and locked me out. I stood on the porch, staring through the screen, as she screamed, "He kidnapped me! And I swear if I don't make it back to Houston immediately, I'm going to have his crazy ass arrested!"

When she was dialing a number from her phone, I knew I shouldn't have put it in the cup holder.

"Hello, police! I've been kid—"

Beaux took Loretta's phone.

"Open the door, Moms! Let me in! Bro, let me in."

Beaux opened the door; then he told Loretta, "Let's go. I'm taking you home."

"You can't do that with my wo—"

Beaux hit me under my chin with his right fist. Didn't take much for us to brawl. I stumbled, but hit his ass back with my left. He staggered; then he fell to the floor.

"Granville and Beaux, stop it. Granville," Mom said, "you can't keep dragging these lil girls who don't deserve you to my house. Get her out of here, Beaux. Granville, sit. I'll fix you something to eat, honey."

"Yes, Mama," I said, watching my brother walk out the door with my woman.

# CHAPTER 5
## MADISON

I was cruising along Kirby Drive in my lustful red convertible, with the retractable hard top down, moaning the lyrics to Janet Jackson's "Any Time, Any Place."

Soon as the light turned green, I slid my sunglasses to the tip of my nose, eyed the guy in the Mustang next to me, then gunned my engine, challenging him to a drag race. He laughed, then shook his head.

Exactly what I thought. He couldn't handle this ride. The sauciness of my seven-speed Ferrari 458 Spider fit me to a tee. Fast. Curvaceous. Jaw-dropping. Dangerous. Powerful. And dare I say, sensuous. We were both in a class reserved exclusively for those who could afford to be bold and beautiful. My whip was a gift from my main man, my dad. He'd spoiled me all of my life and set the bar for men who courted me. A broke man could never be my man.

There were few things money couldn't

buy, but pussy wasn't one of them. My lady lips puckered thinking about my guy. He'd left the office early just for me and I'd done the same for him. Before the break of dawn, I was going to sex him real good. What most women, including my girlfriends, didn't understand, it wasn't exclusively about the punany. It was also about how a woman presented what was between her legs.

My Aphrodite was sweet, with soft, light brown hair. She was everything the name I'd given her represented: love, beauty, desire, and fertility. My inner lips were lady-like and didn't hang beyond my outer lips. My clit was cute as a button and hid under my hood until I got superexcited and en-gorged. Then it swelled to the size of a Tic Tac. I had the kind of goodies men couldn't wait to feast upon. She was pink and tasted delicious.

My special concoction of a teaspoon of white-chocolate extract, two ounces of melted pure shea butter, and a tablespoon of virgin olive oil whipped until creamy, then stored in a jar at room temperature, was my secret recipe for being more savory than Crave Cupcakes.

A call from Tisha registered on my car monitor, interrupting my racing libido. I pressed the answer button on my steering wheel.

"What's up, sexy lady?"

"Where are you?" Tisha's pitch was high, but she was easily excitable and a borderline pessimist, so I instantly discounted her sense of urgency. In elementary school I used to call her "Chicken Little" because every other day her world was falling apart.

"I'm about to pull up in the driveway at Roosevelt's place," I said. There was a smile on my face that I was sure resonated through her receiver.

"Don't get out of your car. I need you to ride with me right now. That asshole Granville kidnapped Loretta and took her to Port Arthur."

"Not my problem," I sang; then I said, "Calm down. Call Loretta and tell her to call my mother. She's down there visiting my grandfather. My mom will give her a ride back."

My grandfather was diagnosed a year ago with stomach cancer. He went under the knife, did radiation and chemotherapy. Mom had begged him to live with her, but he'd refused, telling her, "I was born in Port Arthur, and I'm going to die in Port Arthur."

"Nothing is ever your damn problem.

81

That saying was cute in grade school and college, but it's old now, wouldn't you agree? Besides, what kind of friend are you? You've taken your selfishness to a new plateau. If that idiot kills Loretta, it'll be your fault. You know what. Forget I asked you. I'll go by myself."

I pulled over, giving our conversation time to end before I arrived at my destination. I thought about what my daddy had told me: "Get the facts first. Law applies to every aspect of life, Madison. If you're going to run our family business, you don't have to practice, but you must understand the legal ramifications of the decisions you make."

Somehow I doubted Granville knew if what he'd done was against the law. Neither did I. Unless he showed up at Loretta's job, put a gun to her head, dragged her by the hair, and locked her in his car against her will, I couldn't get involved or fire him for taking my girlfriend on a trip to Port Arthur.

"Tisha, Loretta is generally the calm one, you're the one who always panics first, and I keep it one hundred by balancing the two of you, which makes me a true friend. But what you're saying is nonsense. I'm not about to spend the next four hours on the road, when my mama is already there.

Listen, Tisha. That's the way love goes when you either pick the wrong man or when you can't control your man. You've been with Darryl, off and on, since the ninth grade, and it took twenty years for him to marry you. You divorced a millionaire and you ended up paying for your second wedding. And I paid for your reception. I'm trying to mind my own business, but while we're talking about shiftless men, you need to stop supporting Darryl's broke ass. He needs to get off of unemployment. But knowing him, I'm sure he's going to suck up all ninety-nine payments, then complain about how no one will hire him. Damn, the least he could've done was buy you a bigger ring, since that was *all* he paid for. If he paid for that."

Tisha snapped back, "I love Darryl, and having him in my life is more important than a piece of jewelry. Colin Powell's wife didn't need a ring, and I don't *need* one either. What does it really symbolize — how much money a man has?"

*Not if the chick buys the ring and the groom. Hell, Darryl should've come two for the price of one, with his cheap behind. Tisha should have another man in her bed and Darryl living in the basement, backyard, some damn where since he's barely at home anyway. But no.*

83

*She voluntarily opened her legs for him and let him give her his lame-ass dick. Ain't that much love in my heart for no trifling-ass man.*

I glanced at the diamond Roosevelt put on my finger — my ninth one — thinking they're all larger than my girlfriend's. Hopefully, her marriage would last longer than Loretta's relationship with Granville.

I replied, "But you, my love, did not marry Colin. You've got dead-beat Darryl. And if you love him so much, why didn't you change your and your children's name from Thomas to Jefferson?"

"Are you serious?" Tisha asked.

"Dead," was all I replied as I merged into traffic onto Allen Parkway.

"You know he's not my boys' biological father."

"Exactly. Keep it that way. Don't have any kids for him." I'd never divorce a millionaire and marry a broke man. Tisha was lucky, for now. Her house was paid for and she could live off of the $20,000 a month from her ex. But what was she going to do if her ex stopped paying alimony and Darryl started cashing in her investments? What was the point of putting a cart in front of a horse? So she could carry them both on her back? Wouldn't be me. Not in this or any other lifetime.

"Cool," Tisha said. "I swear, all you people from Port Arthur are touched in the head. Must be the chemicals in the water. I can't deal with you now. I wish he would've kidnapped you instead of Loretta. To be continued."

"Never that." I was on the brink of being annoyed, until I remembered to ask, "Where's Raynell?"

"Not that you care, but she's upstairs with my kids. Her nanny dropped her off at my house after school. Loretta doesn't want Raynard to know about this, so keep your mouth shut. And I hope you're not telling all our business to your latest fiancé."

What business? How Loretta's baby was born out of wedlock? I'm a grown-ass woman and I reserved the right to disclose whatever with whomever. Don't want your business in the street? Keep it in your mouth.

Exhaling, I said, "Look, I wouldn't have asked about my goddaughter if I didn't care. But Loretta made her bed — letting her sleep in it overnight won't kill her. I've got plans for and with my man tonight," I said, handing my keys to the valet attendant.

"Hold on, Madison. It's Loretta."

"Make it quick, Tisha. I've got things to do."

85

The spacious lobby at the Royalton was better than most hotels' and the condo buildings' in Houston. As soon as I entered, the concierge recognized me and phoned Roosevelt. I nodded at him, then smiled as he said, "Yes, Mr. DuBois, Ms. Tyler is here to see you." Moments later the huge frosted double doors parted. I sashayed in, passing by the climate-controlled wine cellar for the homeowners.

Since I was still on hold with Tisha, I decided not to get on the elevator, knowing the call would drop before I made it to the thirty-second floor. I went into the recreational room, got a cup from the complimentary concession area, filled it with Sprite from the fountain, then helped myself to a box of fresh popcorn from the free-standing red popper machine.

The balls were neatly racked on the pool table. The ten-person movie theater was empty. Glancing out at the oval-shaped infinity swimming pool and adjoining Jacuzzi, I could sell my eight-bedroom, ten-bathroom house and comfortably live here. The fitness center had all the equipment, including a steam sauna, that I needed to keep my body slim and tight.

"Madison?"

"Calm down. I'm still here," I said, pouring out the rest of my soda.

"By the grace of God, she's okay. She's riding with Beaux. She should be home in an hour. She wants us to meet her at her place when she gets in."

So I could sit around and listen to her complain about how horrible her day was? I hated hearing anyone whine about their mistakes. "Text me when she makes it home. Roosevelt has an early flight with the team, so I'll stop in at Loretta's in the morning before she goes to work. Bye, girl."

"But —"

I ended the call and made my way to my man's 5,000-square-foot penthouse. The queen portrait in his foyer was all about me. He'd mentioned something about buying it 'cause it reminded him of his mom, but I was the woman of his domain — and the only household his mother was running was hers. She could make it easy on herself by stopping her judging of me, or she could resist and make it hard on herself. Either way she'd learn that I was the number one woman in Roosevelt's life.

"Hey, honey," I said, kissing him.

Roosevelt wrapped his strong arms around my slim waist. Slid his tongue in my minty-fresh mouth, then passionately sucked my lips.

"What took you so long, babe?"

*Nothing worth mentioning.*

"It sure smells good in here. What did your chef prepare for us?" I asked, ignoring his question.

He smiled. His teeth were bright, and his lips were slightly darker than his caramel tone. I rubbed his head. His haircut was professional, nothing fancy. It was trimmed even and close to his head, with an immaculate lining all the way around.

"Actually, I cooked for you," he said, then stared at me. "You okay, baby?"

"I'm fine. It's just Tisha. You know how dramatic I've told you she can be."

"Complaining about Darryl again?"

Roosevelt was the perfect height — six feet two inches — and just the right weight, 190 pounds. He still lifted weights every day to maintain his washboard abs.

"Surprisingly, no. Not this time. I'm hungry and starving." I roared, then fingered his dick. "I've got plans for Tiger." That was my nickname for his manhood.

"Aphrodite, that's my gurl." He kissed two fingertips, placed them on my clit, and slowly slid upward.

"Do that again and we might have to skip dinner."

"I've got something special for her too.

But we are going to eat first, and back to Tisha. If it's not her husband, then what happened this time?" he asked, taking a Pyrex dish out of the oven. "Seafood casserole, just the way you like it."

A man of Roosevelt's caliber should have a woman catering to him. But I trained each of my men to do for me what they expected me to do for them.

"It's nothing serious. Loretta was allegedly kidnapped by Granville."

Fumbling the glassware, he recovered the dish nicely; then he placed it on the cooling rack.

*What the hell?*

"She's okay. I'll check on her in the morning."

Roosevelt set the oven mitt on the counter, detached his cell phone from the charger, then pressed a few buttons.

"Loretta, you all right? Madison just told me something about that guy you told me about taking you against your will."

I stood in the middle of the kitchen and watched my man pace the floor, behaving as if my girlfriend were his.

Turning his back to me, he asked, "You need me to come get you?" Then he paused. "You're sure? Madison and I can come by . . . all right. Then close your eyes," he said. "Lord, thank you for keeping Loretta safe. This could've been a tragedy, but praise Your name it wasn't. I pray You restore Loretta's peace of mind and continue to watch over and protect her. In Jesus' name, amen."

"What the fuck was that?" I asked, staring at Roosevelt's back. "End the damn conversation, right now."

He turned to me. "Madison, please don't. Loretta is our friend. Loretta, I'll check on you in the morning before I leave. If you need me before then, don't hesitate," he said, then ended the call.

"Oh, hell no, Roosevelt. She is not *our* friend, and why do *you* have Loretta's number, and what's this offering to go get her and praying with her over the phone?"

Calmly he answered, "I'll explain over dinner"; then he prepared our plates. "Have a seat, baby."

I didn't want to be one of those females who ruined a positive moment by bitching all night, so I took a few deep breaths, loosened my jaws, and relaxed my shoulders. The dining table had a new black-and-cobalt tablecloth, three vanilla-scented candles were the centerpiece, and his place setting was next to mine. What happened to the things I'd decorated his dining room with?

I sat in my chair and stared out the window at the full moon. We'd never argued over the one year we'd been together, and I didn't want our first fight to be over Loretta.

"I like the new look," I lied.

"Thanks. It's feng shui. I'm learning to create peaceful energy by changing a few things. I might get me an altar too."

"Too?" I said shifting in my seat.

Roosevelt filled our flutes with champagne and then put our plates on the silver mats. The scent of herbs, spices, and marinated vegetables reminded me I hadn't eaten today. I wasn't trying to lose weight, but the constant churning in my stomach could make me drop ten pounds in a week if it didn't stop. I was no fool. I knew exactly where he'd gotten his new ideas. Right now, I didn't have an appetite for food or for Roosevelt.

He sat beside me and held my hand. "Lord, bless this food before us and allow it to nourish us to do Your will. In Jesus' name, amen."

I released his hand. "Roosevelt, let's not pretend that what just happened didn't. I demand to know. How did you get, and why

91

do you have, Loretta's number?"

Lifting his glass, he said, "A toast to the only woman I love. Madison, you are my everything. You complete me. I'd be crazy to cheat on you."

That was the way it was supposed to be, but he hadn't answered the question. Besides, who said anything about cheating?

"I'm listening."

His jaws clenched. "Okay," he relented. "I went to Loretta's house to ask her a few questions about you."

I tossed my napkin on the table. "About me?" The flame ignited the tip. I dipped it in my glass of ice water.

Roosevelt didn't move; he didn't try to help me put out what could've burned his condo down if neither one of us would've done anything. The same could happen to our engagement if I ignored his association with *my* friend.

"I've walked through fire with gasoline drawers on, but never in a relationship. I'm warning you, Madison, don't do this. The reason I put a ring on your finger is because you're drama free. I have a game in a few days and I've got to make sure *everything* is in order for my team."

"Well, it's not in order with your woman, and it won't be if you don't tell me the real reason why you went to her house and why you called her tonight."

"I want to trust you fully, but I've got to be sure that we're not going to end up in divorce court or have the media following us with bad press. I know you have your own money, but —"

"But what? You don't think I have more money than you, or you think I'm marrying you for your money? My family has built an empire —"

"Damn it, Madison!" he yelled. "This isn't about money!"

I was not backing down. He was wrong.

"So you go to her, instead of coming to me! Why?"

"Yes, I did" was all he said.

"What did she tell you? And don't leave out anything."

"She said I should ask you."

Really? Was that all? I knew Loretta didn't want me to marry Roosevelt, so she had to have told him something bad about me. This wasn't adding up.

"She's right. We have to keep other people out of our affairs, including Loretta and your mom."

I'd deal with Loretta in the morning, but now I needed to have sex with my fiancé before he got on and off that plane with groupies nearly half my age trying to suck his dick. I was mad, but I was never too upset to please my man.

A relationship with great sex could survive most heated conversations, but one with bad sex made every negative situation worse because there was no outlet for one's frustrations.

Roosevelt kissed my cheek. "When I get back, we're going to introduce my brother to Loretta."

"Are you serious? As in a double date?"

"Think about it like this. If she's dating Chaz, you don't have to worry about my friendship with her."

*Friendship, my ass.*

"Thanks, baby, for cooking. That was thoughtful of you," I said, kissing him on the lips. "And no worries about your calling Loretta. I forgive you."

*Just don't let it happen again.*

I ate a small bite of shrimp, crabmeat, scallop, and lobster. The onions, cheddar, and celery were mixed to perfection.

"Oh, this is *soooo* delicious. I'm about to have an orgasm in my mouth."

I gave my man a soft peck on his lips to encourage him to make better decisions.

He backed away from me.

"Don't take my love for you as a weakness. It's my strength that allows me to be vulnerable with you. I don't need your forgiveness, Madison. I didn't do anything wrong. If you want a boy, take off my ring, put it on the table, and leave."

*Okay, I can handle this.*

I could've called his bluff, taken off his diamond, and had him begging me to come back before I made it to the door.

*Nah, I have something else in store for you.*

I knew what guys were thinking before they finished formulating their thoughts. He was confirming his masculinity. I had to let him keep that in tact. Eventually I'd convince him not to befriend my friend. For now, for peace sake, I'd have to make him believe my idea was his. It was time to shift gears.

"Baby, why don't you go shower while I clean up the kitchen."

Giving Roosevelt time to regroup from my mild interrogation was wise. I stored the food in the refrigerator, even though I knew that neither of us would eat it. But the casserole was too tasty to trash and doing so would be an insult. His housekeeper could toss it tomorrow after we'd left.

I went into his bedroom. He was still in the shower. I turned down the covers, lit a sandalwood candle, got a glass of cognac for him, poured another champagne for myself, and then dimmed the lights. Surfing through his iPod, I selected his sexy jazz saxophone playlist. The sound and the shape of that horn made me want to do nasty things — some of which were unimaginable to other women.

I went into the bathroom, took his towel, and finished drying his body. Seductively I said, "Get real comfortable, baby. I'm going to freshen up for you."

All my toiletries were on my side of his vanity. I showered, then massaged my body with shea butter. Afterward, I lightly coated Aphrodite with her special-flavored concoction. While the oils soaked into my skin, I flossed and brushed my teeth. I moisturized my face and hair; then I dabbed perfume in the right places. No need for clothes, I had work to do.

Standing at the foot of his customized larger than king-size bed, I peeled away the covers. I drizzled hot massage oil from the candle onto his feet and legs. My hands caressed the crevices of his crotch then slid all the way down to his toes.

"Ah, baby," he moaned. "Yes."

This was my first time doing what I was about to do to him. I slid my breasts over his chest to his erection, over his knees to his ankles. My fingers glided up both legs, to his hip, then back down to his feet. I opened my mouth, wrapped my lips around his big toe, and then passionately sucked.

"Ah, fuck," he whispered.

A whisper was cool, but that wasn't my ultimate goal. I maneuvered my hands up to his pelvis, and then I crawled between his legs. I lifted his knees in the air. His feet were flat against the mattress, but not for long.

Parting his thighs, I tilted his pelvis; then held his ass in the palms of my hands. I gently pressed my lips against his asshole.

"Damn . . ." He exhaled. "Baby, baby." He gripped, then hugged a pillow to his chest.

I circled the tip of my tongue on the outer part of his rectum, kissed him, licked over his perineum, up to his balls, up his hard shaft, then slowly sucked his head. A little of my saliva and his precum escaped for lubrication. Moving my hands from underneath his butt, I firmly gripped his dick and eased him in as far as I could.

His ass lifted higher. "I love you, Madison."

*I know you do, baby.*

Making my way back to his asshole, I passionately sucked it. This time he turned sideways, like he was a wide receiver positioning himself for the perfect play. I followed him, and stayed with him. He started stroking his dick.

I licked his ass for a while longer, touched his hand, and then softly said, "I've got you, baby. Let go."

Easing him in and out of my mouth from the back of my throat to the edge of my lips, I stroked his dick.

He buried his face in the pillow. "Madison!"

"Cum for me, baby."

Waves of semen flooded my mouth. I swallowed each one until his dick stopped throbbing. I held his dick in my mouth for a moment; I waited until his shaft softened.

"That was amazing," he said.

Curling next to Roosevelt, I replied, "No, you are amazing."

I had more mind-blowing sex secrets, but I'd reserve those for emergency situations. In the morning he was going to hit this pussy raw — until all his newly generated seeds spilled inside me.

# CHAPTER 6
## LORETTA

There wasn't a moment when I felt like Granville was going to kill me, but his kidnapping me was the first time I'd feared for my life. Domestic altercations didn't always start off violently. An argument could fuel anger, which caused yelling; and when a man believed he wasn't in control of his woman, he could easily lay an open hand across her face. If that didn't make her obey him, he was capable of curling his fingers into fists and punching her upside the head. I'd never been that woman, and I planned on keeping it that way.

"That's my house right there," I said, pointing from the passenger seat. On the drive back, I had texted Tisha: I'm almost home. Bring my keys and if you have it a hundred dollars.

Beaux pulled into the driveway and turned off his engine. "Wow! You live here by yourself?" he asked, staring up at the second story. "What in the world did you see in my brother?"

Wondering the same thing, I opened my car door and then replied, "Thanks for bringing me home." I wanted to pay him for his time, but my purse was in my locker at work.

"Mommy!" Raynell called out, running toward me. "You're home!" She jumped into my arms and hugged my neck, reacting as though she hadn't seen me in days.

Children derived comfort from consistency. Parents got peace of mind knowing their kids were safe. I didn't know what I'd do without my girlfriends. I said a silent prayer, *Thank you, Jesus, for watching over us.*

"Mommy, who's that man?"

I reminded my daughter, "It's not polite to point at people."

Tisha chimed in, "Gurl, stop being nosy."

"My daddy says I'm 'inquisitive.' "

I chuckled. Thanks to Raynard, Raynell had the largest vocabulary in her first-grade class. My baby was right. We were teaching her to be a thinker and to inquire about what she didn't understand or wanted to know. Raynard might never become my husband, but we did agree on what was in Raynell's best interest. Hopefully, she'd make better relationship choices than her mother did.

The look in Tisha's eyes said she was glad I was home. "This was all I had on me," she said, handing me fifty. "I'll take Raynell inside and put her to bed. She's already taken her bath."

My eyes began to water as I watched Tisha unlock my front door, with my precious daughter by her side.

"Here," I said, handing Beaux the money.

He gently pushed my hand away. "That's not necessary. I apologize on behalf of my idiot brother. You're a really nice woman and he doesn't deserve you. What I can't understand is why come he keeps meeting the good ones."

His comment made me think about Madison's nine engagement rings to my zero.

"Good night, Beaux."

"Is it okay if I keep in touch? Maybe take you out?" he asked.

If it was true that people from Port Arthur married their relatives, I guess brothers sharing women was more common.

"I'm flattered, but it's not okay." I walked inside and closed my door.

Tisha was seated on the sofa. Two flutes filled with champagne were on the coffee table. She handed me one. "I figured you'd need this."

I kicked off my shoes. Exhaling, I took a gulp and then sat next to Tisha.

"He's a fucking moron. Never in my life have I met a man that insane."

"When did you first realize something wasn't right with him?"

Huh? Frowning, I thought about her question for a moment, then said, "I think it was the day I told him I didn't want to see him anymore."

"The red flags had to be there before that. What made you decide you didn't want to see him again?"

Pressing the glass against my lips, I stared at my girlfriend. "He was nice, always wanted to take me out and buy me gifts."

Winding her hand in a circle, Tisha motioned for me to continue.

"He was annoying. Talked too much. Was always gawking over me. That silly gaze wasn't sexy. He was always talking about having a woody, as if his dick defined him. I hated that. He did have a big one and all, but that slobbering in my mouth when we kissed was disgusting. And him buying me an engagement ring, as bad as I want one, made no damn sense."

"A what? After three weeks of going out?"

"You heard me right." I still didn't have a

ring on my finger, but officially I'd been proposed to once.

"Oh yeah! It's a good thing you left his ass alone. But you know he's not done, right?"

"Well, I am. Besides, I made Madison a bet that she couldn't tame Granville, and you know how competitive she is. She accepted the challenge."

Tisha said, "As upset as I am with Madison for not supporting you on this one, I still wouldn't wish anything bad on her. You've got to cancel the bet."

"I can do that, but I already gave Granville her business card and told him she wanted to go out with him. If I call him to call it off, he'll think I want him back."

"What the hell are you doing? This isn't a game. That man is dangerous."

*True. But I didn't know then what I know now.*

I finished my drink quietly. "Reasoning with Madison should be easy, once I give her details about what happened today."

Tisha stood and placed her empty glass on the coaster. "I've got to go put my two to bed. I'll check on you in the morning. Get some rest," she said, then left.

Pouring a second glass of bubbly, I wondered what I'd do different if Chicago introduced me to Chaz. Was there something wrong with how I dealt with men? Did Raynard ever truly love me? I was thirty-five, a single mom, and forget not having a husband — I didn't even have a man.

"I don't want to keep living like this, God. I don't. Give me back Raynard. Give me Chaz. Give me a man who loves me for me, so I can love him!" I cried out. "I'm not desperate, but, Lord, I'm tired of being lonely."

I removed my clothes, stretched out on the sofa, and closed my eyes.

"Mommy, wake up."

"Huh, baby? What?" Opening my eyes, I felt Raynell's small hand on my shoulder. Her silk scarf was tied over her head. I removed it. I hadn't noticed last night, but I was glad that Tisha had combed her hair.

"What time is it?" I asked, picking up my phone from the coffee table. "Seven o'clock. Oh no. Let's get you dressed for school, princess."

"I can dress myself," Raynell said, running upstairs to her room.

Following her to the second floor, I went to my bedroom. I put my phone on the charger, then went to the bathroom. I sat on the toilet and stared at the floor. Yesterday Granville freaked me out. But what

104

really made me trip this morning was my girl. I couldn't believe Madison wasn't willing to drive to Port Arthur to pick me up under the circumstances. I wasn't the type of needy friend to impose upon my girls. I wasn't dramatic like Tisha. Anger filled my spirit. I started praying that Madison got hers one day.

Wiping myself dry, I washed my hands, face, brushed my teeth, then headed to relieve my stress. Kneeling at the altar, I lit three candles. I closed my eyes and cleared my mind. I gave thanks for Tisha, Chicago, and Beaux.

I prayed for Madison, wondering if I hadn't met her in kindergarten, would we be friends? Did time make a person your friend?

I could've died yesterday. I asked that Granville never come near me again; then I blew out the flames.

I went to Raynell's bedroom. "You look beautiful, lil mama."

Thank God for uniforms. The only deviation was short or long sleeves, skirt or pants, cardigan or pullover. The doorbell rang.

I gave Raynell a big hug, then said, "That's your nanny. Let's go."

Opening the door, I was surprised to see Madison.

"Hey, Godmommy," Raynell said, giving Madison a big hug. "Bye, Mommy. I love you." Raynell grabbed Madison's hand. "Let's go."

"Whoa," Madison answered. Just as she explained, "I'm not taking you to school today, Miss Princess," Raynell's nanny drove into the driveway.

I kissed my baby, gave her a tight squeeze, and helped her into the car. "I love you. See you this evening," I said, then told the nanny, "Stop at McDonald's and get her a fruit snack box for breakfast."

Thankful that Raynard had insisted I have a nanny to pick up and drop off Raynell from school, take my baby to her house after school, help with homework, and bring her home, I walked inside, leaving the door open for Madison. She could choose to walk in or leave, but there was no invitation on my part.

"Like that, Loretta?" Madison said, following me. She closed the door, then plopped into the purple chair.

I continued upstairs to my bedroom and selected my basic black slacks and black top from the walk-in closet. My work clothes were even more uniform than Raynell's. That was good and bad. Sometimes I'd like to dress sexy like Madison and put on a pair of stilettos, so I didn't have to keep a change of happy-hour clothes in my travel bag in the trunk of my car. Comfort was more important, though, and flats were necessary for me to briskly move around the pharmacy while standing on my feet for eight, sometimes ten, hours a day.

Madison stood in my doorway. I admired her red pencil skirt, soft cream-colored sleeveless blouse, with a pretty scoop neckline. Her platinum blond hair was so short she could barely pinch it with her nails, but the zigzag style was fitting and ultrafeminine. Maybe I should consider cutting and coloring mine. Try something edgy instead of sporting a chestnut ponytail five days a week.

"Loretta, stop avoiding me."

I put on my pants, shirt, and shoes. I sat at my vanity and put on my raspberry lipstick.

"Fine, Loretta. I just came to tell you I'd appreciate your not talking to my fiancé when I'm not around. Friend or not, you've got to know that's inappropriate behavior."

What was she going to do? Keep her man from talking to every woman? If I were truly her friend, she should trust me with befriending her man.

My cell phone rang. I went to my nightstand, checked the caller ID. If Madison weren't being such a bitch, I would've ignored the call. I picked it up and answered, "Hi, Chicago."

"I was worried about you," he said in a concerned tone.

Looking at my girlfriend, I said, "I'm fine. I'm getting ready for work."

"I hope you don't mind me calling so early, but I wanted to make sure you were okay."

"I'm good. Thanks for checking on me. I've gotta go. Have a nice day and get that *W*. I'll be rooting for you. Bye." A quick prayer with him would've made my day, more so than pissing off Madison, but it wasn't worth continuing the conversation in front of her face.

I knew Madison well. Another minute on the phone and she would've said something loud enough for him to hear. Her face was redder than her skirt. Passing by Madison, I guess she called herself doing to me what I'd done to her at Tisha's reception. She firmly grabbed my biceps.

"Loretta, you don't want to play with me, girlfriend."

"Don't you have a man to conquer," I told her. "The one who almost killed me." Soon as I'd said that, I wished I hadn't. Christians were supposed to lead by example, and I never derived pleasure from another person's pain.

"As a favor to you, I'm going to show you how a real beauty handles a beast. I'll have him eating out of my hand. And don't worry. He'll never kidnap me."

"I don't recommend you get involved with Granville. He's not stable. Although I don't believe you deserve Roosevelt, stick with him. He's a great man."

Madison laughed. "I guess you would know that, wouldn't you, since you've got my man calling you," she said, tossing my arm into my side. "Don't play with me, Loretta. I'm warning you. Discontinue all communication with Roosevelt, as of this second."

For the first time I saw insecurity in Madison's eyes. She wasn't worried about my being attracted to her man; it was worse than that. She thought her man liked me. All during our friendship she felt she was so irresistible that every man wanted her, including Tisha's ex-husband and Darryl. A smirk crossed my face.

I felt in control of something Madison couldn't do anything about. If she could've stopped her precious Roosevelt from calling me, my phone wouldn't have rung. Maybe I really could stop him from marrying her.

"I've got to go to work," I said, escorting Madison out of my house.

"And I've got work to do. I'll let you know how it goes with Granville."

What was Madison trying to prove? She had the potential to take another one of Houston's most eligible bachelors off the market. She'd be foolish to spread her legs for another man. I followed her to the front door of her house. If I were Chicago's fiancée, I'd be faithful to him forever.

"Wait, Madison. As much as I'm hurt about your not caring enough to come get me, I can't let you go through with our bet. Granville really has some sort of mental problem. The bet is off."

She waved her pointing finger in front of my face. "So you can befriend my man, but I can't prove I'm a better woman than you?" She opened her front door and told me, "Too late. The bet is on." Then she closed it in a cute kind of way, sticking her ass out.

What made her so competitive? At this point all I could do was pray for her, but I wasn't going to stop being her friend, nor was I going to ruin her engagement. She'd been competitive over men since all of us started having boyfriends in junior high.

I walked back next door to my house, got

110

in my BMW, and headed to work. Turning right on Post Oak Lane, I glanced in my rearview mirror and saw a Ford emblem on the grille.

My heart started beating fast. The black four-door Super Duty was inches away and Granville was in it. I said aloud, "Okay, he does work at the mixed-use construction site at San Felipe," which was at the next light. I kept my eye on him. Got in the turn lane.

He merged behind me. I turned and kept driving. He should've made a right at Post Oak Road; instead he followed me onto 610-South.

Rather than going to work, I merged onto I-10 East, called in sick, and continued to the District Attorney's Family Criminal Law Division to file a protective order. I parked at a meter, figuring he wouldn't be stupid enough to pursue me.

"Loretta, I apologize. Please don't do this, dear," Granville said, walking two steps behind me.

I ran down Caroline, in front of the Harris County Civil Courthouse. I prayed, *Jesus, please make this man stop stalking me.* Not waiting for the walk sign, I didn't see the cars coming. The first car missed me. I jumped on the curb and started sprinting toward the double doors.

*"Ow!"*

I turned to see Granville's body on top of a car. He fell in the street, got up, and stood on the sidewalk yelling, "Loretta!"

Entering the building, I approached a policeman standing in the lobby. "Please, Officer. Help me. There's a man outside and he chased me here. I'm afraid for my life."

"Calm down," the officer said. "You're in a safe place."

"But if you go outside, you can arrest him. Please! I'm begging you." Tears of fear streamed down my cheeks. I clung to the officer's shirt. My arms and legs trembled uncontrollably.

"I take it you came here to get a protective order against him. Second floor," he said, pointing to the elevators. "And don't be like the other women who come here, waste everybody's time, then end up taking him back."

My stomach churned with disappointment. I wanted to throw up on his uniform. Was he serious?

I placed my purse on the conveyor, cleared security, and went to the second floor. "I need to file a protective order," I said to the clerk, who was sitting behind the security glass.

She pointed to her right. "Take all the pamphlets on domestic violence. Read them carefully, and come back to me if you're still interested or have questions."

I sat in a chair away from the other women in the waiting area. I never thought I'd find myself here. Imagined they felt the same way. I barely knew Granville. Stepping outside in the hallway, I phoned Tisha.

"You okay?" she asked without saying hello.

"No, Granville followed me this morning. I'm at the DA's office downtown getting ready to file an order against him. I'm so scared of this man — I don't know what else to do."

"I'm on my way."

"Don't come," I said. "You have to monitor your kids at home."

Texas Virtual Academy K–12 had become popular for many parents in Houston. The option was awesome. Tisha's kids had laptops. She'd set up a room in her house where they sat at their computer desk while a state-certified teacher — who might not be in the same state — taught the curriculum online. Her children loved interacting with classmates by sending side messages, which the teachers couldn't see.

I thought schooling from home limited

social skills. Raynard agreed, so we enrolled Raynell in a private school, where she could interact face-to-face with adults and children.

Hopefully, Granville would back off, once the order was in place.

"I just wanted you to know where I was. I'll call you when I'm done. Thanks for being a true friend. Bye."

Ending the call, I felt Madison should know. Give her another chance to do the right thing and know how unstable Granville was.

I wanted to call Chicago, but that wouldn't be fair to him. I knew he had business to handle. I didn't want to be responsible if anything went wrong for him or the team. I went back into the room and took a seat in the corner.

If I told my dad, he'd kill Granville. If I told my mom, she'd kill him too.

One thing about most folks in Texas, they didn't go looking for trouble; but if problems came their way, they had the right to bear arms and wouldn't hesitate to pull the trigger. I never wanted a gun in my house. Didn't believe I had a reason . . . until now. The "what if" my child hurts herself or one of her friends bothered me. I couldn't forgive myself if child's play turned into

114

murder. But I'd blame myself if Granville broke into my house and I hadn't done all I could to protect my family.

Walking to the window, I prepared to take the necessary action to get an order; and I'd decided to get a gun.

# CHAPTER 7
## CHICAGO

During my flight I found myself thinking more about Loretta than Madison. How could Loretta have not known the minute she'd met the dude that something wasn't right? That would've never happened to Madison. I understood that people being friends or family didn't mean they could teach one another how to choose the perfect mate. Considering I was one of the most eligible bachelors in Houston, I knew Madison had lucked up. Couldn't say the same for her girlfriends.

There had to be signs. Did Loretta ignore or overlook them, or did she feel she could change Granville? I had to call her as soon as I landed in Cincinnati. Make sure she was okay. When she told me she was good, I relaxed and phoned my fiancée. Instantly I got her voice mail. Dialed her again and got the same.

*Hmm, that's unusual.*

I hoped Loretta hadn't mentioned our conversation. If she had, I hoped she hadn't done it in a way that might have upset Madison.

En route to my suite, I relaxed in the backseat of a luxury Town Car. A call came in from my video manager. I smiled. He was the kind of jovial guy who brightened everyone's day.

"Hey, give me some good news," I answered.

He was always hyped and spoke fast, in a motivating Dick Vitale kind of way. I appreciated this guy so much I wanted to give him a raise. When I made the recommendation, the owners suggested cutting my staff's salaries by 10 percent, I wasn't having it. I would've fought the same if it were 1 percent. Most of them deserved more. No way was I going to pay them less. My job was bigger than balancing the team's budget. There were two players who deserved a pay cut, but not my right-hand employees or the crews that reported to them.

I'd prepared a special report showing the extra hours these guys put in off payroll. They didn't pad their expense reports, abuse their credit card privileges, or complain about being on the road away from their families. I never had to ask them twice to do anything. Fortunately, the owners ended up agreeing with me, and my staff never knew the discussion happened.

"I'm on top of it, baby! Everything is in order. Everything! My video team is here, and the computer equipment is on location, wired, functional, and set up to view whatever footage we need on Cincinnati's games and players."

"That's what I want to hear. You're proof that great leadership starts at the top. We have to do our part to hold on to first place in our division. Can't take it for granted we'll make the play-offs, you know. That's how teams slip up. Underestimating their opponents. Thanks, man. I'll see you after practice today."

"Later, boss."

The driver parked in front of the hotel. I was a generous tipper, but I didn't believe in giving handouts or bonuses to those who didn't earn them. Depending on how my driver handled things between now and my departure, he could only go down from the 25 percent I'd allocated for him.

I answered another incoming call. "Hold on a second," I said, and then instructed the driver, "Have my bags sent up to my room." I let myself out of the car.

The driver hurried to my side. "Mr.

DuBois, please. Let me do my job," he said, holding the door open.

I'd been chauffeured for the last six years. Having someone open doors for me was nice, but not necessary. I believed in making my own way and treating others how I wanted them to respond to me.

"It's all good," I said.

Walking up to the counter, I slid my license and credit card to the front-desk attendant; then I spoke into my Bluetooth.

"What's up, baby?"

"Inventory check is complete," my equipment manager confirmed.

"Special workout machines, weights, vests, everything?" I asked.

"Confirmed," he answered. "Uniforms, helmets, socks, shoes, gloves — all checked, baby."

"That's what's up. Later, man." I ended the call and headed to my suite. Everything down to shoelaces was crucial. Whatever specialized items my players requested — like mouth guards and jockstraps and protective cups — I demanded we had an extra supply on hand.

Once my food manager called, inventory would be complete. Making certain everything was on location was my responsibility. All that took place on game day was Blue

Waters's job, and he let it be known to the owners that he wanted my position of general manager.

Blue's background was best suited for administration, but he was a damn good assistant coach. I held the same position with a different team before I had been hired as general manager. I loved my job. Didn't want to move up, over, and definitely not down in my career. I didn't feel threatened by Blue, but I never allowed myself to get too comfortable with anyone. Hiring him to work on my front line wasn't a consideration. I kept him on the field. If he got one foot in the executive office, he'd probably challenge my authority every day.

There were a few college games I had to watch while in Cincinnati. My eight scouts were amongst the best in the country, but I never took anything for granted. I was the one approving the salaries and maintaining the budget for the coaches and the football players too. Any bad decisions ultimately became mine.

Sitting at the desk in my suite, I scanned my iPad to review a few college players' profiles. I was making sure their grades, health, and stats would benefit us to watch them closely before the draft. I also kept an eye on free agents with other teams — players who would make us stronger, or backups who could replace starting players in the event any of our guys were injured and couldn't return for the season.

My cell interrupted my research. I answered, "Hi, Mom."

"I saw you come in the lobby. You know you're supposed to let us know you made it in safely. Your dad is in our room sleeping, and you know how bad he snores. I'm on my way to your room. Where are you?"

There was no need in debating with my mom; she wasn't *asking* if she could come to my room. I had to stay on top of things for the team, but I was never too busy for her.

"I'm in suite three thousand on the thirtieth floor. I've got a half hour, Mom, before I have to leave."

There was a special feeling a man got when both of his parents loved him unconditionally that could not be replaced by his woman or his wife. Madison added a balance to the mix; she had my heart. But if she started trying to control me, I'd call off the wedding. A real man was a leader, not a dictator and definitely not a follower. Until I said, "I do," I reserved the right to change my mind.

Based on Madison's actions last night, she

121

could be a distraction if I asked her to attend away games with me. I wasn't tripping off our conversation about Loretta, but my fiancée did have valid reasons to be concerned.

Now, Madison licking my asshole, that shit was amazing. I couldn't wait to get some more of that. The sensation was incredible. Her magnificent mouth massage was why I had to leave her in Houston the rest of the season. If my ass was in the air with her lips pressed between my cheeks, those calls I just answered would've gone straight to voicemail.

I was grateful that my family supported me on road trips and at home by attending the games when they could. Chaz was here too. Thinking of my brother reminded me I had to call him.

"Hey, Chicago, I was just getting ready to call you. You got time for dinner tonight with us? I'll pick the restaurant."

"Not tonight, man. Tomorrow, after the players finish video review. But, hey, listen. Have you given serious consideration to meeting Loretta when we get back to Houston? You can pick that restaurant too. Madison and I will meet you guys there."

Chaz laughed. "No way. She's too close to your girl."

"You know I've never set you up with a woman you didn't like. Besides, you seemed open when I mentioned it before."

He was quiet for a moment. "You heard what you wanted to hear. I wasn't serious. I only said that to find out what Madison's hidden agenda is for marrying you."

"Then do that. I just need for you to take Loretta out."

"She sounds desperate."

"Hey, Mom's at the door. I'll talk to you later. Bye."

Opening the door, I was not prepared — but at the same time not surprised — to see two topless females smiling at me. They stood nipples to nipples, with huge, firm breasts exposed.

"Hey, Chicago," they sang in unison. "Can we come in?"

Some things a man couldn't control. My dick started crawling down my thigh.

"If you two bitches don't get the hell away from my son's room, I'll beat your asses like you stole something, handcuff ya, and call the police myself."

My brother and I had gotten enough whippings to know my mom meant what she said. She started swinging her purse in their direction. Mom would've hit one of the girls upside the head if the girl hadn't

123

ducked. I laughed at those females running in their high heels like they were track stars instead of groupies.

"Thanks, Mom," I said, closing the door.

"I can't stand these trifling women. They'll do anything to get a man's money. Chicago, if pussy is that easy —"

" 'It's cheesy, and cheese ain't nothing but bait for a rodent.' I know, Ma." I gave my mother a hug. "Thanks for always being there for me. Have a seat on the sofa. I don't have much time. Would you like something to drink?"

"I'm good. We have the wine you had delivered to our room."

There were a few things my mom did faithfully. She went to church on Sundays, prayed every morning and night, and drank a few glasses of merlot every day. When she had one too many, she'd call Chaz or me and rant on about trivial things. We didn't worry too much about those conversations; but when Mom wanted to talk and she was sober, like she was now, that's when we were concerned.

I sat next to my mom. "What is it, Ma?"

"You know what it is, son. That Madison girl. I've got a bad feeling about her. Have you set a date yet?"

"Ma, you know I would've told you and

124

Dad if we'd done that. No. We haven't."

"Good, put it off for two years. If she last that long, I'll give you my blessings."

"Two *what?*" I laughed.

"I'm serious. You're only thirty-two. You can wait two years to start a family."

"Yes, ma'am," I said, to make my mom stop worrying.

"Good. Now, I was going to tell you and Chaz this next week, but I might as well tell you now."

I stared into my mother's eyes. She didn't blink. That meant what she was about to say was crucial.

"Your grandfather has decided, against my will, to give you and Chaz your ten-million-dollar inheritance before he dies."

"That's great news, Ma! When?"

"When y'all get back to Houston."

Was I hearing my mom right? It wasn't like Chaz and I weren't self-made millionaires. My brother had created lots of cell phone applications that went more viral than Angry Birds and had made himself a millionaire. Chaz wasn't much of an athlete, like I was growing up. He was extremely cerebral, a sort of brainiac. I'd sounded so many ideas off him — including the sports integrity policies I'd presented to the national football committee — Chaz could probably replace me as general manager.

"Why?"

"Why what?" Mom asked. "Why is your grandfather doing this? Or why don't I want him to do it?"

"Both."

"I still think he should wait until you guys are forty or at least put it off for four more years. But he insists on doing it while he's alive. He's so stubborn, he'll probably outlive all of us. I don't agree, but it's his money from his investments in the oil industry. And knowing him, there's a lot more where the twenty mil is coming from."

I leaned over, hugged my mom, and then tightened my embrace. "I'll keep making wise decisions. I promise you, Ma."

Holding on, she said, "It's not you I'm worried about. It's that girl. Do me a favor, and never tell her how much money you have. And make sure she signs a prenup. If she truly loves you for you, she'll sign it."

Perfect timing for my phone to ring.

"Ma, I've got to take this call. Dinner tomorrow with you, Dad, and Chaz. Chaz said he'd make the reservation." I answered the call before it went to voice mail. "Hey, what's up?"

Mom stood. I followed her to the door.

"I'll choose the restaurant," she said.

"Chaz is too over-the-top for my appetite, with all those small plates of strange food. I want a steak."

My brother did have what Mom considered exquisite taste. I'd better make the reservation for our double date with Loretta. I closed the door, then said, "Madison, I have fantastic news, baby!"

# CHAPTER 8
## GRANVILLE

Sitting in the chair at a tattoo parlor on Gulfway in Port Arthur, I knew what I wanted, but I didn't know what to expect. I held my breath with anticipation.

"Breathe, dude. You're too fucking big for me to pick your ass up off of the floor if you pass out."

*Fuck!* I exhaled. The first minute made me almost regret my decision. Once I relaxed, I started enjoying the pain of the needle dragging across my flesh and digging into my skin.

After he got past the *L,* it hurt so good I wanted to piss in my pants. Why did I wait until I was forty-five to do this? I should've done this in my twenties. But then, I'd have a scroll down to my dick with *Regina, Kim, Stacy, Denise, Pam,* and a list of all the other women who had loved and left me. I had to suppress my woody. Didn't want the artist to think his light skin, wavy hair, bulging muscles, wife beater, and saggy jeans were the reason my manhood kept growing. The more that needle dragged, the more it burned and bled, the bigger my shit got. This was going to be all bad if I had to unzip my pants and let the beast out.

"It's okay, boss. This kind of thing happens all the time. Even when I'm tattooing a dick," he said.

A dick? Damn, I should've had *Loretta* put on my woody instead of across my heart, but he was finishing up the *a* and my dick was my best friend. If anything bad happened to my dick, I'd feel worthless.

"You mind if I take a picture?" he asked, holding a digital camera.

"No problem, bro. Take one for me too," I said, handing him my new iPhone.

"I'll take a few for you. Your total is two hundred dollars, cash," he said.

I threw in an extra twenty when I saw how good her name looked. I nodded, then whispered in my sexy voice, "Loretta."

He applied ointment and then covered her name with a bandage. "Thanks, man. Leave this on for three hours. Trust me," he said, scanning through his camera, "you don't want this to happen."

"Damn! What the hell is that?"

"An infection from someone taking off the

bandage too soon. Normally, you could take it off after two hours . . . but with all the refineries constantly pumping pollution into the air, I add on an extra hour. It looks good. This is your first, but you'll be back," he said. "This shit is addictive."

"Nah, you won't be seeing me again," I told him as I buttoned up my shirt.

*Not unless I change my mind about tattooing Loretta's name across my dick.*

"Well, if you ever want to have it removed, I'm the best. I can do that for you for a reduced price, since you had it done here. Or I can turn her name into a fire-breathing dragon. Keep that shit in mind," he said, shoving the money into his front pocket.

"She's the one," I said, dipping my left shoulder as I strolled out of his shop. Loretta was going to love me for this. Pounding on the smooth side of my chest, I gave myself props.

*I did that shit!*

I got into my truck and headed to Mom's, hoping my baby hadn't followed through with trying to get that PO.

Even if she had, filing for a protective order wouldn't deter me. Wasn't like she had it yet. Should I text her a picture of our tat? Nah, I'd wait to surprise her. That way I could see the smile on her face before she smothered her name with raspberry kisses. I'd give Loretta another day or so before contacting her.

Fortunately for me, she wasn't broke, so the system wasn't going to foot the bill for her. By the time she found out all she had to do, she might get discouraged and give up. Then maybe I could convince her to wear my ring.

In Harris County, orders were harder to get than a license to carry a gun. Southern systems were designed to keep attorneys feeding their families. I'm glad I didn't live in California. While on vacation I fell fast and hard for one of those chicks in Oakland; the next thing I knew, some process server named Clarence Randall was knocking on my hotel room door and handing me papers to appear in court. Rather than show up and let her show out, I packed my suitcase and got my black ass on the next flight back to George Bush Intercontinental Airport.

In Texas, Loretta would have to hire a lawyer to prepare and present her case. Then I'd have to be served. Then if I just so happened to be unable to make the assigned date, I could delay the case and request a new date. Eventually I'd have to show up in court; and by then, I'd know for sure if Loretta was done with me for good.

*Honk! Honk!* I blew at the boys standing on the corner, near the Kansas City Southern Railway monument. Still couldn't figure out why they decided to put that rail car in the heart of the hood. In addition to naming our fine city after the railroad genius Arthur E. Stilwell, I'm sure the city could've found a better way to honor him than mounting a real train in an open field, where Beaux and I used to play football when we were kids.

Rolling down the window on my Super Duty, I yelled, "What's up!" and kept going. Damn, my voice was a little too loud and hurt my throat. Can't lie, though. I felt good sitting high in my truck, looking down on those guys. I doubted any of those dudes had stepped foot outside of Port Arthur. From my boots to my roots, I was a country boy. Had a shotgun in the bed of my truck to prove it. But I was better than those guys. Had more money, a better life, and a fiancée. I was happy I'd moved to the big city.

I liked New Orleans, but wouldn't live there. The drive was too far away from my mom. Since I was older than my brother, I was the number one son.

Parking in my mother's yard, I saw Beaux's car was already there. At least this time we didn't have a reason to fight. I lifted the cover on the back of my truck and got the ice cooler full of seafood that I'd packed earlier before leaving Houston.

Mom was sitting in the living room with my brother watching *The Color Purple.* She must've seen that movie a gazillion times.

"Hey, baby. I'm glad you made it. You came by yourself this time?"

Not by choice. "Yeah, Loretta couldn't make it, but she said to tell you hello."

"Liar," Beaux said, jerking the chest from me. "Spare us the" — he silently mouthed, "fucked-up" — then said aloud, "fantasy in your head, dude."

I unbuttoned and then removed my shirt, like I was starring in the lead role in a movie. I peeled away the bandage and curled my fingers into a fist.

"Why would I do this, if she didn't love me, bro?" Deep inside I wanted him to give me a reason to go upside his head.

Beaux looked at my chest; then he laughed in my face.

"Because you're a fool, that's why. I'm the one who dropped her off, remember? Not you. She never wants to see you again, in heaven or on earth. And we both know she won't have to worry about that heaven part, because your" — he mouthed, "black ass" — then said, "is going straight to hell."

133

My eyes narrowed. I moved in his direction, with the intent to strike him down.

Mama said, "Sit down, Granville. You're blocking the television."

"You're disillusioned, man. I'ma go prepare the meal. You keep your behind in here," Beaux said, heading toward the kitchen.

I could still hear him laughing as I sat in what used to be my dad's recliner and kicked up my feet. "How you doing, Mama?" I asked, leaning forward to avoid falling backward in the chair.

"Boy, don't tear up daddy's chair too. You're so clumsy. You're forty-five and you still break up all my stuff."

I went to get up.

"Sit. Next time be more careful. I'm glad you're comfortable in your father's chair. Beaux hasn't sat in it since your daddy died."

"Mama, how did you and daddy stay married for forty years? I mean, I know you never did, but did you ever *think* about leaving him?"

"Boy, hush. Your father would roll over in his grave if he heard you ask me that. We were like Martin and Coretta, one spouse for life. Till death do we part. Your father was a real man, just like you and Beaux.

Don't get married until you're sure you've got the right one. Y'all problem is trying to find the right woman. They don't make 'em like me and Coretta anymore, and that's not y'all's fault. Women these days want to be the man, pay the bills, and tell their husband what to do. Take your time. You'll find the right —"

"I can't afford to keep taking my time mama. In five years I'll be fifty and still might not have a wife and kids. How much long —"

"Hush up all that nonsense. You can still make babies. You don't have to have them. But that Loretta girl ain't worth two pennies rubbed together. And if I were you, I'd remove her name before the ink is dry on that there tattoo."

*Wow, she didn't say nickels this time. But that's not true. And there's no way I'm taking my baby's name off me, because she is the only woman for me.*

I didn't respond to Mom. Whenever we disagreed with her, she thought we were calling her a liar.

"I'm glad Dad moved us out of the projects and into the white house," I said.

When we were growing up, our friends thought we had the worst house on the block; but to us, it was the best. I thought big and named it after the presidents' mansion. Mama used to say, "It's not where you live. It's how you live."

Sure, Loretta had a bigger white house, with a huge paved driveway, large courtyard, and two gigantic evergreen trees, which stood taller than her second-floor bedroom window. Seldom did I see her on the balcony above the living room. I had to download to my new cell one of those satellite applications that I had on my laptop. That way I could spy on Loretta's house whenever I wanted. So far, she was faithful. Raynard was the only man I saw there. I was beginning to love technology.

Mom sighed. "Yeah, he married me and moved us from his parents' project to this here house. I was thirteen and pregnant with you and he was twenty. But now that *I'm* getting older, I wished he hadn't moved us so close to the refineries so soon. They're practically in our backyard. Do you know Mrs. Taylor, Mr. and Mrs. Wallace, Mr. Tucker, Mr. and Mrs. Butler, and the Waltons were all diagnosed with the big C?"

Beaux yelled from the kitchen, "Working at those refineries and living in this house killed Dad. Every year people in our neighborhood die from some form of cancer. Seems like we're all going to die of cancer."

"That's not true, baby. I'm fifty-eight and I don't have it."

Beaux stood in the doorway of Mom's shotgun house. "How would you know, Mother? You haven't been to the doctor since Daddy died."

"I just don't want them putting me on medication I don't need just because of my age. I think the chemo and drugs are the real reason people are dying so fast. One day they walking, and the next day they buried."

I asked Mom, "When was the last time you been to the doctor for a checkup?"

She tightened her lips, tucked her duster between her thighs, and folded her arms over her stomach.

"That's it," Beaux said. "We're taking you to the doctor next week."

"So they can sho'nuff sign my death certificate. I'm not going. Leave well enough alone. When the good Lord is ready to call me home, He'll let me know. And y'all ain't been talkin' this doctor mess for a long time, so hush."

"Let's continue this conversation over dinner," Beaux said.

Beaux had set the table with a platter of fried catfish, dishes full of roasted crab, boiled shrimp, crawfish, and corn on the cob.

"Oh, baby. This sure looks and smells good," Mama said.

I pulled out her chair, waited for her to sit at the table, and then sat across from her. Beaux sat at the end, but no one was in Dad's chair. Mama wanted it that way. The recliner was okay to relax in, but Dad would forever be the only head of Mother's household.

My cell phone rang. I didn't recognize the number, but I hated missing calls. I answered, "Hello."

"Hey, Granville. It's Madison."

"Madison? My boss, Madison?"

"Yes," she said. "I need to see you in my office first thing in the morning. Eight o'clock sharp. Don't be late."

"Sure thing. I'll be there."

"Bye." She ended the call before I could ask any questions.

"Sounds like somebody is getting a promotion," Beaux said.

I guess Loretta wasn't kidding. What was I going to do about her name tattooed on my chest? I'd never had a light-skinned Creole woman like Madison Tyler interested in me. They didn't date my kind. Man, Madison was the wife I'd been dreaming of since I was a little boy.

"Mama, you're going to love my new girl-friend."

# CHAPTER 9
## MADISON

I hate when people say they have great news, and then in the same breath tell me I've got to wait. I don't like delayed surprises! Roosevelt could've kept to himself whatever excited him, and then told me when he saw me — especially since he wouldn't be back for another two days.

To keep my mind off what he had to say, I told Granville to meet me in my office. He should be here any minute. My video camera was set up to record our initial encounter, but mainly it was to school Loretta on how to deal with men. When I show her the tape, she will be shocked. One, because she called and warned me not to make good on our bet. Two, she hadn't given me Granville's cell number. Didn't need her to. He worked for me. I got it from his résumé.

My receptionist buzzed me. I glanced into the oval-shaped mirror on my desk, freshened my red-hot lipstick, then answered,

"Yes, Monica."

"Ms. Tyler, your dad is on line one."

Dad needed a hobby to occupy his time. His calls were coming in earlier each day. Yesterday, it was eight. What did he want at seven forty-five in the morning?

"Thanks," I said, then answered, "Hey, Papa."

His voice trembled. "Good morning, sweetheart. I couldn't sleep last night."

"Stop worrying, Papa. You don't have to call me morning, noon, and night. I promise you, I'm handling things. I just need more time to get it done."

"We're running out of time, Madison. We're down to four months of operating capital and then it's lights out on Tyler Construction for good. I moved from Port Arthur to Houston thirty years ago and started my company with two employees. Me and your mother. You know how many people depend on us now to provide for their families? Two hundred!" he shouted.

*I know. I know. Stop acting like it's my fault that we're financially strapped!*

Over my thirteen years of working for my dad (after graduating from college), I watched him take on more business than we could financially sustain. Why? Ego. Men and their goddamn egos could destroy the world. He saw dollar signs and ignored the warning signs. Spent money before we'd made it. Bought me the Ferrari, Mom a Bentley, and got himself a Porsche before the ink was dry on this last contract.

Mom had begged him not to take on this Westheimer expansion mixed-use project, but he swore he could compete with the big boys. The city had to guarantee two minority firms on this billion-dollar redevelopment deal; we were selected as one of the general contractors.

The potential earnings before expenses were $50 million, and that was all Papa saw. Problem was, we only got a small percentage up front. When the project was over, we'd be lucky to net $10 million over the next several years.

Our resources were being depleted because the city's accounts-payable system didn't coincide with our obligations on our past and present projects. Plus, the mayor was talking about how the city might run out of money if the state cut off their funding. If the city had to lay off employees as a result, we'd have to follow suit.

"Papa, take Mama's advice this one time and sell your jet. We don't need a private plane. We can fly first class. And we'll have enough revenue to meet payroll and expenses for the next two months."

"I'm not going to do that, Madison. What will my fraternity brothers, family, and my friends think about me? I'll tell you what they'll do. They'll talk behind my back and say, 'Johnny Tyler is broke.' I'm not broke, sweetheart. I just don't have the money that's been promised by the city. All you have to do is get access to your fiancé's inheritance and everything will be okay. Ten million is all we need to cover everything, and I'll pay Roosevelt back with interest before he realizes you borrowed it. Do it for Papa, sweetheart. When is your wedding date?"

My mother, Rosalee Tyler, was smarter than my dad. She'd never ask me do such a thing. And if she knew what my dad was up to, she'd stop him.

The muscles in my shoulders tensed. I desperately needed a massage.

"We haven't set one yet."

"Set it two months from now. I'll pay for it."

"What! With what?"

"Lay off a few employees. Better to lay off a few than to let all of them go."

Right now, my dad was going straight to hell.

"I will not! And Roosevelt doesn't even

have his inheritance and might not get it for years."

"But he's not broke. Marry him and find out what he does have. You can make this one less thing for us to worry about."

*Us?*

My receptionist buzzed me. I didn't care who it was; it was a timely exit opportunity.

"Love you, Papa, but I gotta go. Bye."

The eight engagement rings in my jewelry collection were my championship rings for winning at the sport of dating. I refused to pawn any of them. I removed Roosevelt's ring and put it in my drawer. Men bought me expensive gifts because they loved me. I'd never stolen from or cheated anyone out of anything. But this was my dad, and family came first. I had to find a way to save our company.

The knots in my stomach tightened. Exhaling, I answered, "Yes."

"Mr. Washington is here to see you."

"Send him in."

*Yes, indeed.*

Granville entered my office. His cheap cologne reached me as soon as he crossed the doorway. He had on a hard hat, an orange vest, a faded blue, long-sleeved, pullover cotton shirt, fitted jeans, and large steel-toed black boots.

144

"Good morning, boss," he said, squaring his shoulders.

"Glad to finally meet you, Mr. Washington," I replied, giving him another head-to-toe assessment. He had that strapping Mandingo physique like the porn star. He was the kind of man I'd want to take me sexually. I saw how Loretta could've been curious about his manhood.

I stood and extended my hand. His long, thick fingers swallowed mine. I braced myself for a squeeze that might hurt. He surprised me. His shake was firm yet gentle.

"Have a seat."

He damn near knocked over my executive chocolate leather chair, which weighed nearly fifty pounds. He spread his thighs as though he hadn't noticed what he'd done. His dick imprint was huge, like a log of salami.

Wow, no wonder he was crazy. He couldn't possibly think straight when that thing got hard.

I sat on the edge of my desk, crossed my legs, and slid my hands up my creamy smooth thighs. He was stunned, like most men and women when they saw my natural beauty up close.

He stared toward the floor, but it was obvious what he was really trying to look at was the opening in my skirt. I scooted back a few inches.

Blending business with flirting, I said, "Your immediate supervisor told me what a great worker you are and I wanted to personally thank you."

He lowered his head a bit more as he grinned like a ten-year-old with a crush on his teacher. "Thanks. Am I getting a promotion?"

The scratchiness in his voice was kind of sexy. His inability to look into my eyes during our conversation meant he had low self-esteem, or he was focusing on not getting aroused. Either way I was not having a dialogue with a hard hat.

"Please look at me while we're talking."

For the first time, his eyes met mine. "Huh? Okay."

"Granville Washington, tell me, what are your career objectives?"

I gave him a moment to shift mental gears. Then I repeated the question, and added, "Where do you see yourself in two to five years?"

"Here, of course. Working for you, boss. I'm not going anywhere. I'll never leave you."

Now I was confused as to why it took Loretta more than fifteen minutes to leave this fool alone. I glanced up toward my camera and tilted my head sideways. Maybe it was what was lingering between his thighs; it certainly was not what was between his ears.

Redirecting my attention to Granville, I said, "Think about what I just asked you and tell me when you come to my house tonight for dinner." I handed him my address on a piece of paper. "Six o'clock sharp."

Escorting him to the door, I hated how he dipped his left shoulder. That was so ghetto. His pathetic attempt to be hip was not impressive. Loretta should've told him that.

I closed the door, then exhaled. Granville could never measure up to my man. I prayed that whatever good news Roosevelt had, it was related to his inheritance. My image wouldn't survive a foreclosure, and I refused to move back home with my parents and moving in with my fiancé before we were married wasn't happening either. Cohabitation was the demise of many decent relationships.

Daddy had really messed up bad this time. I had to win this bet with Loretta, just in case I needed her to make good on her offer that I could have whatever I wanted if I won. An eye for an eye. Since she wanted me to call off my wedding, I would demand that she sign over the deed to her house, move out, and I'd move in.

I took a few hours to make calls to the city. A partial payment would be issued as soon as they reviewed our invoices; but, of course, they couldn't say exactly when that would happen, since they were understaffed and behind on processing checks for the Westheimer project. I hated how the government could be late with getting us our money with no penalties for them. But if we were late paying our taxes, they piled on late fees, daily compound interest, and penalties.

Monica buzzed, then announced another call from my dad. I looked into the video lens. "Loretta, I'm going to win this bet. And when I do, you owe me big time."

Powering off the video, I answered, "Hi, Papa."

"Madison, how's it going?"

"Why don't you come out of retirement and work for the company? That way you can be on the phone all day with the city and directly get the same answers I keep giving you."

"My blood pressure is already high. Those people will give me a heart attack."

And he'll give me one if he doesn't back off.

"I gotta go. Tell Mama I said hi. And don't call me tonight. I'll be busy. Bye, Papa."

It was three o'clock. I shut down my computer and locked my door. On my way out of the office, I told Monica, "Don't disturb me the rest of the day, especially for my father. I'll be back in the morning."

I stopped at Rice grocery on San Felipe. I picked up fish for me, and steak and lobster for him. He didn't look like a fresh-vegetable guy, so I didn't bother with the kale, broccoli, squash, zucchini, or carrots. Irish potatoes were a better selection. Chives, sour cream, bacon, and butter sounded like toppings he'd enjoy. I tossed in a fresh bag of spinach, in case I was wrong.

On my way home I called Loretta.

"Hey, Madison girl, what's up?"

"Just checking to make sure you haven't been kidnapped," I said, laughing. "Because you're about to get hijacked, my friend."

Flatly she said, "Just make sure you don't spend Chicago's ten million before he gets it next week."

*Next what?* Obviously, she thought that shit was cute. Was that his surprise? Why would he tell Loretta that? She had to be lying. Roosevelt would never tell her something like that before talking with me. "How do you know that?"

"Because I'm about to get hijacked."

Loretta was wasting my time with her sarcasm.

"Look in my driveway tonight at six," I said, then ended the call.

I wanted to dial Roosevelt, but if what she'd said was true, I didn't want to appear anxious. Loretta was beginning to test the limits of our friendship by clinging to my fiancé. That hookup with Chaz now seemed like an ingenious idea. Maybe I could somehow gain access to Chaz's banking information through Loretta. Then I could use his millions and make it look like Loretta was the guilty one. I'd arrange that foursome immediately after properly welcoming my man back home.

Prepping the food, I wrapped the potatoes in foil, placed them on a cookie sheet, then put them in the oven. The main thing I had to do after my bath was cook his meat. I filled my oversized black porcelain tub with steaming hot water; then I added scented essence salts and mineral oils. What was this Granville guy really like? I didn't believe he was the deranged person Loretta had claimed.

I got a warm towel from the dryer in my bathroom, wrapped my wet body in it, then brushed my teeth. I massaged my skin with shea butter and tended to Aphrodite with her special white-chocolate potion.

No bra was necessary. A thong and a sleeveless, loosely tapered, midthigh, short, semiconservative coral-and-blue dress was the perfect fit. It complemented my three-inch pink heels. I wore diamond earrings and a choker, but no ring was on my finger. Damn, I'd forgotten my ring at work. I'd put it on first thing tomorrow. Tonight I was as ready as I could get for this encounter. It was okay that I didn't have my diamond. I wouldn't dare wear Roosevelt's ring while sexing Granville.

Intercourse was what I'd agreed to do to win the bet, and I'd have no regrets. After he put the head in and took it out, I was going to be the biggest winner! A dab of perfume and I was headed to the kitchen to heat up my stovetop grill.

It was six o'clock and Granville was right on time.

*Damn! Is his truck big enough?*

He got out of his pickup and stared at Loretta's place. My eyes trailed his. She wasn't in the doorway or on her balcony above. That was okay. I had a handheld video set up on a tripod in my bedroom.

"You all right?" I asked.

He scratched the left side of his chest.

151

"Yeah. I'm good." He squared his shoulders, then did that stupid thuggish dip as he walked toward me.

I rolled my eyes with disgust. The lyrics for "I'm Too Sexy" played in my mind. What was he out to prove? Who was he trying to impress? If I didn't have a bet, I'd send his ass next door and shut my door in his face.

"Come on in." I had him follow me to the kitchen. Had to keep an eye on him. Wasn't sure if he was the kind that would steal my easy-to-lift valuables. "Have a seat at the bar."

The wet bar was a cozy place for intimate conversations any time of the day. He pulled out the chair; it fell to the floor. He picked it up, jammed it to the floor as though the chair was the problem, then sat down. I wanted to say something, but I didn't. Wished he'd remove that hideous cowboy hat, but he hadn't.

I could tell he was a cheap Jack and Coke or beer man, but I didn't have Jack or beer. I mixed him a Crown Royal Black with Coke, then set it on the bar in front of him.

"I am getting a promotion," he said, swallowing a huge swig.

He wasn't, so I skipped asking him about his goals. "Where do you live in Port Arthur? I'm from there too," I said, putting his steak on the grill.

"Really! We could be cousins." He laughed, hanging the heel of his cowboy boot on the wooden bar on the side of the stool, and then spreading his other leg. Why he didn't use the steel bar in front of him was beyond me.

"Your folks still live there?" I asked, flipping his T-bone. I placed my fish, his lobster, and six strips of bacon on the grill; then I removed the potatoes from the oven.

"My mom lives next to Terminal Road, by the tracks close to Gulfway."

"My parents live here. My grandfather refuses to move from Port Arthur. He lives over that way, close to your mom. He goes to New St. John Missionary."

"My mom goes there too! Seriously, we might be related," he said.

"I hope not," I said. Not because I wasn't going to fuck him, regardless. He was way too dark to be in my family tree. If Roosevelt weren't successful, wealthy, and attractive, his caramel complexion would fail the "spoon of coffee in the cup of milk" test used by Creoles who could pass for white.

Changing subjects, I shared with Granville, "My grandfather has cancer. He'll probably have to move in with my mom pretty soon. How're your folks faring, being so close to the refineries?"

Granville was ten years my senior and not in my league, so I didn't care about who was in his circle, family or otherwise. I was blessed my parents moved me out of that toxic tank when I was five.

Looking at his slumping posture, even if I hadn't viewed his résumé, I could tell he wasn't college educated. And because he didn't have the intellect upstairs, his big dick was what he worshiped. No telling where his dick had been. He was the type that wanted a sophisticated lady, but he would fuck a stripper onstage if the boys cheered him on.

His eyes drooped. He took a huge gulp, tilted his hat, and then said, "My dad died from cancer and my mom won't go to the doctor. Says the chemo and radiation kills faster than cancer. She believes when it's her time to go, God will bring her home."

"I'm sorry to hear that about your father. Look, dinner is ready. We can eat at the bar."

I wasn't asking. I refused to let him ruin the furniture in my formal dining room. The table, chairs, china, and cabinet were antique originals given to me by my grandmother before she died of cancer. Those items were precious to me and impossible to replace. I loaded the baked potatoes, prepared our plates, and then sat beside him.

"This looks great!" he said, carving his steak.

I wasn't one to say grace, but damn he could take that damn hat off! He devoured a fourth of his T-bone before I tasted my fish. Probably best. The sooner we got through this, the better.

"I like you," he said, diving into the potato. "Do you like me too?"

I wished he wouldn't talk with food in his mouth. "What do you like about me?" I asked, shoving my plate aside. Watching him eat like it was his last meal made me lose my appetite.

"You're beautiful, got nice hips, lips, breasts, legs, feet, and a big butt. You smell good, and you're the lightest woman I've dated."

*What? Dated?*

"This is *not* a date."

"Yes, it is. Why else would you invite me to your house and cook for me? Another drink would be nice," he said, staring at me. His eyes drooped like a puppy dog's. He lifted his eyebrows in a flickering kind of way. His nose and upper lip were grossly wet.

"Why don't you wipe your face and we

take the next round of drinks into my bedroom?"

The sooner we got started, I could then
put his ass out.

He stood. Knocked my stool over again.
Picked it up, jabbed it to the floor.

Shaking my head, I made both of us a
double of Crown Royal Black and Coke. I
handed him the drinks and grabbed the
bottle. I had to make this the quickest fuck
ever and I couldn't do it sober. He followed
me. I drank straight from the bottle, swallowed twice.

"Wow! Your bed is the biggest I've ever
seen. This bedroom is nice! You rich? You
are rich, aren't you?"

Granville glanced around. Walked over to
my seventy-inch flat screen mounted to the
wall. Thank goodness, his hands were full. I
picked up the remote and turned on the
television. It was already preset and started
playing a triple-X film.

A beautiful Asian woman was being ser-
viced by a sexy white man. The guy in the
video slowly began licking the woman's gold
stiletto heel. His tongue traveled to her toes
as he kissed each one.

"How much did you pay for that TV? I've
never seen a porn flick this classy," he said,
plopping onto my blue satin comforter. He

was the kind that treated a thousand-dollar comforter the same as one bought on sale for ten bucks. He sipped from one glass and placed the other on the nightstand.

I hurried to pick up mine before he got the two drinks confused.

"Is that video camera on?" he asked. A weird smile crossed his face. "You're going to make me a porn star? I'm ready!"

"It's broken," I lied, pressing the power button. Apparently, he didn't need me to answer any of his questions. Next to his dick he was in love with the sound of his voice, because he wouldn't shut the hell up. He had on too many clothes for me to undress him. "Get comfortable."

He removed his cowboy hat, boots, unfastened his humongous belt buckle, then took off his jeans, underwear, shirt, and kept on his wife beater. *Whatever.* Everything remained exactly where it fell beside the bed. *Trifling.*

I eased my dress over my head; then I laid it across the lounge chair on the other side of the room. His eyes bucked. He licked his lips and started panting with his tongue hanging out of his mouth.

Slowly I walked toward him and peeled back the comforter. Then I lay my body atop the blue satin sheet. Curling my finger,

I said, "Go down on me." Might as well put his tongue to good use.

His big sausage fingers parted my lips. He began lapping like a mutt. I curled my hips toward his mouth. "Slow down and suck her gently."

"You smell good and taste sweet. What is this? I know. Dessert. Yum, yum."

Didn't matter. At least he could follow instructions. After he got my pussy nice and wet, I told him, "Lay down."

When he stood, his dick was long, hard, and beautiful. I prayed he knew what to do with it, but I wasn't taking any chances. I had the right-size condom that covered him completely. I put it on him, then straddled that Mandingo like I was getting ready to mount a horse.

"You're gorgeous. I don't know what I did to deserve you, but I'm going to treat you like my queen."

I placed my finger over his lips. "Don't talk. Please don't talk."

Holding his manhood, I lowered my juicy pussy onto him. Easing a little in at a time, this motherfucker felt amazing. Roosevelt was a good length, but this dick could break record sizes. I was sure of it. My pussy throbbed automatically.

I took it all in and sat there for a moment.

He was doing a good job of not speaking, but I wished he'd stop staring at me with that stupid grin. I bounced with a slow rhythm. Gradually I picked up the pace. Soon I found myself riding the shit out of his dick. It was so good I went into a zone and couldn't stop humping him.

Raising my hips above his dick, I thrust back down and . . . screamed, *"Ahhh!"*

My body lifted in the air. He grabbed my hips, pulled me back onto him. "Yeah, ride your dick. You can take it. You're so pretty."

That dumb fuck had moved when I was riding him. His dick was now in my ass. I was in excruciating pain.

"Let me go!" I wanted to punch him in his face, but my ass hurt too much. I scratched the back of his hands.

"Yeah, I love it! Scratch me harder," he urged, grunting with that disgusting voice. He started ramming his dick inside me as he held my hips in place. I felt blood coming out of my rectum.

"Stop! Stop!"

"That's right. Cum for me," he said, digging deeper. "I love you, dear."

Everything started fading to black. I thought I was going to die. He pushed deeper and I cried, *"Stop! Stop!"*

# CHAPTER 10
## LORETTA

"Hey, little mama. It's time to tuck you in."

Raynell hugged my neck. She didn't have to say it. I felt her love. Squeezing her tightly, I kissed her forehead as I rocked her in my arms. She gave me the inner strength to prioritize what was most important in my life. Her.

I made better decisions because of her, like setting my goal to start a nighttime child care service in five years. That way, before my daughter became a budding teenager, I wouldn't have to take personal days from work to volunteer at her school. Or worry about her cutting class to bring a boy to our house while I was at my job. And I'd be my own boss, like Madison.

"Little angel of mine," I whispered as my eyes swelled with tears.

She was only six, but since conception she'd brought me endless joy. God knew what I needed; and although I didn't have

Raynard, He gave me somebody to love and someone who loved me unconditionally. I constantly craved the relationship my parents had.

"One day we'll be a family."

"Don't cry, Mommy. You're right. I love you, and Daddy loves us."

"I know, baby." I hadn't realized I'd said that aloud.

Raynell looked into my eyes. "I have a secret, Mommy," she said, wiping my face.

"You know there are no secrets between us," I reminded her. "Out with it now."

"Daddy said what you just said, Mommy. He told me one day we'll be a family. Oh, I haven't said good night to my daddy." Raynell spoke as though her secret was a fleeting thought. Easing from underneath the covers, she sat on the edge of her bed.

I handed Raynell her own cell. "Make it quick. You've got five minutes. When I come back in here, no excuses, young lady. You're going to sleep."

Some parents thought a child having a phone at Raynell's age was too young. The teachers at her school wanted to ban cellular devices, but that was a battle they'd never win. Most of the students at her school also had laptops and e-book readers.

"Okay, Mommy." Her face was bright.

Her eyes shined. I left her door open.

"Hi, Daddy!" she said. I imagined the smile on his face was bigger than the one on mine. Raynell was one lucky little girl to have two loving parents in her life.

Thinking of luck . . . Madison was on my mind in an uncomfortable way. I wished she hadn't gone through with sexing Granville. He wasn't worth it. He was the first man I'd met with zero sense of logic — nada, zilch, none — not an ounce. The only things he comprehended were the thoughts in his head.

Tisha and Chicago were right. The signs were there. He had a split personality, would lose his temper, and go from cold to hot and back in a matter of minutes. Whenever he wanted to see me, if I were busy, he'd pressure me until I agreed to go out with him. He didn't care if I was inconvenienced, as long as he got to feed or taste me. His degrading comments were followed up with apologies and compliments. After having sex with him a few times, I avoided putting myself in situations where we were alone, because all he wanted to do behind closed doors was stick his dick inside me.

Madison was grown and could handle herself. "Not my problem," I said, stepping onto my balcony. When Madison said that, she meant it. I said it, but that wasn't true.

I stared next door into Madison's driveway. It was nine o'clock and Granville's truck was still there. I felt so bad for not being able to talk my friend out of that ridiculous bet that I almost threw up. I wasn't jealous. Granville was the kind of man a woman was relieved to get rid of and never see again. He'd been at Madison's for three hours. They must've been having a good time. Two crazy people from Port Arthur probably had a lot in common.

However, if anything bad happened to her, I wasn't sure I'd forgive myself.

Inhaling the fresh air, I stared at the stars. The constellations were mesmerizing. God had a purpose for everything. I wondered if the stars were always in alignment. What did God have planned for me?

I had a huge house, solid bank account, and triple-A credit. I had a beautiful daughter, she had a good father, and I wanted him as my husband. Maybe it wasn't meant for me to marry Raynard or any other man.

My cell rang. It was Chicago. I looked down at Granville's car and decided it was best to ignore his call. What would I say to him? My heart couldn't lie; and whatever was happening in Madison's house may have been my fault, but it wasn't any of my business.

I turned to enter my bedroom and my cell rang again. It was Chicago again. I hesitated, wanting to answer this time. What if it was important? What if he needed his prayer buddy? In the midst of debating, his second call went to voice mail. Probably best. Raynell's five minutes were up, but what if he called —

This time I answered right away. "Hey, is everything all right, Chicago? I was putting Raynell to bed."

"Sorry for bothering you." His voice was flat. "But —"

"Don't apologize. You're never a bother."

"I haven't heard from Madison today. Have you?"

"I spoke with her this morning" was all I said.

"Can you do me a favor and go check on her for me? Tell her I'm worried. I mean, it's not like her not to text and call —"

Right at that moment I heard Madison scream, *"Stop!"*

"Oh, my God!" I blurted.

"What is it?" Chicago asked.

There was no time to respond to him. I dropped my phone in the lounge chair, ran to my baby's room, and snatched up Raynell.

"Mommy, what's wrong?"

*Jesus, help us,* I prayed, carrying my little girl in my arms. My eyes were filled with tears. *Lord, let her be all right!*

"Mommy," Raynell said, then started crying. "You're scaring me."

"Hold on tight to Mommy, princess."

I grabbed my keys to Madison's house; then I headed next door in the opposite direction to Tisha's. I ran as fast as I could. *Bam! Bam! Bam!* I pounded on Tisha's door; then I frantically rang her doorbell.

She swung open her door. "Loretta, what's wrong with you?"

I shoved Raynell inside. "Sweetie, stay here until Mommy gets back." I yanked Tisha's hand and closed her door.

Tisha stood still in protest, then opened her door. "Raynell, go upstairs with my boys and stay there. Everything is okay."

I could hear my baby crying as she walked away.

Tisha demanded to know, "What's going on?"

"Trust me," I cried out. "Granville is at Madison's house and Madison is in trouble. I heard her screaming."

"What!" Tisha said, leading the way.

We started sprinting toward Madison's house. Granville ran out her front door.

165

"You bastard!" I yelled, wishing I had a gun.

He got into his truck, then sped out of the driveway. I knew something horrible had happened.

I didn't need my key because the door was wide open.

"Madison!" we called out.

There was no answer. Felt like my heart missed a beat, but my legs kept moving. We ran upstairs to her bedroom.

"Jesus Christ!" I screamed. "What did he do to you?"

Madison was naked and facedown; her ass was covered with blood. I turned her over, pressed two fingers against her neck.

"Thank you, Jesus, she has a pulse. Call nine-one-one," I told Tisha.

Tisha ran to Madison's home phone. "We have an emergency."

While Tisha was on the phone, I got a closer look at Madison. Her eyelids fluttered. All I saw was white. I wasn't sure if I should cover up her lower body, but I knew I wouldn't want strangers staring at my privates if it were me lying across the bed.

I went to her dresser, rummaged through all of her lace nighties, got a loose-fitting cotton gown, and eased it over her head. I checked again to make sure she had a pulse and was breathing. I held Madison in my arms. Her body was heavy and lifeless.

"I'm so sorry. I told you not to mess with him. It's all my fault."

"It's not your fault. It's Granville's fault. He did this. I hate him!" Tisha cried out, then yelled into the phone, "Hurry! We need an ambulance, *now!*"

I thought about the passage I'd read from T.D. Jakes's Bible: *"Nothing challenges our ability to let go like death. . . ."*

I prayed, *Dear God, don't let her die. Not like this. Please, Lord. I'm begging you. I don't know what I'll do if you take her from me.*

Praying made me think about my cell and how I never ended the call with Chicago. *God, please don't let him still be on the line,* I thought, digging into my pocket. Damn, I forgot I'd dropped my phone in the lounge chair on my balcony.

We heard sirens getting closer, the whirring sound stopped abruptly. Tisha ran downstairs. I heard her say, "She's up there. Hurry."

The paramedics raced in. "Whoa, what happened here?" one guy asked, checking her vital signs. The other paramedic saw the blood and immediately left. A minute later he returned with a gurney. They strapped Madison down and rushed her out of the bedroom.

She'd need decent clothes to wear home from the hospital. Quickly I packed a maxi-length dress and some flats. That was the fastest thing I found. On my way out I noticed her video was on. Instead of removing the tape, I powered it off, detached the camera from the tripod, and took it. She'd done this to prove to me she'd won the bet. There was no telling what was on it; and just in case the police or stupid-ass Granville came back to her house, I wasn't taking any chances. Hopefully, enough evidence was here to have Granville arrested and convicted of rape.

I ran behind the guys. "Where are you taking her?"

Once they told me, I locked Madison's door, ran into my house, placed the camera on my coffee table, grabbed my purse and car keys. Tisha followed me to my house.

"I can't go with you to the hospital," she said. "Call me when you get there."

Looking into my friend's eyes, I knew the answer but asked her, "Why not?"

"Darryl isn't home and I can't leave the kids alone. You go. Call me as soon as you know something," she said, walking away.

I went back inside, got my cell phone, and left.

It seemed like all couples, married and dating, had issues. According to Tisha, Darryl's pattern after they married was to come home around three in the morning after the club closed, go straight to bed, wake up around eight, kiss her and the kids before they started home school, and leave, claiming he was going to look for a job. She wouldn't see him again until three A.M. the next day. I hated to think he married Tisha for a place to live, but he did. Darryl knew exactly what to do to secure a place to lay his head. Maybe I was better off without a man.

En route to the hospital, my cell rang. It was Chicago. Ignoring his call wasn't the right thing to do, but I had to do that. I parked, hurried inside the emergency room, and let the intake person know I was there for Madison Tyler.

Not wanting Chicago to worry, I texted him: Sorry for the confusion. Had an emergency. Will call you tomorrow.

He replied, Is everything all right?

I didn't want to get into an exchange of messages: It will be. GN.

I called Tisha. She answered right away, asking, "Is she okay?"

"I don't know yet, but I'll stay here all night if I have to. I feel responsible."

"What do you think Granville did to her?" Tisha asked.

Shaking my head, I wondered the same. Did he rape her? Force himself inside her anally? I'd heard of women being ripped wide open by guys who either didn't care or were clueless about how to penetrate the anus properly. I prayed Madison didn't have to have surgery. If she offered it to him, he was so dumb. . . . No telling what that asshole had done.

I said, "I have no idea, but I wish I had a gun. I'd go to his house and shoot him dead. He's so stupid."

"Don't say that, Loretta. You're not that kind of person."

"I know I'm not. But some people take you to the edge. You have to fight back or get pushed off of a cliff."

I wasn't leaving until I could hug Madison and let her know how sorry I was. I sat in the hospital lobby, holding the phone and staring at the television screen while listening to Tisha complain about Darryl. I closed my eyes, until I heard an unmistakably scratchy voice.

"I'm here to check on my girlfriend, Madison Tyler."

"Tisha, you are not going to believe what fool just walked in. Girl, I gotta go."

# CHAPTER 11
## CHICAGO

What in the hell was going on?

One minute I was talking to Loretta; twenty minutes later all I heard were sirens; ten minutes after that, the call dropped. Numerous times I called Loretta, no answer. Then I tried Madison, voice mail . . . again.

There wasn't much I could do. The team wasn't flying back from Cincinnati to Houston until the morning. I paced in my suite. Worrying was not getting me answers.

I sat in the middle of the floor, folded my legs, placed the back of my hands on my thighs, opened my palms, then closed my eyes. I inhaled deeply, held my breath. Usually, I'd wait five seconds, but this time I didn't exhale until I could no longer hold it in. Clearing my mind, I concentrated to remove all thoughts. I focused on the large, dark circle until it became a tiny black dot, then disappeared.

Meditation and prayer always helped to

center me, but the two were very different. Prayer gave me strength and faith. Leaving everything in God's hands was easier said than done, knowing He gave me the power to make a difference. Meditating gave me inner peace and clarity.

Right now, I didn't want to think the worst. My breath was all I heard. My body felt lighter. I heard girls giggling outside my door. Whatever they were giddy about didn't concern me, but they broke my concentration.

What else could I do? My parents and Chaz were back at home. "That's it." I sat on the bed and called my brother.

"What's up?" Chaz answered, sounding like he was still excited from our big *W*. That, or he was ready for me to get home so we could collect our $10 million from Granddaddy.

"I need a favor, man."

Without hesitation he said, "Anything. I'm all ears."

"I haven't heard from Madison all day."

"Aw, man, don't tell me you're going to be one of those engaged guys who's freaking out about what his woman is doing when he's not around."

"You know me better than that."

"I know, but don't start getting caught up

like this. You know me, I don't believe in reeling women in, tying them up or down. I'll give a female all the rope she needs. What she does with it is up to her. She can hang herself, have her freedom, play tug-of-war, use it to escape, or hang in there with me. Relationships are simple. Women are complicated. Give her some rope, man. She might be up to no good. You'll be home tomorrow."

Chaz was right. I shouldn't worry about Madison. I didn't think she was sexing some other man, but what if . . .

"Look, man, I was on the phone with Loretta, and —"

"You mean the Loretta that you're hooking me up with? Man, you'd better leave my woman alone." Chaz laughed, then continued, "Y'all cool like that?"

"She's my prayer buddy."

"Your prayer what? Since when? I thought y'all just had that one conversation after you proposed to Madison. You weren't sure about Madison then, and you're not sure now. I know you. But back to Loretta. You know that's how shit starts, right? One minute you're praying, the next minute your dick is in her hand, then you're fucking."

I laughed. Chaz always kept it real.

"You know me better than that, man. I'm

serious. I need you to go to Madison's house right now while I'm on the phone and see if she's there. If she's not, go next door to Loretta's. If you won't do this for me, I'll call and ask Mom."

Chaz knew if I was willing to call our mom to go check on Madison, I had to be desperate. I was. I had to know before I could go to sleep. Otherwise, I'd be up all night.

"Obviously, you're serious. I'm on it," he said.

I loved Madison. One day shouldn't have been that big a deal, but I sensed something was wrong. Would never believe she'd cheat on me. That wasn't it. She always made time to text and call, so for her not to do either was unusual. It was probably the way she'd licked my ass that had me all messed up. When I got home, I was going to do the same for her. Lick her ass the way she'd done mine. Make her scream my name until she came. Then I was going to make love to her like never before, whisper in her ear about the $10 million, then pour champagne on her toes and suck it off. Maybe I'd buy her a diamond waist chain. Maybe she was doing one of those silent-protest things that females do when they want to know something their man won't tell them.

"Chaz?"

"Yeah."

"Where are you?"

"I'm almost there, man. Chill out."

My brother lived at the Royalton too. Our condos were less than fifteen minutes from where Madison, Loretta, and Tisha lived.

"I just drove up. The lights are on, so that's a good sign."

"Go knock on the door," I told him.

"Cool."

I heard Chaz knocking.

"Ring the doorbell."

"I did. She's not answering."

"Go next door to Loretta's."

"I'm on my way. Only for you, dude."

I heard him knocking.

"She's not answering either?"

"Nah, man."

"Go to Tisha's. She lives in the redbrick house with the green shutters on the other side of Loretta."

"You've got it bad. Last chance, man, then I'm out."

I heard him knocking a third time. I prayed she was there.

"The lights came on, so somebody's home," Chaz said.

I took a deep breath. My heart rate slowed. I started pacing again.

I heard Tisha ask, "Who in the hell are

you? And why are you knocking on my door?"

"I'm sorry to disturb you this time of night, Tisha, but Chicago is worried about Madison. I'm his brother, Chaz."

"I'm sorry. It's just that you don't go knocking on strangers' doors this time of morning. Loretta just called. They're keeping Madison overnight for observation."

"What the fuck!" I said. "Overnight for observation? Ask her what happened, and what hospital?"

"What happened? What hospital?" Chaz asked.

"Who are you talking to?" Tisha asked.

"Chicago."

"Oh . . . wow. Um, it's not that serious. I think she ate something she was allergic to."

"Ask her what hospital," I said again.

"Do you know where she's at?"

"She should be home soon. I can't remember where they went, but Loretta is with her. I'll text Loretta to make sure Madison calls Chicago as soon as she can. Tell Chicago not to worry. Madison will be okay." Then I heard Tisha say, "Good night."

My heart pounded. I told my brother, "I heard her. Madison is at the hospital. Now the sirens make sense. Thanks, man. I'll call around and see if I can find out which one she's in."

"If you need me, call me," Chaz said. "But I suggest you get some rest. Even if you find out where she is, there's nothing you can do tonight. At least now you know why she didn't call."

Chaz was wrong. I was sure the second Madison heard my voice, she'd smile, knowing I cared enough to find her.

"I love that woman."

"I know. And I'm happy for you. But she's not a dog. You can't put a microchip in her ass and track her every move the second she doesn't call or text. One day I'd like to feel that way about a woman again," Chaz said. "But ain't no way I'm turning into a private investigator."

My brother was going to fall for Loretta. And when he did, he was going to be the same way, and then I'd remind him of his words.

"You will."

I dropped to my knees. "Thank you, Lord, for keeping Madison safe. I don't know what I'd do without her," I prayed aloud.

"I can put a tracking device on her phone for you. That way you'll always know where she's at," Chaz suggested.

"I'm not doing that. I trust my woman."

"It's not about trust. Think about it. Let

me know if you want me to download a GPS on her cell."

# CHAPTER 12
## MADISON

Tisha coming up with my having allergies was a brilliant idea, but I didn't have any that I knew of. The one food I've hated all my life was coconut. Knowing I'd never slip up and eat it, I'd tell my fiancé that's what I had a bad reaction to. I was relieved Tisha hadn't told Chaz which hospital I was in or the real reason I was there. Her loyalty gave me time to get my lie together.

Being in a small, cold emergency room for five hours, I'd spent most of my time waiting to get seen by a professional. Patients who were shot, stabbed, hit by a car, having or had a heart attack came first. Tired of feeling the blood dry, I ended up cleaning my own ass. Wasn't as though they needed evidence for a rape kit. If I could've inspected myself, I would've done that too.

Finally, when a doctor did come in, he stuck his finger up my ass. Said he had to disimpact my stool in order to determine the extent of the damage. I wasn't sure if I wanted to scream because the pain was more emotional or physical, but I let it all out on both ends. He recommended minor surgery with a few stitches. I refused. He suggested I stay a few days for observation. I declined. He wrote me a prescription for Tylenol 4 with codeine and said, "No vaginal intercourse for six days, and no anal sex for six weeks. You should be okay by then."

I gave myself three days for vaginal and I'd try to refrain from anal, as he'd told me. The dress and shoes Loretta had sent in had to do. I'd put them on after the exam. I was happy the doctor didn't say no sex of any kind for six weeks. I guess having my anal tissues slightly torn wasn't as bad as having a baby. Tisha never waited long after having her kids to have sex, but I wasn't taking any chances with my rectum. I might not have anal sex again until I was married.

When I was released at three in the morning, Loretta was waiting for me. She took me to the pharmacy to get my meds. I cursed out Loretta all the way home. Her apologies didn't mean a damn thing. That bitch making that stupid bet because she was jealous of my engagement was one thing, but her befriending my fiancé had to come to an end. She'd fucked up my life enough already.

I got out of her car, slammed her door, went inside my house, and sat on the sofa. I wasn't mentally prepared to go upstairs and see what condition my bedroom was in. I'd gone to the kitchen, taken two Tylenols, and retuned to the sofa. After an hour my body began to relax. Felt like I was floating and nothing mattered. I closed my eyes. My body was heavy and light at the same time as my back sank into the cushions.

My doorbell rang and awakened me. I had no idea what time it was. The sun shined through my front windows. Seemed as though I'd just fallen asleep. I'd awakened on the sofa. Now my ass and back ached.

"I'm coming," I said. Dragging my feet, I placed my hand on my hip. I still had on the sundress and flats. As I opened the door, there stood the second to last person I wanted in my home. I left the door open, then walked away.

"Madison, we need to talk about what's happening. I am truly sorry." Loretta closed my door and followed me to the living room.

"Sorry enough to stop talking to my man? Sorry I'm the one who got screwed and fucked at the same time? Or sorry you lost the bet?" I said, reminding her I'd won.

181

"I came by to give you your camera before I go to work. That, and to see if you needed anything."

I took the video recorder, but I didn't have a thank-you for her. Had run out of curse words last night and I didn't feel like repeating myself. I opened the camera.

"Where's the tape? Did you forget to put it back after you watched it?"

Her eyes stretched north and south. "I didn't take anything out, I swear, and you know I wouldn't do that. Let me see."

She reached for the camera. I pulled it back. At this point, in my opinion, Loretta was capable of anything.

"Then where is it? I don't know who you are anymore." I paused. Our eyes met. Loretta felt like a stranger who had come to my front door.

"Are you going to press charges against Granville?" she asked. "I'll help you. I have an attorney processing my paperwork for a protective order. I can tell her to do yours too. We can go to court together. That'll make our case stronger. I got you into this. Let me help get you out."

She still didn't get it. Or maybe this was exactly what she wanted me to do. Follow her lead.

"Hell no, I'm not pressing anything. If I

do that, Roosevelt will start questioning me; and knowing you, I'm sure you'll tell him everything and my engagement will be off. Is that what you've been praying for, Miss So-called Christian?"

Her eyes filled with tears.

"Get out of my house." I escorted her to the exit.

She faced me. When she opened her mouth, I slammed the door in her face.

My cell buzzed, indicating I had a text message. I picked up my phone. It was from that asshole! It read: need me to bring you anything dear? you are my boss.

I called Granville's supervisor and told him Granville had violated company policy; then I instructed him to send Granville to human resources. I called HR and gave them my instructions.

His ignorant ass had to go. Tomorrow, when he reported to my office, I'd personally reinforce what I'd instructed HR to do today. Thanks to Loretta, the wrong man was consuming my energy.

Roosevelt was worried about me and I had to keep it that way for six weeks, or until my rectum had recovered from the torn tissues. Something as simple as having a bowel movement was going to hurt like hell. I swallowed two more Tylenols with a large glass of water.

Sitting on the toilet, scared to push, I cried. The emergency doctor had advised me to make a follow-up appointment with my general practitioner. I had to consult with a woman, so I made myself an appointment with my gynecologist, instead. After what had happened, I had to have all my entry points checked out before letting Roosevelt make love to me. There was no telling what Granville had done after I'd passed out.

I'd learned the hard way that some men actually could tell when their woman had been with another man. With my intense anal pain, I couldn't risk having sex and making it worse, or take a chance on losing my man if he found out the truth.

Too afraid to shit, I wiped myself, then flushed the toilet. What if the condom had come off while Granville was inside me? What if that fool took it off on purpose? What if Granville had a disease? At least the one thing I wasn't worried about was having Granville's baby. Maybe this was a good time to stop taking my birth control pills. That way if I got pregnant for Roosevelt, I'd give him a reason to marry me right away.

My phone rang. I smiled. Did a little

dance. It was my baby.

"Hey," I answered seductively.

"You okay?" he asked.

"I'm good. A little sick from the coconut." I was scared to death. What if I had permanent damage? How could I explain that to him?

"I'll make you feel better when I get in. I can't wait to see you. I miss you so much. Our next game is at home, so I'll be around to take care of you personally. No more coconut for you, young lady."

"Why don't you call your concierge and give him permission to let me in," I suggested.

"Soon as we hang up, it's done. I have to board our plane. . . . Madison?"

"Yes, baby."

He whispered, "I was worried all day and night. Next time, baby, answer your phone, send me a quick text, or have Loretta contact me."

I was pissed her name kept coming out of his mouth. "Okay" was all I said.

"I love you."

Making a kissing sound in his ear, I told him the truth. "I love you too."

Soon as I hung up, I screamed, *"Ahhh!"* A sharp pain pierced my rectum forcing me to fall to my knees.

Between the anger about Loretta and the pain in my ass, I didn't know which one was worse. The meds were making me sluggish, but I had to go. I showered, dressed, and left my house. I stopped at Rice grocery store, picked up a few things to cook, along with some Epsom salt, and then headed to Roosevelt's.

I wanted to call Loretta and curse that bitch out again. Since she talked to God so much, she'd better pray this situation turned out okay or she'd be begging Him for me to stop beating her ass.

# CHAPTER 13
## GRANVILLE

When was Loretta going to learn that trying to get me arrested wasn't working for her? Soon as she heard my voice, she started yelling and ran out of the emergency room to the police officer on duty. I calmly took a seat and waited. The cop came in; he detained and questioned me.

I explained to the officer it was an accident. I didn't give him any details because I didn't want Loretta to overhear. What had happened was between me and my woman. Not him. And definitely not Loretta. She was my ex. Didn't miss a good man until I was gone. Now she was tripping because she'd never get any more of my big woody.

My dick slid inside Madison so fast that I had no idea I was in her ass until after I came the second time, pulled out, then saw all the blood. She was so small I was impressed that she could aggressively ride this old cowboy. I was her horse; she was my jockey. And she was much better in bed than Loretta.

After the officer checked with Madison, I wasn't sure what she'd told him, but I was released immediately. I felt he owed me an apology, which I didn't get. Why people kept doing me wrong, I had no idea.

Just in case Madison tried to act like Loretta and deny what we had was real, I'd rushed and installed a GPS tracking device on Madison's iPhone before I'd ran out of her house. I registered her information, got the code from her e-mail account, which was open and running, confirmed myself as an approved person, and then hid the application in her utilities file. I barely got out in time. As Loretta and Tisha came running toward the house, I got in my truck and sped off.

Taking a quick break, I went to my truck to check on my woman. We weren't permitted to have cell phones on-site, so I was risking getting a written warning if I got caught. If that happened, it would be my first. Now that I was dating the owner, I gave myself this special privilege, knowing she'd have my back.

Madison hadn't called me since she'd left the hospital. My tracker indicated that she was at home, but how did I know for sure?

I'm certain she didn't have her iPhone at the hospital; because by the time I'd found her, I'd been to three different emergency rooms. Well, I couldn't worry about that now. She'd get her phone eventually. Between home and hospital I'd find her when I got off work.

I called her. Pressed *face time* on my cell. Reading the message, I frowned. The option wasn't available. *Hmm. Gotta figure out why that didn't work.*

I texted her: need me to bring you anything dear? you are my boss.

Laughing out loud, I cracked myself up. What woman could resist my infectious humor?

My supervisor tapped on my window. "It's not break time, Washington. Get your ass out your truck and report to me."

He'd better be careful how he talked to me. After I marry Madison, he'd have to answer to me.

"Sure thing," I said, checking for a reply to my text. There wasn't one.

She was probably blowing off a little steam by ignoring me. I'd pick her up some flowers after I got off and take them to her house. That kind of stuff cheered women up. Dropping my phone in the middle compartment, I locked the door; then I trotted back to the site and got back to work. Didn't want both of my bosses to be mad.

My supervisor walked over to me. I'd never seen that look on his face. His teeth were tight like a pit bull about to bite off my head.

"What's wrong with you, man?" I curled my fingers tightly. If I didn't hesitate to knock Beaux on his ass, I wasn't going to let this dude catch me off guard.

"I should ask you that. I told you to report to me, not back to work. Washington, I've been instructed to give you the rest of the day off. Report to human resources immediately."

I laughed so hard that my throat hurt.

"I'm serious, Washington. Leave now," he said.

Removing my hard hat, I slammed it to the ground. "Be careful how you treat the people you meet on your way up, dude. You . . ." I scratched my head.

*Wait a minute. This could be a good thing. Maybe Madison forgot to tell me last night that I'm getting promoted.*

I picked up my hat and skipped to my truck. There were no messages from Madison, so this had to be a big surprise. I happily headed to HR.

When I arrived, they were obviously

expecting me, for I was escorted to a conference room, with three women seated around the table. I wasn't turned on by any of those females. I was so loyal to my woman that I didn't even get a woody. Something good was going to come out of this, I felt it.

"Good morning, ladies."

"Have a seat, Mr. Washington," one of them said with authority.

I curled my lips down and stared at her as she looked at me over her glasses; then I wobbled my head, thinking, *You're not the boss of me.*

"Give me the news. I finally made supervisor." I laughed, then smiled.

Hopefully, Madison hadn't changed her mind and decided to file charges. I hadn't done anything to feel bad about, but women didn't care if a man was right when they felt wronged. Afraid a cop might walk in, I glanced over my shoulder.

"Mr. Washington, your employment here at Tyler Construction is terminated, effective immediately."

*Terminated?* My head snapped in her direction. *Did Madison set me up? She wouldn't make love to me, then let me go, would she?*

"Why? What did I do?"

"You walked off the job this morning. We

have to let you go. Your absence could've cost injuries to other employees."

"But it didn't."

"But it could have. You're a liability, Mr. Washington. We're also downsizing due to budget cuts and we have to determine who's reliable. What you did was a violation to" — she slid a sheet of paper in front of me — "our policy."

I ripped it up. "I'll talk to the owner about this."

"I was going to get to that next," she said. "You need to report to Miss Tyler's office at eight in the morning. If you show up at the work site, you'll be arrested for trespassing."

Madison sure had a strange way of showing her love. *I guess she's one of those independent women used to doing things her way.*

"I'm sure this misunderstanding will be cleared up *mañana*," I said in my best Al Pacino voice, then left the conference room.

I got into my truck, checked my phone. Madison was at . . . on Allen Parkway. Why was she there? I headed to her location — the Royalton. That was a big, fancy condominium building. I parked in the large circular driveway with an oversized water fountain. I wasn't buying anything here, so

192

I didn't park in the spaces marked FUTURE HOMEOWNER.

A valet came out. "Who are you here to see?" he asked.

I deepened my voice, then said, "Madison Tyler."

"Who? I can't understand you. Who are you here to see?" he asked again.

Letting go of my macho baritone, which didn't impress him, I repeated, "Madison Tyler."

"We don't have a Madison Tyler who *resides* here."

"But I know she's here," I said. "My tracking device shows her at this address."

"Are you stalking someone?" he asked. He walked to the rear of my truck and took a picture of my license plate with his phone. "Unless you know someone who lives here and you have their permission to enter this property, stay away from this building," he said, taking a photo of me.

*Fuck him!* I sped out of the driveway, got on the interstate, and then headed to Port Arthur to have Loretta's name turned into that fire-breathing dragon.

The cover-up hurt more than getting the original tattoo. I was so angry, and I took the pain like a man. It was my fault Madison was avoiding me, but she'd better not be seeing another man. I'd made Madison suffer, and I deserved to hurt too.

"Dig deeper, dude. Make me bleed until the blood runs down my chest." I couldn't hold back my tears. I started crying. I wanted to lay my head on his shoulder. I wasn't gay, but I needed someone to feel sorry for me in order for me to feel better.

The artist took a picture, put ointment on my chest, then bandaged my new tat. "Be happy, dude. You said neither Loretta nor Madison ever saw the tat. That's a good thing. You can't be sportin' a dragon and be acting like a girl."

"You're right. Thanks, man," I said, handing the tattoo artist three hundred dollars.

"If you need that fire-breathing dragon turned into fireworks, I'm your man."

Putting on my shirt, I asked him, "What don't you do?"

"Men," he said.

I got into my truck and headed to where I knew I always had a shoulder to lean on. Couldn't come this close without seeing my mom.

I didn't want to believe I was really fired. *That's it!* A smile crossed my face. Now I understood why she was letting me go.

I couldn't be her employee *and* her lover.

# CHAPTER 14
## MADISON

The neck pillow that I usually put behind my head while taking a bath was underneath my butt. The elevation relieved some of the pressure. I rested my neck on a folded towel, reassuring myself it wasn't that bad. If I were a praying woman, I'd ask for forgiveness of all my sins. It wasn't like I didn't believe in a Higher Power.

Something or someone had to have created the universe, galaxy, and spirit that existed inside me. Atheists and Christians could walk side by side and you'd never know who was what, unless they told you, because some of the people who called themselves Christians treated people worse than I have.

My friends didn't have to take my advice, do as I'd done, or follow in my direction. I wasn't trying to lead them or anybody else. I was reared to express myself and never shrink for others. My high standards and high self-esteem came naturally.

The power of positive thinking had served me well over the years. My optimistic attitude toward men earned me a collection of rings, which I was proud of. Many women would live their entire lives and never have diamonds put on their fingers or have husbands. Truth was, those women weren't very smart, especially the ones who bought their own engagement or wedding ring.

My outlook on business had saved my dad's company from prior potential catastrophes. And my friendships with Loretta and Tisha had survived three decades. I didn't want new friends, but I didn't want my girlfriends too close to my man either. I definitely didn't want them to know I was struggling not to lose my status in the corporate world.

Thirty minutes soaking made a huge difference. I toweled off, called in-house housekeeping, and had them come clean the bathroom. I'd have to submerge my body again, right before Roosevelt arrived, but now it was time to swallow two more Tylenols and keep things moving.

Unpacking the groceries, I chopped chives, onions, and red and yellow bell peppers. I diced the tomatoes and ham, fried then crumbled the bacon, sliced the mushroom, then shredded the American and Swiss cheese. I wasn't much of a baker, so I placed five Pillsbury cinnamon rolls on a baking sheet and preset the oven to 375. The champagne was on ice and the orange and cranberry juices were in the fridge chilling.

I didn't care much for cooking, but I was great at it. I was damn near perfect at everything I'd done. Whisking the eggs for omelets, I imagined Raynard's wife, Gloria, was the same way. A glamorous perfectionist. That's probably how she snagged him from Loretta. Women who were brainwashed that love was enough, or love would make their relationship last, didn't understand men. A man didn't always intend to break a woman's heart, but he did. So a woman had to have a plan to get and keep her man.

My priorities were similar to my mother's. I had to have financial stability, emotional security (which was different from love), and a man with family values. The religious side of Roosevelt was a bonus. I was no hypocrite. I'd never gone to church with him. But if Loretta didn't back off, I might have to join Second Baptist.

Suddenly my stomach hurt more than my

ass. I'd taken four painkillers and hadn't eaten a thing. I toasted a slice of bread, scrambled an egg, and ate it while standing in the kitchen.

After I finished my light meal, the doorbell buzzed the same time as my cell. I opened the door and let the maid in.

"The master bath," I said, then answered Roosevelt's call.

"I'm almost home. You need me to pick up anything from the store?"

"Thanks, babe, but I've got it covered. I think my allergies are trying to act up again, but I'll be fine. I'm preparing brunch for us." My intent was to keep him in empathy mode.

"Go lay down and rest. I'll call my chef right now. He can cook for us."

"That's why I love you so much. You take such good care of me. Don't bother calling your chef. I've got a surprise for you. I love you, honey."

"I like that. I love you too. See you in a few."

"Okay, bye." I ended the call with a smile on my face.

*Oh shit!* A needlelike penetration darted up my rectum to my spine and brought me to my knees. *God, please take away this pain.* Perhaps I was a Christian in my own way. I crawled to his bed and lay underneath the covers. I had so much on my mind.

"I'm done, miss," the maid said.

Rolling onto my stomach, I told her, "Thanks," but I didn't get out of bed. I listened until I heard the door close.

"Hey, baby. Daddy's home," Roosevelt said, entering the room shortly after the maid had left.

Obviously, his path had crossed with the maid's exit. I carefully propped my back against the headboard. "Hey, you," I whispered.

He sat on the side of the bed, kissed my forehead, and then touched my hair. "I missed you so much, Madison. How're you feeling?"

"I'll be okay. I just need to relax for a moment."

"Well, I have some news that might cheer you up a bit."

With all the craziness happening, I'd forgotten about his surprise. I smiled.

"I wish I could hold things in like you, baby."

"I don't want you to ever keep anything from me ever. You ready for our surprise?"

" 'Our'?"

"*Our* . . . the ten million my grandfather is giving me." Before he completed his sentence, my eyes lit up. "We'll have it in two days. He decided not to wait until after he dies to give it to us. He's giving Chaz his and I'll get mine."

I wasn't sure if the "we" and "us" included me, or if he was referring to Chaz; but as far as I was concerned, his money was ours. I was going to make my dad so happy when I gave him the news.

Holding his face in my palms, I said, "We should think about getting married right after the season is over." Then I planted a sloppy kiss on him.

"Baby, what's the rush? That's two months away. My mom wants me to wait two years."

"I'm not marrying your mom and I'm not waiting that long to start having your babies."

"You're right. I agree. Two years is too long. Let's talk about this later. I'm going to take a shower so I can get in bed with my baby and Aphrodite and start practicing on having our first."

My eyes widened. Sex wasn't what I had in mind.

"First things first," I said.

"That's the chef. I didn't know you'd cooked, so I'd called him anyway. Let me get rid of him and I'll be right back," Roosevelt said, disappearing out of view.

I was so overjoyed I forgot about my ass hurting. Maybe sex would help me feel better. If I could ignore a cramp in my leg during sex, then overlooking a pain in my ass should be easier. I'd have to make sure Roosevelt took it slow, and there was no way I was getting on top at any point soon.

He came back in the bedroom. "Invite Loretta, Tisha, and their kids to my suite for this Sunday's game so we can announce our wedding date in three months," he said, holding up three fingers.

"Really!" I said, holding up two fingers.

"Really, babe. You're right. You love me. I feel the same about you. What's the point of waiting? Where's my ring? Put it on and don't take it off again," he said, entering the bathroom.

Roosevelt had just made me the happiest woman in the world, but I was not inviting Loretta anywhere.

# CHAPTER 15
## MADISON

Brunch was wonderful yesterday. Afterward, we curled up in bed and watched Kevin Hart's standup concert movie while eating popcorn and enjoying a few cocktails. Consuming alcohol with meds wasn't recommended; but for the first time since the incident with Granville, I was feeling pleasant. And I was thankful I'd made it through the night without having sex with Roosevelt.

Usually, we spooned where he held me in his arms, but this time I cradled my breasts to his back and slept peacefully. The position was my way of avoiding tempting him to have intercourse. I couldn't risk having him getting an erection and trying to penetrate me in the middle of the night. I didn't want to lie about why we couldn't. I wasn't ready.

Opening my eyes, I kissed the nape of his neck.

Roosevelt faced me and pressed his lips to

mine. "Good morning, sunshine."

"Morning, my love."

"How'd you sleep?" he asked.

"So good," I moaned. "I appreciate you, baby. The way you love me makes me feel like the luckiest woman in the world." This time I pressed my lips to his.

"What's on your schedule today?"

"I have to go into the office," I said, easing out of bed. "Then, this afternoon, I have a doctor's appointment."

"For your allergies?"

"Yes," I lied.

My butt ached, but not nearly as much. I was actually able to walk normally to the bathroom. I drew bathwater, went to the kitchen, ate a cinnamon roll from the day before, and then swallowed two Tylenols with a glass of water. Didn't want any unnecessary pains hitting me unexpectedly.

Roosevelt had tucked himself underneath the covers up to his neck. I closed the bathroom door and enjoyed another Epsom salt soak. Moisturizing my body, I massaged leave-in conditioner into my hair; then I used a wide tooth comb to create a swerve pattern in my short platinum hair.

Representing power and highlighting my Creole beauty, red was the color for today. I put on my low-rise fitted skirt, a camisole, my short-sleeved buttoned jacket, and matching stilettos.

"Bye, babe. You going into the office?" I asked.

"Yeah, I need to get up. How about lunch? You have time?"

"I always have time for you. Call me," I said, leaving his place.

Waiting for the valet to get my car, I thumbed through my iPhone. Twelve new text messages and they were all from . . . Was he serious?

i love you madison.

please call me dear.

i can't wait until tomorrow to see you.

what are you doing at the royalton?

are you seeing another man?

am i being promoted?

please please call me dear.

what are you doing?

you want to have coffee before our meeting?

why have you been at the royalton all night?

are you cheating on me?

who did you spend the night with?

This fool was stalking me. How did he know where I was? I set a pass code to lock my phone. Couldn't take any chances on Roosevelt accidentally seeing text messages from Granville.

Before getting into my Ferrari, I glanced around the circular driveway; then I put on my sunglasses. It was sunny and unusually warm for this time of year. This was the kind of weather where Roosevelt and I would have sex outside in my pool. His balcony faced the street; and although he was in the penthouse, we couldn't risk anyone taking nude photos and putting them on the Internet. If I continued getting healthy, I would be able to make love to my man in a few days.

I let down my retractable hard top. My office wasn't far from Roosevelt's condo, but I wanted to inhale the fresh air. The wind grazed my scalp. Two blocks down the street and Granville's truck was behind my car.

He pulled alongside me at the red light.

"Madison," he shouted in that disgusting, scratchy voice. "Where were you?"

As soon as the light changed to green, I sped off. Damn near running every light, I put up my top. I used my corporate pass to enter the parking garage. Thank goodness, he didn't have the same privilege. He had to use a separate entrance into the visitors' lot.

I hurried to my office.

"Monica, when Mr. Washington arrives,

after he comes into my office, wait ten minutes, then have security come up to escort him out of the building. Advise them that he's not allowed access to my floor in the future."

"Sure, Ms. Tyler. Your dad called as you were walking in. He's on hold."

"Tell him I'll call him later," I said, shutting my door. I sat behind my desk and phoned Loretta.

She answered, "Hey, how are you?"

"Fucking pissed. That's how I am. How did Granville know where I was yesterday, last night, and this morning?"

"I have no idea."

"Liar! You told him."

"I tried to warn you."

"No, your ass set me up. That's what the fuck you did. Roosevelt wanted me to invite you and Raynell to his suite on Sunday to watch the game, but I'm uninviting you."

"Fine, Madison. I'm tired of trying to prove myself to you. If you need me, I'm here for you. But if all you intend to do is insult me, don't call me. And be careful. Granville is a dangerous man."

I ended the call without saying bye. Monica buzzed me.

"Yes."

"Mr. Granville Washington is here."

"Send him in, and do what I asked."

That fool entered dressed like he was on his way to a rodeo. He had one hand behind his back, his cowboy hat over the left side of his chest, and he had that stupid smirk on his face. Someone needed to tell him that skinny mustache was repulsive. He needed to shave it off.

"Here, dear, I brought these for you," he said, handing me the most repulsive bunch of flowers I'd ever seen. Where'd he get those? From a grave site after they'd sat in the sun for two weeks and dried up?

I snatched the bouquet and slammed it in the trash.

"Have a seat," I told him.

"Yes, dear," he said, plopping into the leather seat and damn near knocking it over again. He stared at the flowers; then he hung his head toward his lap as he pouted. "I'm sorry."

"Granville, I wanted you to understand that you are fired from Tyler Construction. You are not allowed on the construction site or on this floor. I wish I could ban you from this entire building."

"What did I do wrong?" he asked, still staring down.

"Everything. Where do you want me to start? You kidnapped Loretta. You violated me. You —"

His head lifted and his eyes narrowed as he cut me off. Wiping his wet nose, he said, "You haven't mentioned anything work related. Last time I was here, you said I was doing a good job. Loretta is history. You invited me to your house. You pursued me. You obviously want to be my woman. I accept, dear."

My voice escalated. "I am not your damn woman!" I flashed my finger in his face. "I'm engaged."

*Oh damn!* I opened my drawer. *Jesus, no, where is it?* I fumbled through the pencils, pens, writing pads, and . . . exhaled. I slid it on my finger and held it toward Granville's face. "You can't afford this or me. Unemployment won't pay you enough."

I wanted to pick up my paperweight and knock him on his ignorant head. What a waste.

"I don't care about your ring. You are my woman."

I pushed back my chair, stood, and yelled, "Get your retarded ass out!" Then I pointed toward the door. "And don't ever come back here! And stop stalking me!"

He stood and flicked his eyebrows. "Yes, dear," he said, then laughed. "I crack myself up."

Never had I wanted to beat a man down until now. "And stop being so stupid!"

He placed his hat on his head and stopped in the doorway. He rubbed his chest and hoisted his big brass buckle. "I haven't broken any laws or policies. If you go through with firing me, I'll charge you with sexual harassment. And if you're wondering where that video of us is, I've got it, dear," he said, then laughed again.

"You filthy, dirty bastard," I hissed. "Return that tape to me immediately. That's mine. I'll sue you for defamation if that gets out. Security! Get him out of here," I demanded. I couldn't stand the sight of him. "And make sure he never comes back."

*Slam!* I closed my door. *That fool! Ugh! I hate him! I hate Loretta.* I called her back.

"What now?" she answered.

"You're going to pay for this shit!"

"What are you talking about?" she asked, sounding clueless.

"I've decided what I want from you."

"Madison, I'm at work. What are you talking about?"

"Since you lost the bet, I want you to sign over the deed to your property to me and move out by the end of the month. I don't even want to have you as my neighbor. I hate you!"

Loretta became quiet for a moment; then she said, "God hasn't given you any power over me. You have a right to feel however you want, but you lost the bet."

Was she serious? Was she in cahoots with Granville?

"I had sex with him. I won the bet."

"Prove it. How do I know you had sex with him? And for the record you haven't tamed him . . . and you won't. I just pray God keeps you safe. You're so consumed with making everybody around you feel like they're beneath you that you don't know how to be a friend. Don't call me again, Madison. Good-bye and God bless."

*That bitch! How dare she turn this on me!*

# CHAPTER 16
## MADISON

Revenge was mine. Stunned, I sat at my desk. Those dreadful flowers were stinking up my office.

Monica buzzed a few minutes later. "Your dad is on the line."

"I'll take his call. Send in a janitor to empty my trash."

Might as well take my dad's call. If I didn't, he'd phone back in a few minutes. "Hi, Papa."

"Good morning, sweetheart. Were you able to set a wedding date?" he asked.

"He agreed to do it after the season in three months."

"Three? They probably won't make the AFC championship game. Can you move it up to two? We really need to save the company."

"No! I can't! I won't! And we will make the play-offs! Am I not doing enough for you? It's not my responsibility to make sure you have a private plane to fly around in, while I bust my behind. Leave me alone!" I said, then ended the call.

Damn! I had to rethink who and what was most important to me. I made a few calls to the city. If I could light a fire under the city, I wouldn't have to access Roosevelt's money.

I learned that our invoices had not been processed and it would be at least another few weeks. Translation: probably months. I had no idea when they'd cut us a check, but I could meet payroll until the wedding — if I walked down the aisle in my father's time.

Shutting down my computer, I needed a dose of positivity. I called Roosevelt.

"Hey, babe. I was just getting ready to call you. I'm finishing up. You ready?"

I smiled on the inside, then whispered, "Yes, I am."

"Damn, sounds like we might have to get a room and have lunch delivered to us. You want to meet at Hotel ZaZa?"

"Oh yes," I moaned. I needed an escape and sex, even if it was just oral. "Wait until I get my hands on Tiger. I'ma make him roar like never before."

Roosevelt cleared his throat. "Should I reserve our favorite Magnificent Suite, with the tub on the balcony?"

Roosevelt was the type of man with money that I loved. Our preferred Black Label suite, if it were available, might cost upward of $1,500 for the night. Soaking in their outdoor sunken tub was one of the most romantic experiences I'd had in Houston. Hot summer nights by candlelight, sipping champagne and leaning my head back on my man's chest as we gazed up at the stars, were some of my fondest memories.

An idiot like Granville couldn't comfortably spend that amount on a regular basis without worrying about how to pay his rent. The $90,000 a year I paid him couldn't pay my state — let alone federal — taxes.

"Why don't we meet at Monarch for lunch?" I said, smiling. That man made me so happy.

There was a tap on my door. "Janitor," a voice said.

"Come in," I said, pointing at the wastebasket next to my desk.

"So you're teasing me, huh?"

"Oh, I haven't teased you yet, baby. But I do have to go to the doctor at three, so I can't feast on you in the room. Rain check?"

I had to keep this appointment. My rectum felt a lot better. It was tolerably sore, but I'd feel more comfortable with a professional assessment.

"That's right," he said. "I can be there in thirty."

"Okay, babe. I'll see you then."

I started to take two more Tylenols, as prescribed, with a bottle of water but changed my mind. The suggested two tablets four times a day was making me light-headed. Plus, I didn't want to get addicted to a prescription medication. I grabbed my purse, and exited my office.

"Monica, I'll be out the rest of the day. If anyone calls, text me the message."

"Have a great afternoon, Miss Tyler."

Driving out of the garage, I checked my rearview and side mirrors. My eyes widened in anticipation of seeing that jerk. What was it going to take to get rid of Granville? I was positive I hadn't seen the last of him. If I had brothers, I'd have them silence Granville with a good old-fashioned ass whuppin'. The kind that would send *him* to the emergency room with a few broken bones.

I valet parked at Hotel ZaZa, entered the Monarch, and requested a table for two on the patio. The sun had warmed the city up to seventy degrees. While I was waiting for Roosevelt, I checked my messages. I had a text from Tisha: OMG! How are you? Loretta told me you two aren't speaking. We've got to squash this feud. Stop by my house when you get home. Love you.

Well, it was good to know I had one girlfriend in my life.

"Can I get you something to drink?" the waiter asked.

I had a taste for one of those black apple-tinis, but mixing Crown whiskey with the meds I'd taken this morning wouldn't settle well on my empty stomach.

"A bottle of your best champagne," I said, knowing a few sips of bubbly wouldn't hurt and it would complement whatever we ordered to eat.

"Hey, baby," I said, standing to press my breasts next to my soon-to-be multimil-lionaire husband.

He smiled, placed a bouquet of orange, pink, red, and yellow hybrid roses on the table, lifted me off my feet, and then kissed me. Roosevelt sat next to me.

"Did Loretta tell you she's going out on a date with Chaz?"

*F her.* Why did her name have to be the first to come out of my man's mouth? He still didn't get it. I should pick up the flow-ers and hit him over the head. Instead, I sniffed them.

"They're going out without us? What hap-pened to our double date?"

*OMG. What if Chaz falls in love with Loretta and marries her? Then she'd be my sister-in-law.* No way was I going to let that happen. If Chaz went out on a second date with my ex-girlfriend, I'd show her how it felt to have someone ruin her relationship.

"They're grown. They'll be fine. I'm concerned about us, not them," he said, staring at me as if he knew my secret.

If Loretta told him, I'd kill her for sure.

"What's on your mind?" I asked, inhaling the fresh air. I gently touched my roses. Looking at them helped calm me. I sniffed them again.

"Things seem too good to be true," he said. "Rumor has it Blue Waters may get a GM position in Oakland."

"Really? Well, we wish him well on that. That way he can stop kissing the owners' asses for your job."

"I've never loved a woman as much as I love you."

That was the way it was supposed to be. "I love you the same. Don't jinx us."

"No, I'm serious. I'm not trying to shake this up, but I'm scared."

"Did you talk with your mom about our decision to move the date up to two months?"

"Three. And of course, but she's not the

reason I'm scared. I don't know why I've got this uneasy feeling. It's like God is trying to tell me something — for me to be patient. It's like He's going to reveal something to me."

I kept quiet because I didn't know how to compete with what God was trying to tell him. Did God really talk to people or were Roosevelt's thoughts an illusion in his head?

"Maybe it's because it feels like we're rushing this. Perhaps Mom is right. We should wait two years."

Looking into his eyes, I saw a fear I'd never witnessed. Even when his team was down and it appeared there was no chance to win, I hadn't seen this expression.

The champagne arrived on time to shift the mood. The waiter poured two glasses. "Ready to order?"

Roosevelt shook his head. "Give us a moment."

"Yes, sir. Congrats on the win in Cincinnati," the waiter said.

Roosevelt nodded, then smiled. "Thanks, man."

I held my man's hand. "Baby, don't get cold feet. Don't be scared. This is what we want and we are ready," I said, trying to reassure him. "A toast, to love, trust, and happiness."

Our glasses touched, I took a sip, glanced toward the bar, and almost spilled my drink. Not again.

"You okay, baby?"

"I'm good." I unlocked my phone. "I need to get going to my gynecologist."

Granville had texted: why are you here with him?

I gulped my champagne.

"Gyne-who? For allergies?" Roosevelt asked.

Praying my fiancé trusted me, I said, "Aphrodite might be having a reaction too. It was a recommended precaution by the doctor in the emergency room. I have to make sure every part of me is healthy. I'll see you at the condo as soon as I'm done with a full report," I lied. I set my glass on the table and kissed my man. "I love you."

"I'll go with you. My driver can take us. After we're done, he can bring you back here to get your car."

"Who's going to take care of me when you're on the road? I'm a big girl. I have to learn to take care of myself. Don't spoil me too much," I said, walking in the opposite direction of Granville, who was posted at the bar drinking a beer. His glass was almost empty. How long had he been watching us?

I requested my car from the valet. While I

was waiting, that fool approached me.

"So you are cheating on me. And with the general manager of my favorite team! You tramp. You stank-ass tramp," Granville said.

Truly afraid, I moved away from him. Didn't respond. I couldn't get into my car fast enough. He didn't seem to be in a hurry to follow me, but how in the hell did he know where I was?

Parking in the lot at the hospital, I kept looking over my shoulder as I entered my doctor's office and registered with the receptionist. The nurse stood in the doorway, called my name, escorted me into the doctor's room, then took my blood pressure. Watching the machine, it was 140 over 92.

"Madison, we'd like to see this much lower. Undress and put this on. The doctor will be in shortly. I'll retake your pressure before you leave," she said, closing the door.

I removed my clothes. A small bloodstain was in the lining of my white lace panties. I prayed my cycle wasn't starting. I balled them up and stuffed them in my purse. Putting on the robe, I lay atop the examination chair and placed my feet in the stirrups.

"Well, hello, Madison. You're a little early for your annual. Is everything okay?"

"I hope so." I wanted to lie and say I had

an allergic reaction, but that would under-
mine her intelligence. "I had an anal slip
and fell on my man's dick. I'm feeling much
better, but I want you to check everything
from 'the rooter to the tooter,' as my mom
would say. And give me a blood test for
everything too."

No telling what Granville had done to me
while I was passed out. I had to make sure I
wasn't bringing any diseases into my engagement or I'd never make it to the altar.

"Have you had or suspect that your partner has had multiple partners?"

"Absolutely not. And he's my fiancé," I
said, flashing my ring.

"Well, congratulations. Let's see here," she
said, putting on a pair of rubber gloves. The
doctor examined my labia, then squeezed
gel on my outer lips. She spread my vagina,
inserted the cold speculum, twirled a few
cotton tips inside me, and then asked, "How
long has this been inside you?"

I raised up. "Let me see that."

*Oh, Jesus.* She held a condom in front of
my face. I didn't feel it come off. Why didn't
I know it was inside me? Probably too many
meds.

She used her foot to open the trash, then
tossed the rubber. The doctor smeared a
few slides, before removing the plastic

disposable device and dropping it in the garbage.

Replacing her gloves, she said, "I'm going to check your womb by inserting my fingers, then squirting more lube."

I wished she could examine my head. The probing inside and pressing on my stomach was normal, but I was freaking out. *Don't trip,* I told myself. If they checked my pressure again, it was undoubtedly going to be higher if I'd contracted anything.

She removed her gloves and put on a third pair. "Now I'm going to check your rectum. Does it hurt?" she asked before touching me in that area.

"No." The painkillers had kicked in nicely, but I had to slow down on taking so many before I fell asleep behind the wheel. What on earth would've happened if I'd had sex with Roosevelt and he'd found another man's protection in my pussy?

She squirted more lubrication, then gently touched the outside of my anus. "Yeah, it's irritated down here. I'm not going to disturb your insides."

"I need you to swab that end too," I said, bracing myself.

"Are you sure?"

"Positive," I said.

"You've got to be careful, young lady." The

221

extended cotton-tip stick slid inside.

I relaxed and maintained my composure.

"If that didn't hurt, you should be back to normal in a few days. If you experience severe pain, come back. Now I'm going to check your breasts and we're all done."

I knew the routine, so I placed my hand behind my head as her fingers danced in small circular motions. Starting near my areola, she worked her way outward. She pressed around my other breasts, then revisited the left.

"All done?" I asked.

"I'm afraid not. After you leave the laboratory, I need to send you over for a mammogram. You have lumps in both breasts. But you do have slightly lumpy breasts, so it might not be serious. If they find any lumps, request an ultrasound. And if the ultrasound shows any possible signs, get biopsies done on both breasts. I recommend my patients get everything done the same day, if they have time."

"I only came in for an exam. I'm not mentally prepared for this."

"I understand. But it's best to be sure. If the mammogram doesn't show anything, you can leave. But everything happens for a reason. That slip and fall may have saved your life."

My day had gone from bad to good to worse. Why in hell was she speaking as though she knew what I didn't? There was no way that at thirty-five years old there was anything wrong with my perfect, perky double D's.

# CHAPTER 17
## LORETTA

A day turned into a week, then into a month, then months; and before you knew it, you'd been celibate for a year. Then you meet a man and you're ready to have sex, so you do it. Then immediately afterward, you wished you hadn't.

In the pit of your pussy, as you feel his ejaculation, you immediately know he wasn't worth it.

You have regrets, wishing you would've held out for someone who actually cared about more than just the fuck. A man with passion prior to penetration would've been nice. Or a man with skills, who could've read and responded to your body language, would've been good. A man who could give you a head-to-toe orgasm would've made it worth the wait.

Today was all about me. I wish I could meditate like Chicago. Clear my mind each morning and start out with a fresh mind-set. Leave the negativity where it belonged, in the past.

You don't stop loving your friends because they've done you wrong, but I was tired of kissing Madison's ass. Did she win the bet? Honestly, I wasn't sure. Maybe. Was it fair to give her a two-part, one-sided bet — to tame Granville and have sex with him — while I stood on the sideline in search of a loophole?

Not my problem.

What I was 100 percent clear on, she could move if she didn't want to be my neighbor, but she was not getting owner-ship of the house Raynard had bought and deeded to me. I'd decided to distance myself from Madison for a while. Stay out of her business completely; and as much as I hated it, that included conversations with Chicago.

Finally I had an opportunity to wear one of my dresses that had the price tag on it. I scanned my wardrobe. Chocolate was too boring. White was flat. I couldn't go wrong with black, but I wasn't feeling that. Was a bustier over the top for a first date? Lime, tangerine, pink, purple, gold . . . no.

I tried on a dark green, sleeveless dress that stopped above my knees. If I added a pair of pearls, my attire would be appropriate for a White House tea party. The one color I avoided ended up being my selection. The little red dress was perfect with my raspberry lip gloss. No ponytail tonight, I let down my hair.

"Mommy, you look pretty. Where are you going?" Raynell asked.

Not sure, I told her, "Mommy has a date, princess."

"With Daddy? That's why you're happy? Can I go?"

I smiled, then shook my head. "Not this time, and it's not with your dad."

"Am I going to T-Tisha's or Godmommy's?"

"No, your dad is on his way to pick you up."

Raynell's eyes beamed. She fell backward onto the dozens of pillows on my king-size bed. "Don't forget, we're going to be a family one day," she sang.

Had my little girl made that up? Or was there still a chance?

It was time for me to move on. Making sure I was hot, sexy, and in a good mood, I sipped my lemon drop martini. I hadn't felt desirable in years. Granville definitely did not make me feel like a woman.

If only for one night, I had an incentive tonight to let go of my marital hopes with

Raynard and start focusing on a new man. Shaking my head, I reminded myself to enjoy my date, not to think about Raynard, and to speak my mind the way Madison does. I wasn't trying to impress Chaz, but I didn't want him to think I was desperate.

My pussy twitched in protest. *We are desperate. We need a dick. A real one that's attached to a man with a pulse.*

I quietly told her, "We have plenty of dicks on the top shelf in the closet."

I had a solid six more years before I'd have to find another hiding place for my sex toys so Raynell wouldn't find them. Hopefully, by then, I'd have a husband and wouldn't have to pleasure myself.

Raynell leapt from the bed. "Mommy, the doorbell!"

"What did I tell you?" I reminded her as I followed her downstairs.

Raynell stepped aside. I fluffed my hair, then opened the door, ready for whichever man was on the other side.

"Hey, Loretta. You look nice."

"Go to your room, Raynell, and don't come out until I come to get you."

"Okay, Mommy."

I waited until she was upstairs; then I clenched my teeth. "You bastard."

"That seems to be the word of the day,"

he said, with that same stupid grin on his face.

"What the hell are you doing here? Leave now, and don't you *ever* come back here."

"Okay. I just came to tell you, you lost a good man. It's over between us. Thought you may have wanted closure," Granville said. "You women like that kind of stuff, don't cha?"

Thank God, Chaz had pulled into the driveway and parked.

"Hey, come on in!" I called out.

Granville glanced over his shoulder and then looked at me.

"Oh, you got someone too? Well, Madison and I consummated our relationship. We had sex, and Madison is my woman now," he said in that disgusting, scratchy voice.

"What was that?" Chaz asked. "Whose name did he say?" Chaz extended his hand to Granville. "I'm Chaz, and you are?"

"Leaving," I said, guiding Chaz inside, then slamming the door in Granville's face.

"That was rude," Chaz said.

"No, that was appropriate. End of that conversation."

I didn't want to alarm my date that I had a psycho standing outside my door. That was the last time I'd suggest a girlfriend of mine should have sex with any of my exes.

That fool could screw up my first opportunity in years to date a real man and sabotage Madison's engagement at the same time. We had to get rid of him.

"My daughter's father should be here in a minute. Would you like a lemon drop martini or something else?"

"I'm good until we get to the restaurant," he said, staring around my living room. "You have excellent taste. My brother does too. Y'all have the same type of artwork."

"Same artist," I said.

The doorbell rang and I prayed that that idiot wasn't on the other side. This time I peeped through the hole, then opened the door. A sigh of relief escaped my lips.

"Come in. I'll go get Raynell."

Raynard stood close to the door. His eyes traveled from my head to my feet and back to my face.

"You look nice," he said, then looked at Chaz.

I made a point to acknowledge Chaz first. "Chaz, this is Raynard. Raynard, this is Chaz."

Extending his hand, Chaz said, "Pleased to meet you, man."

That was my cue to exit quickly. I darted to my altar and said a silent prayer. *Thank you, Jesus. Let Chaz be the one. And if he's not the one, let him stay with me for a while. Don't let him be crazy, or a womanizer, or disrespectful, or judgmental, because I need to hold that man in my arms tonight. And, Lord, no matter what Raynard is feeling, don't put my heart in the middle of two men. Amen.*

I went to Raynell's room. She wasn't there. I went to the living room. Raynell, Raynard, and Chaz were gone. My heart dropped. What had happened? Tears of confusion swelled, blurring my vision.

*Lord, I guess you know best, but I'd like an explanation.*

"You ready?"

I screamed.

"Sorry, I didn't mean to startle you. I had to use the restroom. Raynard and Raynell left. You okay?" Chaz asked.

I opened my front door. Raynard's SUV was gone. I didn't like that he'd taken our daughter without letting her say good-bye to me. I smiled at Chaz. "I'm good. Let's go."

After he closed my car door, he got in on the driver's side of his black-on-black luxury sedan.

"Will Raynell be back in time for the game tomorrow?" Chaz asked.

"I forgot to tell Raynard. I'll text him."

*Chaz is taking us to the game tomorrow. He*

230

invited us to his brother's suite. His brother is Chicago DuBois. Raynell needs to be back by noon.

Raynard replied, Damn! Does that we include me and my son?

Afraid not, I texted back. I should've made a snide remark about Gloria. It wasn't necessary. He had who he wanted.

Okay. BTW, you looked beautiful.

Noon, Raynard.

He replied, OK.

"She'll be back in time." I wanted to ask if Tisha could bring her two boys and her husband, but I decided to wait. Didn't want to impose.

"Are you still involved with Raynard?"

"No. I'm not."

"But you want him."

"I want to have a great evening with you and not discuss my past relationships. I'm completely single, with no attachments. Not by choice. Like I told Chicago, it's hard to find a good man, but I haven't given up hope."

Damn, I wasn't supposed to mention that last part out loud. Now he was going to think I was talking about him.

"I feel the same way about women," he said.

I laughed. Why was I being guarded?

"What's funny?"

"Men and women always say the same things we just said. But when those people meet, they start off good, but sooner or later they can't stand each other."

He laughed. "You're right."

Chaz had a different kind of swag from Chicago. He was more laidback. He nodded, then pulled into the parking lot at Pappadeaux Seafood Kitchen. When he opened my door, I couldn't help but notice his basic black square-toed shoes were spotless.

"I love this place. At first, I was thinking you were going to take me to a fancy restaurant with snails on the menu."

Madison bragged about the five-star restaurants that Chicago had taken her to over the years. I figured his brother liked the same. I couldn't wait to wrap my lips around a Swampthing now and Chaz's thing later. My pussy was puckering out of control.

"They've got something better than escargot," he said. "As a matter of fact, since you don't seem to be open to new things, you're trying alligator tonight."

*WWMD? What would Madison do?* She wouldn't go out on a second date with a man who took her to Pappadeaux on their first. She'd brag about how many countries she'd eaten escargot in and where to find the best.

I recalled a Facebook post Mary HoneyB Morrison put on her fan page: *Have you ever dated or married someone you had sex with on the first date?* The question had a resounding "yes" from over 90 percent of the responses. People proudly commented on how they'd been married, some for decades; and others said they were engaged to partners they gave it up to on the first date.

She made me rethink the significance of holding out. Being a Christian, I should say I'd wait until marriage, but my reality was I already had a baby and no husband.

"I'll taste the alligator," I told Chaz.

But that wasn't all I was going to eat tonight.

# CHAPTER 18
## LORETTA

Sitting across the table from Chaz, I told myself, *Listen more. Talk less.*

He didn't have much to say, once we were seated. Wish I were telepathic so I could read his mind. I began to wonder if he had finally had an opportunity to see me and saw what Raynard had seen and was having a change of heart. I didn't want Chaz going through the motions while watching minutes tick away.

Not sure if we'd be at the restaurant long enough to eat. I wondered if I should drink this frozen Swampthing sitting in front of me or send it back? He'd ordered cognac straight. What if he loosened up after he indulged in alcohol and the liquor spoke for him?

*Loretta, relax. Don't ruin a potentially good date unfolding the what-ifs in your head. Drink the damn drink.*

"So how old are you?" I asked to break

the silence.

The crimson collared pullover with three buttons — the bottom two fastened — complemented his light brown complexion. His black-rimmed, rectangular-shaped glasses gave him a distinguished flair. Chaz appeared two inches shorter than Chicago, which would put him at an even six feet. My three-inch heels made me two inches shorter.

"How old do you think I am?"

I smiled, knowing he was younger than I, but I didn't want to guess.

"What do you do for a living?"

"Breathe," he said.

Giving up, I laughed this time, but I offered no information about myself. The awkwardness quickly returned. I sipped my cocktail, gazed around. It was half full in the dining area, but the bar section was standing room only. If this didn't work out with Chaz, I wouldn't be discouraged. I'd start getting out and socializing more often.

Who would I hang out with? Tisha had slowed down since she married Darryl. My other friend wasn't speaking to me. I didn't want my coworkers in my business, and I wasn't the type to go to a bar alone.

"What's up with your girl Madison?" he asked.

I frowned. "What?"

"Is she legit? Should my brother Chicago marry her?"

"Back up off of me with that. If your reason for being out with me is to drill me about Madison, you can take me home now. I thought you were interested in me."

"And you're the one who asked my brother to ask me to take you out? Interesting." Chaz motioned for the waiter.

My heart sank. Another reminder that I wasn't Madison. She would've hand-fed him a sarcastic reply. Why was I protecting her? What was in it for me? Why couldn't I have said, "She's more interested in Chicago's money than Chicago. Engagements are a game to her. Tell Chicago not to marry her." That would've been the truth.

Gesturing toward me, he said, "Please take the lady's order."

"Are you eating?" I asked.

He nodded.

"As an appetizer we'd like to have a medium-crispy-fried alligator."

"All right. So you are adventurous."

He was clueless that I'd tried alligator before. Escargot too. Both were good. I continued, "And I'll have the lobster and shrimp salad as my entrée." The appetizer was $9.95 and the salad was $17.95. I also wanted the Chilean sea bass, but that was almost thirty-three dollars — the most expensive item I saw. I couldn't imagine running up a seventy-five-dollar tab by myself.

"Anything else?" Chaz asked.

"That's all for me." I didn't want to take advantage of ordering up just because I assumed he could afford it.

"You're sure?"

"Positive," I said.

"I'll have the oyster duo, boudin Cajun sausage, a cup of andouille sausage and seafood gumbo, and for my entrée I'll have the Chilean sea bass. Extra lemon for the oysters. Bring the appetizers out one at a time so we can enjoy them while they're hot. Thanks."

HoneyB should have a "dating dos and don'ts" application for the cell phone so women like me who aren't comfortable or accustomed to dating men with money wouldn't deny themselves something as simple as a hot meal. Maybe that was the difference between Gloria and me. I didn't care how much money Raynard earned. When we were together, I respected his wallet. Truth was, while we were dating, I worried about what Raynard would think of me if I started spending his money. Some men didn't mind doing, as long as a woman didn't ask. Maybe he'd bought me the house because I hadn't asked him for anything. But if a woman didn't ask, he might not get her a basic mani and pedi.

"Why, Loretta?"

"Why what?"

"Why didn't you order everything you wanted?"

Right now, this Swampthing was my friend. I wrapped my lips around the straw and sucked a long time. Exhaling, I said, "I did."

"You know, the one thing I can't stand is a liar. If you ever lie to me again, I don't want to see you again. If you'll lie about something as simple as this, you'll lie about anything — including what's up with your girl Madison."

I felt small, embarrassed, and disgusted. I also began to believe none of this was about me. I hadn't thought of my answer as a lie; but in a way he was right.

"I apologize."

"You apologize for mistakes like stepping on someone's foot. Make this your last time apologizing to me for your not being honest. Liars apologize because they're not keeping it one hundred with themselves, or they get caught being dishonest. Regardless

238

of why a person lies, it's premeditated and intentional. I don't have time to waste listening to a liar try to justify why she chose to fuck up. When you're authentic and original, you never have to say you're sorry. You're a Christian. You should know this. I don't know how Chicago considers you his prayer partner."

*Power to the people!* Shoot 'em in the head with words execution-style, if you have to. Chaz had the take-no-prisoners spirit of a Black Panther. His truth hurt so bad that all I could say was "You can take me home now."

"I can do that. And you can keep wondering why you don't have a man or a husband. Happy with what you're getting, keep doing what you're doing."

What was I doing?

"Or," he added, "we can grow past your revelation and enjoy the rest of our evening. I don't know about you, but the dessert I want to taste is not on this menu."

Chaz gave me a quick wink, then smiled.

I sighed, laughed, then exhaled. "And why aren't you married, if you're such a great catch?"

"Because I'm thirty-one and I develop software applications for the iPhone. I'm sure I'm going to say something else to annoy or piss you off, so we can leave anytime you're ready. Third time is a charm. Just let me know."

# CHAPTER 19
## LORETTA
___

Wow. One date with a secure, self-made millionaire and I felt richer than him. Chaz gave new meaning to the saying "Common sense isn't all that common."

Chaz parked in my driveway, turned off his car, opened the door, and escorted me to mine. As obnoxious as he was at times, I oddly enjoyed his company and didn't want our date to end with a good-night kiss on my cheek. Didn't want to appear easy, desperate, or anxious, but my pussy was trembling with anticipation of feeling his head enter my vaginal canal. I craved that fine-ass black man. I wanted a head that was connected to a warm body and not a mechanical device in my bed tonight.

Slowly I put the key in the lock. "Would you like to come?" I asked him.

He smiled. "Would you like for me to come . . . *inside?*" he asked, placing the emphasis on "inside."

Suddenly my face became flushed with embarrassment. I hadn't said what I'd intended, but I said exactly what was on my mind. After our conversation at dinner, I wasn't going to end our date with a lie.

Confidently I said, "Yes. And yes." Then I entered my house.

He pressed a button on his remote, locked his sedan, and closed my door.

"Thanks for inviting me in. I was hoping that you would. I wasn't ready for our date to end either," he said, sitting in the purple chair. "I see you don't have a television in your living room. Is there one in your bed-room?"

I couldn't pretend I was offended, quote him the Bible, and tell him I was Christian, or refuse to take him upstairs. Tonight I was willing to live a little and take a risk.

I could get used to a man being direct. "Never ask of me or expect me to give you more than you're willing to give me," I said, realizing I could fall hard for Chaz.

Chaz stood. Opened his arms wide. Hugged me close to his hard body. "I could be willing to give you the world, and end up giving you nothing. Stop trying so hard. Next time, if you're going to ask me or any other man for something, speak in the af-firmative."

I shivered. Maybe this was the wisdom Madison had tried to impart upon Tisha and me. Madison was like a teacher who knew the subject well, but her way of getting others to understand what was in her head provoked more questions than answers. Perhaps Madison was complex because she always had a hidden or personal agenda. The way Chaz said things made sense the first time.

"Loretta, look at me."

He placed his hand under my chin. "If it's meant for us to be together, it will happen naturally. I'm not my brother. I don't do anything in a rush, and I don't let women make decisions for me or tell me what or what not to do."

I struggled to keep eye contact. I wanted to look and pull away, but I stood still.

His lips touched mine for the first time. He opened his mouth. I responded in kind. His tongue was sweet, soft, and felt like it was melting my entire body. I closed my eyes. Chaz planted more kisses on my outer lips as he nibbled and bit with passion. I'd never forget our first kiss. I didn't want it to end.

"I like you, Loretta. Let's go get out of these clothes. But first, I'd like to see your place."

Leading the way, I said, "As you can see, this is my living room. I like to sit and chat here with friends or sit alone. Sometimes in the dark with a cocktail."

"Is that your way of meditating?"

I hadn't thought of it like that, but . . . "I don't meditate," I said, walking into the formal dining room. "I use this room for dinner with my daughter and we eat break-fast in the kitchen nook, when we have time."

I started to tell him that Raynell has a nanny, but I felt that was too much informa-tion. And since he analyzed everything that came out of my mouth, I didn't want him to think I was bragging about having paid help.

"I made this bedroom my prayer room."

"This is different. I'm impressed," he said. "This is really nice. My mom would like to have one of these in her house. Has Chicago seen this?"

"Yes" was all I said in response to his question. "Let's go upstairs."

"Before I forget, you can invite Tisha and her family to the game."

"Thanks, I'll do that." I smiled, then showed him the two guest bedrooms, Raynell's room, and then invited Chaz into my "large enough for two, occupied by one" lavish master space.

"Chicago has that same painting in his living room," he said, pointing above my bed.

"I know" was all I said in response to his comment. "Here's the remote. You can watch whatever you'd like. The bathroom is in there," I said, pointing. "And I have a minibar over there. Would you like another cognac?"

"Yes, please, and thanks. You have impeccable taste."

"Who said I decorated my house?"

"Not me. But did you?"

"Yes," I said, smiling. I thought I'd cornered him; but I quickly saw how if I pushed to make a point, he was the type of man that always had a comeback.

Shaking his head, he said, "If you wouldn't mind helping me with my bachelor's condo, I'd pay you for your time."

"We'll see," I said, entering the bathroom. "I'm going to shower. There's more than enough room for us or you can wait until I'm done."

"I'll wait," he said, sitting on the sofa and turning on the flat screen.

Stepping into the shower, I could not believe I had a man in my bedroom. I scrubbed everything three times. Flossed, brushed my teeth, gargled, styled my hair, slipped into a short and sexy blue nightie, and put on perfume. I was ready.

When I strutted into my bedroom, I couldn't believe my eyes. Chaz was under the cover and asleep. I eased in beside him, lay my head on his chest, and stared at the ceiling.

*Damn.*

# CHAPTER 20
## CHICAGO

Today we'd make our big announcement.

I knew my mom wasn't going to be happy. Dad would remain neutral. I wasn't sure how Chaz would respond. My grandfather liked Madison, so the wedding date shouldn't concern him.

*Actually, hmm.*

In the middle of my thoughts, I had a brilliant idea.

I stood in my office and stared out the window. Thousands of fans were lining up at the gate to enter the stadium for today's game. By the time the sold-out audience arrived, over 71,000 would be here to watch us defeat Oakland. I wasn't underestimating our California opponents because we were favored to win. I was being optimistic; I had every reason to. I was soaring higher than the eagles.

Scanning the VIP parking lot, I saw Chaz get out of his sedan, then open the passenger-side doors. Loretta got out, wearing our team jersey with the quarterback's number, denim shorts, and tennis shoes. Madison would never wear athletic attire, unless she was exercising.

A beautiful little girl, who had a dozen red and blue ribbons dangling from her hair, got out of the backseat. Chaz closed the doors. Well, that was probably why I hadn't heard from him last night or this morning.

Loretta didn't seem like the type of girl to have sex on the first date, but the way she was smiling indicated they might have gone all the way. I didn't expect Chaz to give them a ride. He said he was giving her a pass. I could've given VIP parking access to someone else.

Honestly, I didn't imagine he'd like Loretta. Hooking them up was my way of doing Loretta that favor she'd asked for. I mean, of course he'd like the nice side of her. What man wouldn't? But she wasn't his type. Neither of us had dated a woman with a kid.

I didn't understand why Loretta had stopped praying with me. She wouldn't answer my calls or reply to my text messages. I missed communicating with her. If she became Chaz's friend or, worse, his lady, then I'd have to find another prayer partner. When Chaz cared for a woman, he was like Madison, possessive.

Yeah, he preached how he wouldn't chase behind a woman; but if he loved her deeply, he was the same as I was. He wanted to know where his woman was, when she wasn't with him.

Tisha, her husband, and her kids got out of an SUV next to them. I didn't see Madison's red Ferrari. I sat behind my desk and picked up the framed photo of us. My very own Amber Rose. Knowing my baby, I was certain she had to make sure everything was proper for what we had to tell our families and her friends. I put the picture back in its place.

I hadn't shared many moments with Madison's parents, and this would be the first time Mr. Johnny and Mrs. Rosalee would meet my mom, Helen, my dad, Martin, and my grandfather Wallace, who preferred to be called Wally. Over the year Madison and I dated, we spent most of our time in one another's company. The few times I'd met her people, her folks truly liked me, especially her dad.

Game day wasn't my responsibility, but I'd checked in to see if there was anything I could do to assist the operations manager.

As usual, he had everything under control. My secretary buzzed me.

"Blue Waters is here to see you."

I didn't want that arrogant dude to put a damper on my good mood. He'd never come to my office on game day. He never approached me in the respectful manner I deserved. I had no idea what he wanted. He should be on the field or in the locker room with the team.

"Send him in."

Strolling in, he said, "Hey, Chicago," like we were on the same level. "I need a favor, man."

*Say what?* He wanted me to do a good deed for him? Gesturing for him to have a seat at my conference table, I couldn't wait to hear what his five-foot ten-inch, almost too big to fit inside the stadium, ego had to say.

"What's up?" I relocated from my desk and sat across from him.

"I have the utmost respect for you, Chicago. I'll get straight to it. One, I'd like to use you as a reference on my application for a general manager position in Oakland."

His asking was a real Scorpio move. All I had to do now was wait to get stung.

"What you really want is for me to hand over my job to you because you think you can do it better, when you've never been a GM or VP in your life."

I despised this dude. He thought we were cut from the same cloth, because I was once an assistant coach. He was wrong. Yes, at the end of the day, we both got the job done; but at the end of mine, people respected me. Blue couldn't replace me if he shadowed me for a lifetime. The guy lacked character. And no one could teach him that. Not even me.

"Man, I just told you I'm applying elsewhere. But I understand. Just because you're the youngest VP/GM in the league, you don't want to help another brother come up. I came to you because I respected you. What do you think of me?"

"Respected," as in past tense. That was about right. "You don't want me to answer that. You said, 'One.' What else?"

Blue nodded and clenched his jaw. "You don't know me. You're tripping because your girl was trying to get with me. Forget I asked for your help. And if you should ever need mine, remember this moment. The other thing I was going to tell you — although it's none of my business — you're making a huge mistake if you marry Madison."

"Why? Because she wouldn't date you?"

"You're entitled to your opinion. Open your eyes and close your nose. She's . . . Never mind. Madison might be your woman, but she's on my team. Congratulations. Thanks for your help."

Blue pushed back his chair.

"I hope you do get a GM position so I don't have to fire your ass. And if you should find your way back to my office, or want to talk with me, check your damn ego before stepping into my office. Now get out."

Blue stood, shook his head, then left. I returned to the window. Mom, Dad, and my grandfather had arrived. I waited ten minutes, but Madison's car wasn't in the lot. What did he mean Madison was on his team? That was his way of trying to get inside my head. I wasn't having it. I was taking Chaz's advice. I didn't call her. I headed to my suite to greet my family and guests.

"Welcome, I'm glad y'all made it. Help yourselves to anything you want." I kissed my mother on the cheek and hugged my dad and grandfather.

"Hi, Chicago," Loretta said. "Thanks for having us."

"Yeah, man. My family really appreciates this," Darryl said.

Chaz pulled me to the side. "Thanks for introducing me to Loretta. She's cool."

"So you couldn't wait to peel her panties off? You had to do that on the first date?" I asked him.

Chaz's eyes shifted side to side as he stared into mine. "If I didn't know better, I'd think you wanted more than a prayer partner, partner."

"Not at all, my man. Not at all," I reassured my brother as I patted him on the back.

"Hello, everybody," Madison said, stepping into the room.

My jaw dropped. Chaz's did too. I told him, "That's the only woman I want to do more than pray with."

"Hi, baby," Madison said, kissing me.

I wasn't one of those guys who avoided lipstick, but whatever red product was on her lips never got on me. I liked that. That gloss that Loretta came in with had already lost its shine.

My fiancée smelled irresistible. She had on red high heels, a sleeveless, fitted blue dress, with red trim, diamond earrings, necklace, and my ring.

"You look amazing, baby." I hugged her for a while before letting go.

"Why is Loretta here? I thought we agreed

she was not to come."

Chaz replied, "She's my guest. If you have a problem with that, it's just that. Your problem."

Madison looked Chaz up and down. "So not worth it," she said, then greeted Tisha. "Hey, girl. I'm glad you and the boys made it. Hey, Darryl. I thought you'd be at work. Oops, I forgot. You still don't have a job and you're obviously not looking for one today. Probably waiting for your ninety-ninth unemployment check from Obama before you do the right thing. Not man enough to earn your keep. You gotta lay up on your woman. Oops, that's right. You're not home long enough to lay on her. Guess some other woman or man has got her spot. At least Tisha gets to see you for a few hours with your eyes open. Enjoy the game."

Darryl was speechless. We all were. What had gotten into my baby? Since Tisha didn't respond, I kept quiet.

Madison walked away from Darryl, but exchanged no words with Loretta the entire first half. I introduced my parents to Madison's mom and dad. Within the hour my mom had assessed she didn't like Johnny. She whispered in my ear, "I see where Madison gets her ugly ways from."

Pulling Madison outside the room, I said,

"Baby, I don't think this is the right time to make our announcement. You're not supposed to insult our guests."

"Like it or not, what I said was the truth. That's why no one responded. And I say, now is just as good a time as any other. We only have two months, and while both of our families are together, I'll do it."

There was no sense in arguing with her. I'd already given in to having the wedding in two versus three months. "You're right. Let's go back in."

"Oh, one more thing. I have to go back to the doctor tomorrow," she said. "Nothing serious, so I don't want you worrying. It's a routine follow-up. Now let's go."

When we went inside, Madison asked, "Why is your mother talking to Loretta? Are they discussing us?"

Mom and Loretta were hitting it off well. My mother didn't take to too many people right away, but Raynell was sitting next to my mom and she was straightening Raynell's ribbons.

I requested the suite attendant to prepare and deliver a glass of champagne to each of the adults and apple cider to the kids. "Madison, all you have to do is stand by my side at halftime and make the announcement."

"Okay, baby," she said, heading in Loretta's direction.

Women were complicated. I prayed she didn't say anything demeaning to Loretta like she'd done to Darryl. I sat next to Chaz. "Do you like Loretta?"

"Well, Mom seems to, but you know me. I think so but it's too soon to tell. Most women start out extra nice. I've got to do something to piss Loretta off big-time. Make her really upset. If she acts a fool — starts cursing, hitting me, breaking things, or blowing up my phone — does any of that, it's a wrap."

The attendant handed Chaz and me the last two glasses of champagne.

"Roosevelt, baby, it's time," Madison said, standing in front of the window with her back to the football field. We were ahead by ten. The teams had gone into the locker rooms.

We stood close to one another. I placed my hand on Madison's waist.

She spoke loud and clear. "We would like to thank each of you for joining us."

My mother's lips tightened immediately. I knew what she was thinking: *How dare she stand before us and insult us, acting like we are her guests, when it's the other way around.*

I made eye contact with my mom, then shook my head, pleading for her to remain silent.

"We have a very special announcement to make." Madison gazed into my eyes, then kissed me. "Roosevelt and I have set our wedding date and we're requesting your presence. We will exchange vows at church in exactly two" — she tipped her flute to mine — "months. The reception will be poolside at our favorite hotel, where we'll spend the night, then fly out the next morning for our cruise along the French Riviera. We decided we didn't want to wait two years to exchange our vows."

"More like *you* decided *you* didn't want to wait. You've got the whole thing mapped out," Chaz said, moving toward our mom. He placed his arm around her shoulder. "You cool with this, bro?"

"Your brother is right, Roosevelt. You do not have my blessings for this," my mom lamented. "I don't like that girl, and now she's giving me a reason to hate her." Mother pointed at Madison, then shook her finger hard and fast. "What do you want from my son, you gold digger?"

Madison exhaled. "Not this again. Look, Helen. I love Roosevelt. He's grown. He doesn't need your permission."

"Well, you have my blessings," Mr. Tyler said, holding his drink in the air.

"Johnny, tell Madison to stop being disrespectful," Mrs. Tyler commented. "We didn't raise her this way."

"Mama, I don't mean any disrespect, but nothing that I do pleases Helen. You heard her. She hates me. I'm not marrying her, Mama. I'm marrying her son."

Loretta approached me and whispered in my ear, "Congratulations, Chicago"; then she grabbed Raynell's hand and told Chaz, "Friend or no friend, I can't watch Madison disrespect your mom like this. Whenever you're ready, let's go."

My mom's eyes narrowed. She didn't blink. Mom rolled her eyes at Madison; then she looked at me; then my mother walked out. Dad followed Mom.

Chaz followed Loretta. Darryl sat down and began watching the second half of the game. "Congratulations, Chicago and Madison. I may never get this chance again. Tisha, we are not going anywhere until the last second ticks off the clock."

"Cheers," Madison said. "As soon as the shock wears off, everyone will be okay."

I was disgusted and delighted at the same time. The fallouts between my Mom and my fiancée had to stop.

"Baby, I know you have a hard time with my mother, but make this your last time disrespecting her, or there will be no wedding."

# CHAPTER 21
## GRANVILLE

Open your blinds wider so i can see you better.

Madison was in her family room with him. She'd gone to the game. Chicago had followed her to her house afterward. He'd been there for three hours, watching television. How much longer was she going to make me stand by like a voyeur? I was her man. Not him!

They moved away from the sofa by the window.

now i can't see you at all bitch!

I yelled, "I don't care how much money he has! He's not better than me."

Sitting in front of my computer, which was on a TV tray that I used as my desk, I was happy and sad when I spotted them in her backyard. I was happy because I could see them again, but I was pissed off at what I saw. Madison and Chicago were lounging naked by her pool. Her lips were all over his body. She didn't do that to me. I didn't know she had a pool, until I installed this awesome program.

my dick is bigger than chicago's. wouldn't you agree dear?

Having a large sausage made lots of women take their clothes off, just to feel me inside them. They wanted to taste and ride a big one. I was the man, and I knew it. Madison couldn't deny she enjoyed my dick.

My problem wasn't attracting women who made more than me; it was keeping them. I refused to have a relationship with a girl on welfare or one making minimum wage — no matter how fine she was. They were nice enough to have sex with, but who would envy me if I married one of them? I wasn't getting any younger. Why couldn't Madison understand that I wanted to marry her and then have her have our baby, in that order?

I stared at the screen; satellite gave me better vision than an eight-eyed spider. I could see whatever was outside; and if the curtains were opened, inside was visible too. The tracker device I installed on Madison's phone and the spyware on my laptop gave me constant access to my cheating woman.

I had feelings too. I hated what she was doing to me. Doing with him. She was tearing my heart apart.

The stank-ass ho made me want to go back to Loretta. That's right. Miss Raspberry Lips had a man. Everyone who knew anything about our football team knew Chaz DuBois was Chicago's brother. I was competing with rich men. That meant I was in their league.

Just as I texted, i hope y'all drown, I heard a knock at my door.

I didn't move. I called out, "Who is it?"

"Beaux, dude. Open the damn door."

What did he want? I left my program running and went to the door.

"What's up? I hope you didn't come to get me to go to Mom's," I said, letting him in.

"Nah, I came to check on your unemployed behind. You ever thought about applying with one of the bigger construction companies? A worker with your impeccable record, they'd hire you right away," Beaux said, helping himself to a cold bottle of beer from the fridge. He handed me one. I opened it with my teeth. We sat in the living room.

I took my usual seat on the sofa, back in front of my computer. Beaux sat in the big chair.

"What you gon' do, man?" he asked.

Picking up my laptop, I showed my

brother what was happening at Madison's. He seemed hypnotized by the raw action.

"Is this some type of cam shit, dude, where couples let you watch them? I've heard about this, man. This is fucking hot. Got my shit hard."

Beaux followed me to the couch as I put my laptop back on the stand. "I wish it were a fucking cam. That's my ex-boss, my woman. She's cheating on me."

"Man, that's Chicago bagging a ho big-time. He's kind of loose, putting himself out there like that. He could lose his job," Beaux said, sitting on the edge, staring at the screen as though he hadn't heard a word of what I'd said.

Why didn't I think of that? I got my iPhone and started recording a video. Beaux moved closer to me and kept watching. I was never happier to see my brother.

After a half hour of recording, Beaux said, "Man, I'm out. I'ma drop in at the Piano Bar for a brew or two. Take in some good jazz — and if I'm lucky, I'll let you know tomorrow."

Beaux let himself out. Between my two videos I was onto something huge! I took off my clothes, threw them on the floor, went to the bedroom, and got my sleeve and lube out of the drawer.

I reclined on the sofa, filled my sleeve with gel, grabbed my woody, then rolled the silicone cover down my shaft. My eyes rolled to the back of my head. The sleeve felt better than pussy sometimes.

"Ahh, yeah. Fuck the shit out of her," I said, still watching them.

Each time Chicago penetrated my woman, I stroked my dick. It felt like I was inside her too. When Madison came, I came with her.

# Chapter 22
## Madison

*Bam! Bam! Bam!*

Two seconds later.

*Bam! Bam! Bam!*

Loretta snatched open her door.

"You're going to have to do something about Granville," I demanded, trying to pass by her.

Loretta stood in her doorway, blocking my access. She stepped outside, then partially closed her door.

"Keep your voice down. I know you see that." She shifted her eyes toward Chaz's black sedan in her driveway.

"I don't give a damn about him! He's just using you. Don't fool yourself into believing Chaz wants a relationship with *you*. You gave up the pussy too soon."

She tried slamming the door in my face. I shoved her and the door back. She'd better not let my electric green, fitted dress and orange stilettos fool her. I'd kick these shoes off and drag her ass outside by her hair before I allowed her to dismiss me. I wasn't having it.

"Besides, he's not in *your* house. Chaz is in *my* house. I could put him and you out. Don't forget who won the bet, Loretta. You started this mess. You should be dressed for work, and his ass should be gone."

"You mean like Chicago is gone?" she said, darting her eyes to my driveway.

"Look, this isn't about either of them. This is about the quicksand pit you've gotten me into. You're going to get me out of it, or I'm pulling you in."

She had no idea that I'd fired Granville. Now he had too much time on his hands. Stalking me 24/7. I had to pawn his crazy ass back off on Loretta, or have her help me with a plan to get rid of him for good.

"You're going to be late," Loretta said.

"Unlike you, I'm my own boss. I'm always on time. I have to go to my doctor for my test results."

I hated lying to Roosevelt, telling him, "It's a routine follow-up," knowing it wasn't. I had to get the results of my biopsies today. But I was optimistic nothing was wrong with my beautiful breasts. Thankfully, the needle they used was small and the tiny scars were barely visible. Nothing a little waterproof makeup couldn't cover up whenever Roosevelt saw me naked with the lights on.

Loretta's eyes opened wide. "Madison, no. What kind of test? Did he cum inside you?"

"Since you're obviously taking off today, meet me at Houston's on Westheimer, at three o'clock, and bring Tisha. Someone has to be the voice of reason, and the madness must stop today. I'll see you then."

Chaz opened the door, wearing the same clothes he had on yesterday from the game. I turned my nose up at him, hoping he hadn't heard what Loretta said. What if he was standing behind the door, eavesdropping?

He stared down at me, then walked away. That was the kind of shit females allowed that I hated. Chaz was not the man of Loretta's house, but already he was acting like it.

"Three o'clock, Loretta, or you can kiss Chaz's ass good-bye for good," I said, then left.

I got into my car, retracted the top, put on my sunglasses, and drove toward Post Oak. Soon as I got to San Felipe, there he was, right behind me, in that oversized truck. I decided to ignore Granville.

He pulled alongside me and shouted out

his window, "Madison, we need to talk!"

I waited for the light to change, then drove off at a normal speed. Continuing to my destination, I parked at the hospital. He parked next to me. I put up my top, grabbed my purse, and headed to the elevator.

"Madison, I know you heard me. I forgive you, dear. We need to talk," he said. "If you're sick, I can put you on my insurance. All we have to do is get a marriage license. We don't have to file it. We both sign it and I'll give it to my —"

He stopped midsentence. It finally dawned on him he didn't have an employer. I made a mental note to see if he'd illegally added anyone to his insurance while he was working for me. I walked up to the receptionist and handed her my medical card and identification.

"Thanks, you can have a seat. We'll call you shortly," she said.

Granville sat next to me. "This is obstetrics. You getting a checkup? You pregnant with my baby?"

I scanned the room; there was no place else to sit. I needed a distraction, so I scrolled through the applications on my cell phone.

"What are you doing?" he asked, staring at my screen. "Are you ignoring me? I have something more interesting to show you. Look what I have on my phone," he said.

My jaw dropped when I saw footage of me riding him. I shook my head. I slapped his phone out of his hand, hoping it would shatter into a million pieces.

He picked it up, wiping it off. "I've backed it up. Look what else I have, dear."

This time it was Roosevelt and I making love poolside. Great, now he was spying on me while I was in my own home. I didn't overreact. I remained silent. I touched my utilities icon. *GPS tracking? What the hell is this?* I pressed the icon. *Granville is an accepted user? I'd approved him to do what? Track my every move?*

A woman stood in the doorway. "Madison Tyler."

I held my phone in front of his face. "You dirty bastard." I deleted the application, then stood.

"I'll be right here waiting for you, dear," Granville said as I walked away.

If I could kill him and get away with it, I'd do it now. I couldn't believe he'd installed a tracking device on my phone and he was spying on me in my home. How was he doing that?

"I need to check your blood pressure," the nurse said.

"Don't bother. Trust me. It's off the chart. Just take me to the room."

Usually, I had to wait a few minutes for the doctor, but this time she entered right behind me. "Hi, Madison. Have a seat. How are you feeling, dear?"

"Please don't call me that."

"Call you what? 'Dear'?"

"Long story, but yes," I told her.

"Okay. So how are you?"

"You tell me," I said, placing my purse in my lap.

"I'm sorry to report that it's not good news, Madison."

"I'm listening," I told her, hugging my purse to my stomach.

"Your tests for cancer are positive in both breasts. We need to schedule you for an MRI and for surgery right away."

Was I hearing her correctly? "Did you say both?"

The doctor nodded.

"How severe is it?" I asked, not really wanting to know. Tears streamed down my cheeks before she answered.

"Stage two, level B. We need to do the MRI to determine if it's contained or if the cancer has spread to other parts of your body. You can't afford to put this off. If you do, it can only get worse."

Just when I thought my life couldn't get any worse, it did. At this point I started sobbing.

*Why me? I don't have a family history of breast cancer. God, please let this be a misdiagnosis.*

My head started spinning like I had a hangover.

"Are you sure you didn't get my results mixed up with someone else's?"

"Dear . . . oops, I apologize. Madison, they're your results."

More tears poured. "Okay, if you're sure they're mine, I'll schedule the MRI immediately after my wedding. It's only two months away. Then I'll come in —"

"You can't wait that long, Madison."

"I said, 'two months.' That's exactly eight weeks. If I already have it, what difference is it going to make to wait? I'm stressed-out enough."

"Do it this week. I can get you in, in a few days. By then, I can assemble your team of doctors. The surgeon, the medical and radiation oncologist, and I'll have a plastic surgeon present to discuss your reconstructive options. And you'll need chemo."

This wasn't happening to Madison Tyler. "Why is this happening to me? Why can't I do the MRI after my wedding?"

"You can do whatever you'd like. I can't force you to come in, but I highly recommend we get on top of this right away. Lots of women are cancer survivors. You can be one too."

*I could be one too. Great. What are my other options? Dying in two to five years? Living without my breasts?*

"One more thing. An important thing, Madison. Perhaps the most important," the doctor said.

"If it were just you that I was worried about, I'd still tell you to do it now. But, Madison, you have to think for two."

"Don't worry about my telling my fiancé about my having breast cancer. Roosevelt will be fine. I promise I'll let him know him right after our honeymoon."

The doctor held my hand. Stared into my eyes. "I'm not talking about your fiancé. You can tell him when you're ready. Madison, you're pregnant. You have to think about your health status and your baby's."

# Chapter 23
## Loretta

As I lay flat on my back, Chaz eased on top of me and wedged his erection between my thighs. "Okay, we've waited long enough. Breakfast was wonderful, but I want you for lunch."

I was glad we'd moved past his questions about Madison. He knew something wasn't right, but I refused to tell him what was wrong. I couldn't tell Madison's side without showing my own hand. I learned in order not to lie to him, my new line was "I'm not going to discuss it." Not, "I don't want to," or, "I don't think we should." Direct was the best way to deal with him.

"You sure you're ready for this dick," he whispered in a sexy tone, which made me take a deep breath like I was going underwater for a full lap in an Olympic-size pool.

I gazed into his eyes and exhaled. "Yes."

"Cool. Consider yourself warned. This dick is so good, you'll be begging for it."

"Wait. Let me see what you're working with." I turned on the light.

Pleasantly surprised, I held his erection in my hands; then I kissed his glistening head. His dick was at least eight inches, hard. When I wrapped my fingers around his shaft, my thumb couldn't touch my middle fingertip. The circumcision was perfect. There was no extra skin underneath the frenulum.

"Okay, you've seen enough. Lay back and relax."

He spread my thighs with his knees, maneuvered his dick until he found my opening, then slid his manhood all the way in. My heart pounded with pleasure. It had been far too long since I'd experienced the kind of electric charge Chaz gave my entire body when he penetrated me.

I moved my hips down, trying to take in more of him.

He kept still as he grunted, "This is your dick, girl," then he kissed me.

Rotating my pelvis to the left, tightening my pussy, I was on a mission to devour him. God only knew when I'd have this opportunity again. I had to get the first orgasm out of the way so I could finish the ride on top with both hands in the air.

"Take your time," he said, kissing me.

"He's not going anywhere."

Time wasn't what I had. In an hour Raynell would be here. *Damn, I almost forgot! The nanny was dropping her off at Raynard's today.* But I still had to meet Madison and Tisha at three.

"I need you here with me," he said. "I should be the only one on your mind right now."

He was right. Rolling my hips in the opposite direction, a slow orgasm pulsated along my cervix. I paused for a moment, fearing a bigger one was brewing and about to erupt like a volcano. I didn't want to cum hard. Cumming fast was different. Fast was okay — as long as I didn't lose my intensity to climax back-to-back. A hard orgasm would zap my libido, diminish my enthusiasm, and I'd fall on my face before having the chance to mount him.

I lifted my legs and interlocked my feet behind his butt, hoping a different position would balance me out. I was wrong. When Chaz pressed deeper, I came again.

"It's okay, baby. I got you. Relax." He sucked my bottom lip.

This time I opened my mouth, encouraging him to continue with a French connection. Why did I crave the comfort of a man, like without one I'd be miserable forever? I

275

didn't know Chaz that well, but I never wanted him to leave me. Did that make sense? I'd have to figure out the answer later. Right now, I had to concentrate on staying in the moment.

He raised my legs over his shoulders. I submitted, giving him an all-access pass to my mind, body, and soul. He squeezed my thighs close together, then penetrated me to the core. I felt his pubic hairs grazing my clit. His balls were against my asshole. His grinding gradually increased. His strokes went from one every five seconds to four to three to two; and before I could catch my breath, he was pounding me every second.

I screamed with massive pleasure. He stopped. I grabbed his ass and yelled, "Don't stop! Please don't stop!"

My pussy exploded with one big orgasm after another. It felt like fireworks bursting. I closed my eyes and it seemed as though my body floated into midair; all that was left on the mattress was a feeling I'd never had before. How could one man do all this to me in a matter of minutes?

Getting on top, I said, "I want to please you to your satisfaction."

"There's plenty of time for that. Remember when I told you the dessert I wanted was not on the menu? I wasn't lying. I'm

276

just getting started. Lie down and relax."

I thought I'd died and gone to heaven, when his lips touched mine. To use the Lord's name in vain was a sin; but the way that man was eating my pussy, I couldn't help myself. I screamed "Oh, my God" so many times that I was sure God understood. Why else would He have allowed for me to feel this way?

I didn't want to meet Madison for lunch. God knew that too. But I also realized that Granville could screw things up for both of us. Exhausted, I somehow found the words to say, "Baby, I don't want to, but I have got to go."

"That makes two of us," he said, heading to my bathroom.

I used the shower in one of my guest bedrooms. The hot water streamed down my back. Lowering the temperature, I let the water massage my face.

"There you are," Chaz said, joining me.

I thought he was freshening up in my bathroom. "Out, you. We have to get going."

"Let me get this last nut out of the way. It won't take but a few minutes."

He penetrated me from behind and started thrusting long, deep, and hard, until we both came at the same time.

"I'll meet you back in the bedroom," he said, getting out of the shower.

I washed my body twice, dried off, and headed to my closet for a pair of jeans and a T-shirt. Chaz was sprawled faceup on my bed. His dick was standing tall.

"One for the road," he said, motioning with his dick.

Not sure when I'd get this opportunity again, I decided the girls could wait a few minutes. Hell, both of them had accessible dick. I did not.

I mounted Chaz. He guided my hips to a nice pace.

"This could go on forever."

"And it will," he said. "When I'm in a relationship, I want my woman all the time. When I'm not committed, I'm a workaholic. Can you handle it twenty-four/seven?"

Men liked to play games. I was not about to try and decode what was in his head, especially after having mind-blowing sex. He could've meant, sexing him all the time or being his woman. Or he could've been asking me, could I handle him working all the time? Another way of saying, "Don't get attached, because you won't get this dick on a regular." He could've been trying to feel me out to see if I liked him enough to be his woman.

"Handle what?" I asked, staring into his eyes.

"What do you think?" he said, thrusting his dick deeper inside me.

I stopped fucking him. "Get up. Get dressed. And let's go. When you're ready to tell me exactly what's on your mind, let me know."

I might end up signing my house over to that man if I didn't get up off his dick.

# CHAPTER 24
## MADISON

Thankful I'd found an exit out the back door, I trotted downstairs to the garage level to avoid Granville. His dumb ass would probably sit in the waiting area until the office closed before he realized I was gone. I had no regrets for firing him.

At some point today I had to find out what surveillance equipment or application he was using to video record me in my house. Maybe I could ask Loretta to ask Chaz. Until I figured it out, I'd keep my windows closed and stay inside.

I left the hospital with no real destination. Entering the freeway, I must've driven around the 610 Loop four times or more. I'd lost count.

The song by Martina McBride about a thirty-eight-year-old woman discovering she had breast cancer made me burst into tears. I could hardly see the road ahead. The lyrics made me feel if I told Roosevelt what was happening, he'd be there for me. But this was a song and I didn't feel strong. I felt alone.

My mind was in a quandary. If I hadn't almost run out of gas, I might still be going in circles.

In shock, exhausted mentally and physically, I knew this was not the demise of my life. People lived without arms, legs, hands, and feet . . . but my breasts. *Jesus, why?* I started to cry as gasoline pumped into my tank. Tears stained my green dress. I didn't care. The scent of the fumes reminded me of Port Arthur's refineries.

I wondered how many fumes caused people in my hometown to have what I'd gotten. Maybe I could take up a cause, start a revolution, or create a nonprofit to educate residents in Port Arthur about their toxic environment. Was God trying to tell me something? Maybe my condition was supposed to spark my greater humanitarian purpose.

Sitting behind the wheel, with three hundred fresh miles, I could head east to New Orleans or west to Los Angeles. I needed to get away. My cell phone rang. It was Roosevelt. I ignored his call. A text was best.

Headed to the office. Will call you in a few, I lied.

He texted back, We need to talk. Call me asap.

I messaged him, ttyasap baby. Give me a sec.

What was his urgency?

Better yet. After I leave work, I'll pick you up for dinner.

Everything okay?

Hell nah. ttywicu.

I was clueless as to what had upset Roosevelt. Whatever it was, it wasn't more important than the potentially terminal illness confronting me. I had to talk with someone. The one person who wouldn't judge me was my mother. Telling her would break her heart. She'd worry day and night, but she had a right to know. As I knocked on my parents' door, tears filled my eyes before the door opened. I dried them and put on the best smile I could.

"Hey, honey, I'm glad you stopped by," my mom said. "I wanted to talk to you about your announcement. You sure you're not moving too fast?"

"Not now, Ma." I stepped foot in her house. She hugged me and I wept uncontrollably on her shoulder. "Mama, I'm dying."

She ushered me to the sofa. I didn't let go of her. We sat at the same time. Her eyes filled with tears as she rocked me. "What are you talking about, Madison? Why would you say something like that? What's wrong, honey? Did he call off the wedding?"

Sniffling, I said, "Everything is messed up now." I was feeling like a little girl instead of a woman.

"It'll be all right. Mama is here. Start from the beginning. Wait," she said, then called out, "Johnny! Come in here!"

"No, Ma. I didn't want —"

"Rosalee, why you yelling for me? What's going . . . oh, hey, sweetheart."

"Hi, Papa." I dried my face. Sat up straight. I dug under my fingernails with my nails.

Mama gently held one of my hands. "Have a seat on the other side of your daughter. I think we have a family crisis."

"Don't tell me the wedding is off," Dad said.

I hesitated. Unable to face my truth, I stared toward my lap. Pulling away my hand, Mama held on more tightly. I pushed back my middle finger's cuticle with my thumb. I didn't know what news to give them first.

"Take your time, sweetheart. We're not going anywhere," Mama said.

Finally, after five minutes of silence, I said,

"I'm pregnant."

Mama exhaled. "Oh, honey. That's okay. You'll be married before the baby is born. Bringing a baby into the world is a blessing from God. Oh, Johnny, we're going to be grandparents." My mother beamed and touched my stomach. "I can't believe it. This is the best news I've had all year." She kissed me, then held me close. "I pray it's a girl."

"Good job, sweetheart. A baby is called marriage security. Think of it this way. Better you than some other woman having his baby."

I confessed. "The baby might not be his." I couldn't tell them about Granville or the condom the gynecologist pulled out of me. Depending on when I conceived, my unborn could be for that fool.

Mama scooted away from me. "Madison Tyler, I raised you better than this."

Papa chimed in, "Does Chicago know?"

With both hands free, I peeled parts of my cuticle. "Not yet. I plan on telling him tonight."

"Don't tell him. Get rid of it," Papa said. "You have to have an abortion. Next time you make sure it's his."

"Not so fast, Johnny. The Bible says, 'Thou shall not kill.' Abortion is murder.

284

Regardless of who the father is, we're talking about an innocent baby."

"We're talking about saving our business, Rosalee. And," Papa added, as if it were an afterthought, "Madison's wedding."

I mumbled, "I knew I should've kept my mouth shut."

"No, what you should've done was kept your legs shut, but that's water under the bridge. I'll go with you to the doctor." I was shocked to hear my dad say he'd go. His motivation was out of concern for his construction company.

"Don't talk to our daughter like that. And you're not going to take her anywhere to take away this precious baby's life."

Interrupting them, I said, "That's not all. I have stage two breast cancer."

"Dear God, the things we fear the most shall come upon us," Mama said, leaning my head on her shoulder. "I'm here for you, honey. I'll be here every second for you. Have you told Roosevelt?"

"No! I haven't told him! I just found out about it all today. He doesn't know anything." I hoped what I'd said was true and what he had to tell me at dinner wasn't related to Granville.

My mind raced with scenarios of how he could have found out. Granville could've called Roosevelt at this office. The number was available to the public. Or Loretta could've told him her suspicions. I was totally paranoid. Neither Loretta nor Granville knew for sure that I was pregnant.

"And that's the way we're going to keep this situation until after the wedding. You go telling that man you've got a baby who might not be his, and you have to have surgery, and he'll leave you for sure."

My body went numb. I couldn't feel my legs. I leaned back on the sofa.

"He'll find out eventually, Johnny, because she has to have both the surgery and the baby."

"Waiting two months to tell him ain't gon' hurt her."

"But it could kill her. Did you hear her say 'stage two'?"

"One, two, three, I'm a man. I don't know what that means. All I know is you survived breast cancer, your mother, and her mother too. And breasts or no breasts, you still look good to me."

My jaw dropped. I stared in disbelief at my mom. The fluid in my stomach rose to my throat. I swallowed to suppress throwing up on her. "Is this true?"

She nodded. "Yeah, baby. It's true."

"Why? Why didn't you tell me?" I was too

angry to cry.

"That's why I got you out of Port Arthur. I thought it was the environment, and I prayed to God that you'd never have to deal with this. I'm so sorry."

I pushed my body from the sofa with my hands. *Don't pass out, Madison.* I stood still for a moment, then said, "I've got to go. Dad, don't call me. Ma, I'll call you later."

My dad would sell his soul to the Devil, and my mother would try to barter with God to save him. Why would my mother not tell me my family history? Because I didn't ask? Because she never thought I'd get it? She didn't want me to worry. Would I have been better off knowing sooner? I think so. I could've gotten tested years ago and possibly found out if it was genetic. I had lots of questions, but the answers wouldn't do me any good at this point.

# Chapter 25
## Madison

I got into my car and headed to Houston's. Sitting at the bar, I ordered, "A bottle of your best champagne."

"Are you expecting anyone?" the bartender asked.

None of her damn business. "Do you care?" The way I felt, I could've done a baller move and drunk straight from the bottle. "And give me a tall glass of water." It was time to take two more meds.

Gazing at the metal basket filled with fresh lemons and limes, I didn't look over my shoulder, but I swore if Granville approached me that champagne bottle was going to be a weapon. I was going to bust him in his mouth. And I'd keep breaking bottles on his head until every wine and beer bottle I could reach behind the bar was smashed into his skull. How could a man make me hate him that much?

I'd always been careful. No abortions,

Plan B pills, or miscarriages. How was I pregnant and I took birth control pills? That was unbelievable that I was in that small percentage that could conceive on contraceptives. This baby inside of me had to be for Roosevelt.

Taking a sip of champagne, slowly, I let the bubbles trickle down my throat. Loretta and Tisha strolled in together.

"We're going to move to the table in the corner," I told the bartender as I picked up my drink from the caramel-and-charcoal granite countertop.

"I'll have your Moët and two glasses sent right over."

"Hey, how're you feeling?" Tisha asked, greeting me with open arms.

Not answering the question, I gave her a soft hug. "Hey, Tisha. Loretta," I said, leading the way.

Loretta was all bouncy. Obviously, she'd gotten some dick. I was not going to ask her anything about Chaz. That relationship was not going to last.

The booth area was dimly lit. A stationary lamp was attached to the wall. A large white candle encased in glass was the centerpiece. I slid it to the edge of the table. A different bartender delivered our bottle, filled two flutes, then topped mine off.

Exhaling, I said, "I really don't know where to start."

"By learning how to be a loyal friend," Loretta said, smiling. "That would be a good place. You're —"

Tisha interrupted. "Loretta, don't start. That's not why we're here. If we don't stick together, that idiot Granville can do some serious damage. Madison, you speak first. Loretta, wait until Madison is finished, then say what you have to." Tisha looked at me. "When Loretta starts, don't say a word until she's done. And remember we're friends, and we're going to remain friends — no matter what."

Didn't seem like anything the doctor told me earlier was real. I was hoping it would all go away, or I'd get a call from her saying it was a mistake. I hung on to the hope that they got my results mixed up with someone else's.

Loretta said, "Before you start, I'm close to getting my protective order and I'm getting a license to carry a gun. Madison, you should do the same."

I was not walking around armed and on the edge. If I had a piece in my purse and Loretta messed with me on a bad day, I might shoot her ass. I had more important business to handle. Granville was not going to consume my time.

"With the wedding being two months away, I'm hiring a planner to take care of all the details. It will be elegant and small. A matron and a maid of honor — that's you two — and the best man and one groom. That's Roosevelt's decision. I just want this over and done."

"Over and done?" Loretta commented. "These guys fall for your fake Southern ways, high-yellow skin, blond hair, big breasts, tiny waist, and phat ass. You say 'Jump,' and they don't even ask how high. They just do it like fools. A ring doesn't mean anything to you. Is that your symbolism of self-worth?"

I paused for a moment. I wanted her to get all that she had to say out before I slammed her ass. "And what's yours? Huh? Miss Holy, you ho. You open your legs. Let a man fuck you raw. And what do you have to show for it? A wet ass and his baby? Another woman *like me* has got a ring on her finger! She's got Raynard jumping through hoops, and your sorry ass wants him so bad you're wasting your life crying over a nigga who won't even speak to you when he picks up his daughter."

"Madison, all I'm saying is, you're marrying the most eligible bachelor in Houston and you act like you're doing paperwork to adopt a dog."

"At least I have a dog, bitch. This is all your damn fault. You're so fucking jealous. Maybe you should marry my fiancé, since you can't get one of your own. Is that what you want?" I wasn't dumb to take off my ring and throw it at her. I wiggled my fingers in front of her face.

Tisha interrupted. "It's Madison's wedding. Not yours, Loretta. She's making it easier on us by paying a professional."

"Thanks, Tisha. Moving on. Granville. He's been showing up everywhere I go. On dates with Roosevelt. Even at my doctor's appointment today. Sitting next to him in the waiting room, I found a tracking device that fool installed on my cell phone that night after I passed out."

"I'd better search my apps," Loretta said, picking up her cell phone.

I gave them details of Granville following me to the hospital, including when I deleted the application earlier. I went on to tell them about the condom the doctor found inside me during my exam. "And to top shit off, he threatened to sue me for sexual harassment after I fired him."

Loretta and Tisha were silent for a while.

"Does Chicago know?" Loretta asked.

"Know what, bitch? You would open your fucking mouth and ask about him first!" I banged my palm on the table. "What the fuck is wrong with you!"

Tisha opened her mouth.

"Don't say shit! I want to know what's her obsession with my fiancé! I'll tell you what. Bitch, if you breathe a word of this to Roosevelt, I will tell Raynard about your being kidnapped and tell him to take Raynell away from you because you're unfit as a friend and a mother! See how you like that. And stop playing dumb. You know I won our bet."

I was fed up. My blood boiled. I wouldn't dare tell Loretta about my pregnancy and cancer. I couldn't let Tisha know either, because that would be the same as saying it to Loretta.

"You wouldn't stoop that low," Loretta said.

"The question is, why shouldn't I stoop to your level? I was happy until you made that stupid-ass bet!" Before I ended up punching Loretta in her face, I got up and left. They could pick up the tab.

If I hadn't had sex with Granville, I'd tell Roosevelt about my having breast cancer. I believed he'd understand. And like in the Martina McBride song, I knew my man would be my rock. I regretted what I'd done. But all the regret in the world couldn't reverse my bad decisions.

While I was on a roll, I might as well go home and brace myself for what Roosevelt had to get off his chest.

# CHAPTER 26
## GRANVILLE

I'll teach her to delete my tracking app from her phone.

I'd sat in the lobby and waited for hours. Eventually I became worried. I'd watched the receptionist leave for lunch and return thirty minutes later. Still, there was no Madison. Did they admit her? No one stays four hours in a doctor's office for a visit.

Finally I asked the receptionist, "Can you check on my girlfriend? She's been back there forever."

"Who's your girlfriend?" she asked, as if she hadn't noticed me sitting next to the most beautiful woman in the room this morning.

"Madison Tyler," I proudly said, squaring my shoulders.

She tapped on a few keys. "Madison Tyler? She had an early appointment."

"I know what time she came in. Don't you remember us coming in together? I sat right beside her."

" 'Along came a spider, who sat down beside her.' We both know how this story ends." She shook her head. "I do recall seeing you next to her. She didn't say much to you. And when she did, she seemed annoyed. Some girlfriend. But I don't believe you, sir. And I can't give you any information on her. . . . That's confidential. Next," she said, looking at the person standing behind me.

Was that trick reciting a nursery rhyme and telling me I'd frightened Madison away? Was that what Madison had told them? I nodded. "That's cool." My only option at this point was to go to the garage and wait in my car. She'd eventually have to get in hers.

The lady on the elevator was cute. She had on one of those scrub outfits. "You going to or coming from surgery?" I asked, trying not to stare at her hard nipples. I wasn't a pervert, but who could miss them?

She didn't answer. Women were a trip. Bet if she was stranded on a dark highway, she'd be happy if I stopped to help her. I finally got to the garage.

"Whoa, buddy. What happened here?" The space next to my Super Duty was empty.

How did I miss her? I didn't doze off. I

barely blinked. Madison's car was gone. Where was she? I started sweating, trying to figure out what to do next. I wiped my nose and upper lip with the back of my hand. I wish I had a way to track her.

"Fuck!" I yelled, getting into my truck. I slammed the door, paid for parking, and drove off.

Maybe I should visit Mama. Hadn't been to see her since Madison fired me. Now that I didn't have a job, I should spend the night and take her to the doctor for a checkup. Usually, my visit with her was a turnaround. I didn't like staying in Port Arthur for more than a few hours at a time. There was nothing there for me anymore. No women that I liked. No friends I'd kept in touch with. If Mom didn't live there, I'd have no reason to go back. I wasn't up for the drive today. Perhaps I'd go tomorrow.

I turned on my radio to listen to some country music on KILT-FM 100.3. "Yeah!" I shouted as loud as I could.

Massaging my throat, I bobbed my head. I blasted my volume to "Turn It Up" and started singing along with Roger Creager as I thrust my fist in the air.

"Yeah! That's my theme song!" At times country music made me feel like losing control, going wild, and living in a reckless kind of way. Now was one of those moments.

I got an instant woody, which made me think about Madison riding my dick that night. At least my johnson wasn't depressed. I sped onto the freeway, headed I-10 East toward Port Arthur.

Music made me feel alive! Listening to Roger made me realize that turning it up with Madison was exactly what I had to do to keep her.

She wanted me to take control. That's why she didn't speak to me.

*Damn. Why didn't I smother her with my irresistible charm while we were at the hospital?*

Soon as my song went off, and a commercial came on, I was sad again. I missed Madison. I loved her.

"Call eight-eight-eight . . . Call eight-eight-eight . . . Again, that's eight-eight-eight . . ."

"Enough already!" I reached to change the station. Just before I pressed the button, I paused.

"Have you been wrongfully terminated?"

"Yes."

"Has your employer fired you without cause?"

"Yes," I said again.

"As a result, you're one paycheck away

298

from being homeless."

My response should've been "No," but it was "Maybe," if I didn't find a new boss soon. What did I do with the ninety grand a year Madison paid me?

With no head of household, no dependents, no exemptions, no retirement contributions, I was like other hardworking Americans. Almost broke. By the time the state and feds got paid off the top, I forked out money for my car note, gas, rent, food, cell phone, cable, Internet, electricity, credit cards, and dating; my savings account was a joke. That was why I'd closed it years ago.

Competing with my thoughts was the continuance of the announcement. "Well, Turner and Turner are here to let you know you have rights too. If you believe you've been wrongfully terminated, call us at eight-eight-eight . . . we can help you."

This time I was glad they repeated the number aloud so many times. It took me that long to memorize it. I'd heard the commercial before. Always thought, *That's for other dudes. I got a damn good job.* But this time it applied to me. Madison didn't have a legitimate reason for firing me. She couldn't give up the pussy on the first date, then act like we were strangers. I'd do whatever it took to keep her. I'd even drop the case if she gave me back my job.

I took the next exit and called the number.

"Turner and Turner, how may we help you?"

I cleared my throat. "You're not going to believe why I was wrongfully terminated."

"We're here to help you. What's your name?" the woman asked, sounding as though she was taking calls at a drug rehab facility. The only thing I was addicted to was Madison.

"Hi there. My name is Granville Washington."

"Mr. Washington, we need to have you come in for a consultation."

"I'm on my way," I said, ready to rock and roll. "What's the address?"

"We do have a protocol. Let me check the schedule."

I impatiently waited.

"How's next week?"

"How's today?" I asked. "This is serious business. I can call someone else if I have to."

"Hold on," she said. "Let me see if we have any cancellations."

"Okay." I banged on my steering wheel as she did her job. At least she had one.

"Can you be here in twenty minutes?"

"You bet. I'm on my way."

The rush-hour traffic was getting heavy. Afraid they'd make me come back another day if I wasn't on time, I drove off and on in the emergency lane. As I merged to the left, my exit was next. I made it to their office in twenty-five. Hoping I wasn't too late, I parked at a meter but didn't pay. I'd take my chance on getting a ticket.

I sat in the lobby. Filled out the intake sheet I was given, then handed it to the receptionist. She told me the hourly rate was $150, with a one-hour minimum. She billed my credit card, then said, "An attorney will be with you momentarily."

Thirty minutes later I was still waiting. Ten potential clients walked in with no appointment. They had to come back next week. Guess I was lucky.

"Mr. Washington, the attorney is ready for you," she said, then escorted me to a conference room with glass walls.

An attractive woman in a nice gray suit extended her hand. "Welcome, Mr. Washington." She gave me a firm shake. "Please have a seat."

I grinned at her. I could get used to being addressed formally. She made me feel important. When we split the dough I was about to get, she might be my new woman, if Madison didn't get her stuff together.

The attorney glanced over her glasses. Why did people wear eyeglasses when they were constantly looking above the rim? I hated that.

"So let's get to it. Do I have a case?"

"I've reviewed your form. Tell me why you feel your termination is worth ten million dollars."

I stared at her and wiped my nose. "Well . . ." Should I have asked for more? My skull popped sweat like popcorn. "I'd never been fired. My boss got rid of me after we had sex. I was going to ask her to marry me, but then she showed me an engagement ring I couldn't afford to buy her. She cooked for me. Steak. Potatoes. Expensive stuff. I thought I was going to get a raise. I even ate her pussy. She might be jealous because I proposed to her girlfriend, but her friend wasn't as good in bed. I guess what I'm trying to say is I —"

The attorney interrupted me. "Thanks for coming in. We won't be representing you," she said, standing while extending her hand.

This was not over. "Why not? This is money in the bank. It's a slam dunk. We will get paid big-time. You single? I —"

"You don't have a case of wrongful termination, Mr. Washington. You have . . . How can I say this without insulting you?" She paused, then told me, "You don't need a lawyer. You need a professional psychiatric evaluation." She opened the door.

"Oh, so you gon' take my hundred and fifty, give me ten minutes of your time, then kick me out?"

*Fuck this bitch. She doesn't know me.* I saw her sneaking a peek at my dick.

"We don't do refunds, Mr. Washington. Have a good day."

Was that trick serious? I'd just wasted my time and money on a scam. I got into my truck, went home, turned on my computer, and then clicked on the satellite program. I grabbed a cold beer from the fridge. Sat in front of my laptop and waited to see my woman. I opened a new page, wondering how to figure out when and where Madison was getting married.

I had to stop her from making the biggest mistake of our lives.

# CHAPTER 27
## CHICAGO

---

*Dear God . . .*

Exhaling, I sat in my car in front of Madison's place. Here I was, Roosevelt DuBois, the executive vice president and general manager of one of the best football teams in America. The envy of millions of men. The sexual desire of too many women. Was engaged to the most beautiful woman in the world. Being handsome and successful was a blessing and a curse. A week ago I was the man. Today I was uncertain of my future.

Right now, I was pissed off to the point that I couldn't focus beyond the first few words of my prayer. I looked at Loretta's house. I preferred to talk with her before speaking with Madison. Loretta had this inner peace that balanced me. Hearing her voice was calming and gave me the sensation of a Swedish massage. Her words soothed my brain. When she exhaled, the sound relaxed my muscles. Her tongue sliding across those raspberry lips wedged excitement between the crevices of my fingers and toes.

It didn't matter that Loretta was avoiding my calls. Or that Chaz was telling me how much he missed her company. I didn't understand why he wouldn't allow himself to be vulnerable with Loretta. She wasn't the type of woman to use a man. He had his way of dating and I had mine. Chaz's pride kept him away from what might be the best woman he'd met in years. Respect for Loretta made me reluctant to contact her.

I silently told myself, *She won't turn you away if you stand before her. Go knock on her door.*

In the short time that I'd known Loretta, she was what we referred to in sports as a sleeper. She was one of the best women out there, but no man had seemed to notice, including my brother. Why was that? She had all the qualities of a perfect wife: Loyalty. Kindness. Consideration for others. She was a protective mother.

*Chicago, dude, you've got to make a move.*

My soles rested on the cement driveway. I could restart my engine, go home, and give it a day. Not reacting immediately usually

305

helped me to respond in a rational manner. I realized that most situations weren't as bad as they seemed, once you heard the other person's side of the story.

"Roosevelt," Madison called from her doorway in a loving way. "How long are you going to sit out there, baby?"

I didn't want to see her face right this minute. Not turning toward her, I said, "I'll be in shortly." I struggled to shift my anger to acceptance. I couldn't undo whatever was done.

I got out of the car, slammed the door, entered her house, and slammed that door.

"We need to talk."

As usual, she was dressed elegantly. Not a single hair was out of place. Her cherry-red-colored lips popped. The electric blue halter top showed her mouthwatering breasts. Her nipples were so hard that I wanted to bite them through her blouse. My eyes traveled to her silky legs and lower thighs. A mustard skirt loosely caressed her hips. I wasn't interested in taking her to dinner, but I'd be lying if I told myself I didn't want to bend her over the couch and fuck her doggie-style. I sat in the living room in case I got emotionally overheated and needed to get away from her fast.

"Baby, what's wrong?" she asked, touching me.

Her hands were cold. She was barely breathing. I wanted to lay my head in her cleavage for comfort, but earlier today I'd discovered I couldn't trust anyone except my family. And since Madison wasn't my wife yet, she might as well be where she was probably going to end up, on the sideline.

Clenching my teeth, I told my fiancée, "Don't touch me"; then I moved her hand to her lap. "Madison, whatever you do, don't lie to me."

"I'd never lie to you about anything. What is it, baby?"

Hearing her say the word "baby" made me cringe. Her sexy Houstonian accent wasn't going to work on me this time.

"Someone e-mailed me a link to an X-rated video. Do you have any — and I mean *any* — idea how this video got to me? If this gets out, I could lose my job."

I watched her face become ghost white, like there was no blood in her body.

"Baby, what happened? Am I hearing you right?"

I paused and gripped my chin, then let go.

"I'm not marrying a slut. When and why did you do this?"

307

Her face went from white to red. She shook her head.

"I don't know what you're talking about." Her voice trembled, along with her legs. "Can I see it?"

"No. No, you can't. Why should I show it to you when you're in it? What's your association with this dude?"

"Are you accusing or asking Roosevelt? You're all over the place. You're not the only man I've been engaged to."

Maybe I was overreacting. What if the video was made before we'd met? I hadn't considered that.

"This motherfucker was eating your pussy and you were loving that shit."

Her body tensed, and she said, "What you're doing isn't fair. I don't deserve this."

"Just tell me you haven't had any kind of attraction or sex with another man since we've met and I'll let it go."

Tears flowed down her cheeks. I wiped them away. She looked me in the eyes and said, "I haven't, and I never will. I love you too much. In fact, I don't want to see the video. It doesn't matter. All that's important to me is us."

There'd be no trust if I didn't believe her, but there was something else I had to know the truth about, and that was whatever Blue was talking about when he was in my office. I didn't want to find out he'd been with Madison before me.

"Blue Waters says we shouldn't get married. Any reason why he'd make a special trip to my office to tell me that? If you've ever fucked him, you'd better tell me now."

As a man I did not want to work with or near any man who had fucked my fiancée. I'd have to let her go for that one.

Madison exhaled, like a weight was lifted. "Is that what this is about? Blue? He's so jealous of you, he'll tell you anything to get inside your head so he can get your job."

I knew that was true, but why was I so angry?

"Madison, I need you to tell me the truth. Have you been sexually or romantically involved with Blue or any man since we started dating?"

She shook her head. "You just asked me that."

"I need an answer from your mouth."

"No, Roosevelt, I already told you that I haven't."

"Have you ever dated, engaged in oral, anal, or intercourse with Blue Waters?"

Politely she said, "No, Roosevelt."

"Madison, have you ever dated, engaged in oral, anal, or intercourse with any man since we started dating?"

"Again, no. I haven't. How many times do I have to answer the same question?"

Clenching my teeth, I said, "Until I get tired of asking. Is there anything personal, financial, or otherwise that you're hiding from me that I should know about before we get married?"

The questions I wanted answers to made me realize that I was in the right place. Having this conversation with Loretta would've not only been inappropriate, it wouldn't have been helpful.

"No" was all she said this time.

"You think we should get a prenup?"

"At this point, Roosevelt, I think we should do whatever you'd like. If you want to call off the wedding, let me know and I'll call the planner first thing in the morning."

I knew I should've given it another day to discuss my concerns.

"That's not what I'm saying. I just feel something isn't right. I need time to think about this, Madison."

"You're getting cold feet, baby. That's natural. Why don't you go home and sleep on it. Take as much time as you want and let me know if you'd like your ring back," she said. Heading upstairs, Madison glanced over her shoulder. "You can let yourself out."

I walked outside and saw Chaz sitting in his car in Loretta's driveway. There was an SUV parked in front of his BMW. I headed next door to make sure everything was okay. I wanted to show him the video of Madison on my iPad, but what good would that do?

Either I was marrying her or I wasn't.

# CHAPTER 28
## LORETTA

Sometimes a man's purpose in a woman's life was to make her feel again.

Chaz had done that for me. I was still on a sexual high from the multiple orgasms he'd given me. I missed him so much that my heart ached. I wasn't trying to play power-of-the-sexes tug-of-war with him. If he wanted to see me again, he'd have to make the call. One thing Madison taught me was, when a man was seriously interested, he'd initiate pursuit.

Kneeling at my altar, I lit three candles, for Tisha, Madison, and me. I turned my Bible to Matthew 18: 21–23 and read, *Then Peter came to Him and said, "Lord, how often shall my brother sin against me, and I forgive him? Up to seven times?" Jesus said to him, "I do not say to you, up to seven times, but up to seventy times seven."*

That was a total of four hundred and ninety times. I hadn't kept count; but it felt like during our friendship, I'd forgiven Madison more often than that.

I prayed, *Lord, please let me continue to find the strength to love Madison and Tisha for an eternity. I know she didn't mean all the horrible things she said to me. If I could take one thing back, it would be the bet. Help me to find a way to get her out of this situation. And thank you, Lord, for Tisha. I don't know what I'd do without her friend—*

The doorbell rang.

"Mommy, Mommy, my daddy is here!" Raynell shouted, running down the stairs. I heard her race toward the living room.

I blew out the candles and hurried to the foyer. "Lil girl, you'd better not," I said, stepping in front of her. I peeped through the hole. Didn't want any uninvited guests showing up the way Granville had.

I opened my front door. Before Raynell stepped outside, Raynard was inside.

Handing me a Nordstrom shopping bag, he said, "You got a minute. We need to talk"; then he shut my door. He helped himself to a seat.

Raynell sat on the sofa next to her dad. I gave the bag to our daughter. "Princess, take your clothes to the room and stay there until Mommy comes to get you."

"Can I try them on?" she asked.

"Of course you can. And pick out the one you like the most," I told her.

"Okay, Mommy," she said, dancing up the stairs.

Raynard had no idea I donated most of the dresses and items he'd bought. He didn't need to know. He wouldn't understand why his daughter shouldn't have a closet full of clothes she'd never wear.

I sat on the opposite end of the sofa. "What's up? Does Gloria know you're actually talking to me?"

"Look, Loretta, I'm not here to be your friend. I'm here because of this dude you're going out with. Just because he's Chicago's brother doesn't mean I'm okay with him being around Raynell or your having him in my house. Are they sitting outside in that BMW waiting for me to leave?"

My jaw dropped; my mouth was wide open. "Are you serious? You bought it. My name is on it. That legally makes this my house."

I was pissed at Raynard, but I was happy to hear Chaz had come to see me. He knew Raynard was coming and waited, instead of calling. . . . Damn, I had asked him not to come to my house without letting me know. But I was also excited and could hardly wait to see him and get some.

314

*I'm gonna get laid.*

"Oh, I'm real serious. You took her to the game. Had her in a suite around people she didn't know."

"You mean like Tisha, her kids, her husband, and Madison? People like that?"

"I'm not here to argue with you, Loretta. If you're going to keep seeing that dude, I want full custody of my daughter."

"You bastard," I hissed. "You're jealous. You never thought I'd meet a man wealthier and more powerful than you. You show up at my house every week flaunting Gloria. You brought her to Raynell's first birthday party and she's been with you ever since. You didn't even give me a reason for leaving us. You can have your trophy wife, but I can't have a man who happens to be a multi-millionaire?"

"I don't care how much money he has. It's different for me, you know that. I'm Raynell's dad. I'd never touch her inappropriately. You don't know what that dude is capable of."

More like I didn't know what Raynard was up to. I went to the kitchen, grabbed a pack of Lemonheads from the dish, and made my way back to him. I handed Raynard the candy. "Here. All good dogs deserve a treat. I don't run your house and you will not piss

315

on mine. Go home and mark your territory. Oh, that's right. I almost forgot. Your bitch has already done that."

Raynard stood toe-to-toe with me. "So now you have balls."

I stepped closer and stared up at him. "One of us needs to have some, don't you think? If Gloria is putting you up to this, I will give you and her the fight of your lives if you try to take Raynell away from me."

He backed away. "Just stop seeing him and nothing will change."

"I'm going upstairs to get our daughter. For five years you've done a real good job of being Gloria's pet. Tuck your tail and go back to doing just that. And since you're all up in my business, for the record that little boy looks nothing like you," I said, stomping up the stairs.

When I returned to the living room, Raynard and Chaz were there.

"Hey, baby. Sorry for dropping by without calling," Chaz said.

"Hey, Mr. C.," Raynell said, giving Chaz a big hug around his thighs. "I want to go to another game. That was fun."

"Anytime for you, princess," Chaz said.

Raynard pried her away and shifted his eyes to me.

I escorted Raynard out the door with our

daughter. "Bye, princess. Mommy loves you."

"I love you too, Mommy," Raynell said, holding her dad's hand as she skipped to his SUV. "Bye, Mr. C.!"

"Bye, Raynell."

Closing the door, I stared at Chaz.

"Don't say it. I'm guilty. Yes, my visit is premeditated. I'm not going to apologize for missing you like crazy," he said, hugging me tightly.

I couldn't lie. It felt so good to have that man's arms wrapped around me. I deserved his affection. "I miss you too, boo."

"You have time to take a ride?" he asked.

"What kind of ride?"

"If I tell you, you might not want to go. I need you to trust me on this one. You can ride this," he said, touching his dick, "when we get back."

I didn't like surprises. "How about a quickie to take the edge off?"

"I warned you." He pulled out his dick.

I removed my pants.

"You're going to need something to hold on to," he said.

I grabbed the railing to the stairway and leaned forward. When Chaz penetrated me, my entire body trembled. He pounded me with pleasure.

"Hold on, girl, I'm just getting warmed up."

"Oh, my God. I missed you so much." I wanted to tell him, "I love you," but it was too soon.

"Don't keep my pussy from me this long again." *Smack!* He slapped my ass.

It hurt so good that it didn't take long for me to explode all over him. After we came together, he pulled out. "I'm not done with you, but we've got to go."

"I'll be ready in a moment. Help yourself to something to drink and you can freshen up in the guest bathroom."

I jogged upstairs, showered, brushed my teeth, let my hair down, put on jeans and a cute tapered pink T-shirt, with cropped sleeves, then finished with my raspberry gloss.

Chaz was in the living room. He stood and gave me a hug. "Wow, you look and smell good," he said, kissing me. "Let's go, my lady."

# CHAPTER 29
## LORETTA

My lady? What did that mean?

I wanted to tell Chaz what Raynard had said earlier, but that would create unnecessary tension between two men who didn't know one another and put me in the middle. Chaz had no idea Raynard was jealous of him, or maybe I was the one Raynard was pissed off at because there was a man sexing me in the house he'd paid for.

Raynard had his chance to have me. I still loved him, but I might die waiting for him to divorce Gloria. And even if he left her, there was no guarantee he'd come back to me.

It was time to give my attention to the right man. Get to know him. Let him get to explore my deepest fantasies. If I desired a future with Chaz, I had to give him my undivided devotion.

"Relax. Say something. I'm not taking you to a funeral," he said, opening the car door.

His laughter wasn't infectious.

Softly I exhaled. What was wrong with me? We'd just had fantastic, spontaneous sex. In my heart, though, I'd rather be with Raynard.

Settling into Chaz's passenger seat, I fastened the belt. He merged onto Interstate 610, drove onto Highway 59, then took the tollway toward Sugar Land.

"I like you," I told him, wishing I could take it back. Not because it wasn't true. I'd bet Madison would never reveal her feelings for a man before he expressed how he felt about her.

"I like you too. You're cool."

"Cool"? What did he mean by that? Was I cool like a buddy type of friend? Or did he want more? Was I really his lady? Or did the words roll off his tongue without commitment? I wasn't in it for a sex mate. I wanted to get married.

I hated that I loved Raynard. My emotions were totally irrational. So why couldn't I move on? How long would my heart ache for him? I regretted calling him a "dog" and referring to Gloria as a "bitch." Not that I didn't believe that. I did. But I'd never said it to his face.

I lashed out at him the way Madison had done to me. My words proved that I'd lost respect for Raynard. And once a woman lost respect for a man, it was time for her to let go. I fought to keep the tears behind my eyes. I didn't want Chaz to sense how I felt about my daughter's father.

"You okay?" Chaz asked, holding my hand.

"I'm good," I said, blinking repeatedly. I didn't care if he challenged my answer. What made me so emotional? I wasn't on my cycle, or depressed, or sad, or in love. I was confused.

Staring through the windshield, we were approaching the mall. They had good restaurants in this part of town. The Cheesecake Factory was one of my favorites. A slice of red velvet cheesecake, with extra whip, could put me in a seductive mood. Raynard's name was stirring in my mouth. Our last real date was at a Cheesecake Factory.

I told myself, *If you think you're confused now, do not have a conversation about Raynard with Chaz. You'll regret it.*

I'd learned that the way I freely noted negative things about people could make my friends and lovers dislike the people before they'd ever met them. Once I influenced others to form a dislike, I couldn't erase those images.

The time had come for me to make myself

a priority. I was the artist of my life. I held the paintbrush in my hand. Every stroke had meaning. What people saw in me depended upon how I portrayed myself. I was solely responsible for creating my masterpiece. Paintings reminded me of Chicago. Sadness marked an upside-down smiling face on my heart. I missed praying with him.

I wanted Chaz to respect Raynard, and vice versa. Raynard was overreacting and I hoped Madison hadn't influenced him. I'd never left Raynell alone with any man other than my father and her dad. But if Chaz was going to be in our lives, I'd have to eventually trust him with my princess.

Chaz had been patient. He'd left me alone with my thoughts. Perhaps he was emerged in his own.

"I'm not going to ask where we're going, but I am going to say don't show up at my house again unannounced. I don't like that. I'm not going to do that to you, and I demand the same respect."

As long as I was lonely, Raynard was content. He probably felt like, regardless of the few men I'd dated, my pussy was reserved for him. The fact that we hadn't been intimate since I'd given birth was irrelevant. Now that I might get serious with another man, he wanted *sole* custody. Forget Raynard. The only case he'd have against me would be assault with a deadly weapon if he took away my parental rights. I didn't interfere with the way he raised his son; but if he messed with my kid, he had it coming. I was an extremely fit mother.

"Fair. It won't happen again," Chaz said, cruising Sugar Land's upscale neighborhood. Parking in the circular driveway of a residence twice the size of mine, he opened my door. "My parents live here." He interlocked his fingers with mine and led the way to the front door. "My mom asked me to bring you by."

There was no time to find out why he'd done this without my permission. I shook my head, smiled at him with closed lips, then said, "I don't think this is good. I'm not prepared."

"For what? It's my mother. Not my dog. Besides, you've already met her. She likes you. That's more than I can say about your girlfriend."

"You have a dog?"

"No."

I had to laugh.

"I said that to throw you off, which proves you do have a sense of humor. It'll be okay."

I prayed this wasn't about Madison. "This isn't funny and you know it. Why would you bring me here and not tell me first?" Coming to his parents' was too formal. This was impromptu. Men only formally introduced women to their mothers if they were serious. The sex was great, but we barely knew each other.

"Hey, son. Hi, Loretta. I'm glad you agreed to come by," Mrs. DuBois said, hugging me. "Escort Loretta to the family room, honey. I'll get your father."

Everything was in place, except me. I wasn't ready to visit with his folks. The coffee table was neatly set with four tall glasses of fresh lemonade. The crystal was hardly sweating and the ice hadn't melted. She'd probably just poured when she heard Chaz drive up.

Cheese, crackers, and nuts were on four small plates. A platter with more of the same was next to the container half full of fresh, floating lemon slices. I watched a few beads of condensation form, connect, and roll along the outside of the pitcher. Perspiration gathered under my armpits and between my thighs.

I hissed, "This is embarrassing. I'm sweating like a dog."

"Don't be nervous. It's okay. By the way, dogs don't sweat. My mom wanted to talk with you about some things that are impor-

tant to my family. We won't be here long."
His lips gently pressed to mine. He grazed
my nipple, then my cheek. "Don't eat too
much. Save room for dessert." He winked
at his dick.

Panting, shallow breaths consumed me as
I whispered, "Do you know what kind of
things?"

"You are so darn cute. Yes, I do know."

"I guess that's your way of not telling me,
huh? You have some explaining to do when
we leave here."

We sat together on the love seat, but there
was enough space for Raynell to sit in the
middle if she was here. I picked up a cream-
colored porcelain plate and started snacking
on the thin wheat crackers. Not because I
was hungry. It was a good way to occupy
my mouth and redirect my thoughts from
the wet stains I felt underneath my arms. If
I had driven us here, I'd set the plate on the
table and leave.

His dad entered the room and sat in a
chair at the end of the coffee table closest
to Chaz. Mr. DuBois was a tall, slender,
handsome man, with a flat stomach. A
white-and-blue striped shirt was neatly
tucked into his black slacks. The thin leather
belt was fitted. His face and head were
smooth; no mustache or goatee.

As Chaz's mother sat in the chair facing her husband, her blue dress, which matched her husband's stripes, raised slightly above her knees. Her silver hair was full of wide, sweeping waves that neatly aligned with her jaw and the nape of her neck. I handed Chaz my plate, crossed my ankles, and folded my arms.

"Loretta, I know this may seem a bit awkward, but I asked my son to bring you here, dear. This won't take long," Mrs. DuBois articulated. "I'm concerned about my Chicago marrying your best friend, Madison. Now, you and I hit it off at the game. That's why I felt comfortable with your coming over. I know you've gone out with Chaz."

His dad added, "We like you, Loretta. And we like you for Chaz."

It was important that his family accept me. Raynard's parents had said I was welcome in their house anytime, but breaking up with Raynard meant I had to distance myself from them too. It was hard seeing Gloria, Raynard, and their son together at his folks' place. Gloria didn't speak to me. Raynard wouldn't say a word to me. And his parents acted as though nothing was wrong. Holidays and Raynell's birthday were the exception. Raynell stayed as long as she'd liked, but I visited them for one hour.

Mrs. DuBois continued speaking. "Now I'll be frank. I don't care for Madison at all. Never have. As her friend, and as Chicago's prayer partner —"

Mr. DuBois interrupted, "We would like to —"

It was my turn to chime in. "I used to be Chicago's prayer partner. I'm not anymore."

"And why is that?" Mr. DuBois asked.

"It just wasn't a good idea."

Sure, I could've said Madison didn't want us praying together, but I wasn't going to let them use me to get rid of her.

Chaz asked, "Whose idea was that?"

I stared him square in his eyes, pressed my lips together, and exhaled. My neck became tense; I shoved my back against the sofa. I could've told them things that might have given Chaz's parents a heart attack or a reason to persuade Chicago to take back his ring. Madison wasn't right, but her fuckup was also mine. That, and I was no snitch.

Looking at Mrs. DuBois, I said, "No disrespect, ma'am, but Madison is *my* friend. And friendship means something to me. I imagine you have a loving, caring, and trusting relationship with both of your sons, but Chicago isn't committing to you. He's not marrying your husband or Chaz. He's grown and capable of making his own decisions. He told me that he loves Madison. That's all that matters. If you don't care about his happiness or don't want him to walk down the aisle, take it to the Lord in prayer. Regardless of what you do, don't do this to me again. Chaz, whenever you'd like to take me home, I'm ready."

We'd been out three times and each date ended with my insisting on leaving. I could consider this strike three and not see Chaz again, but that would mean I'd be alone, once more.

"She's right, Ma. This is not the way to go about this. Loretta, you don't have to say what it is, but let us know if we're wrong for feeling this way about Madison."

"You have the right to feel however you want." Firmly I said, "No more questions. I'm ready to go right now."

I didn't care if they liked or disliked me. What they'd done was disrespectful. I excused myself and waited for him at his mother's front door. I was glad I'd had sex with Chaz before we left. If we cleared up the confusion on the way to my house, he could stay the night and make love to me until the sun shined on our naked flesh through my skylight.

Since I'd gotten a good dose of a real dick, I didn't want to go back to making dildo selections from my pleasure chest.

Soon as we got into the car, I said, "I'm ready for dessert."

# CHAPTER 30
## MADISON

Desperation didn't win football games, jackpots on a crap table at a casino, negotiations in litigation, and it sure as hell didn't save relationships or mend broken hearts.

The more that a woman clung to a man, she empowered him to dictate her destiny. Eventually he'd cheat or leave her for a younger, prettier, smarter, sexier, or wealthier female. Although the other woman's pussy could be, it didn't have to be better.

For men it was the fantasy of the unfamiliar that excited them. A man's mouth salivated to taste forbidden fruit. The main reason he'd lie in the arms of another was because he was weak and weary. Something in his life was missing and he hadn't found it in his mate. Women with no backbone were unattractive in every way imaginable.

Fall down, and he'd trample all over her. The time he'd stay before walking out hinged on the inevitable . . . disillusion of an illusion called karma. Payback wasn't fair, but neither was his life. She would grant him more time and permission to mistreat her, digging herself deeper into depression. Whenever he left, she should thank him, not beg him to stay. I pitied the woman who would say "I do" to Granville Washington and was happy I'd made it a whole month without him stalking me.

No thanks to Granville, I'd admit that Roosevelt was close to getting some sort of confession out of me about that video, until I straightened my spine and took control. I didn't need a verbal response from Roosevelt. I knew he wasn't calling off our engagement.

Sitting in my office, I had to ensure nothing and no one would sabotage my wedding, especially his mother. I'd decided to make my special-day invitation only; and if Helen weren't his mother, she would not be at the ceremony. I scanned my address list and located the planner's number.

Just as I was about to dial her, Monica buzzed me. "Ms. Tyler, your father is on the line, and Mr. DuBois is here to see you."

I smiled. In a month, I was going to be his wife. Although he'd never done so before, I guess I had to get used to him stopping by whenever he wanted. Roosevelt had the key to my heart, not my house. Was he spying on me? Outside of my hiccup with Granville, I was a one-man type of woman. At times I might not have been a lady, but I certainly wasn't a tramp.

Placing my phone on the desk, I wasn't expecting to see my man this early, and definitely not at my office. Roosevelt wasn't the type of guy to interfere with another person's livelihood. A conversation during working hours for him was usually short and to the point.

Wondering what had brought him in, just in case he had more drama, from Blue, Loretta, or Granville, I swallowed two painkillers to mellow my mood. Chased it with a bottle of water. I'd begun enjoying the way the meds gave me an escape from what I refused to believe: I'd been unfaithful based on a dare.

I'd take that horrific night with that imbecile Granville to my grave. I had to. Loretta had to as well. My ass would eventually have a full recovery from his big-ass, salami-size dick. I wasn't sure what was happening inside my breasts. I couldn't feel anything abnormal. Sure, I had lumps, but what woman didn't? What if I went in for surgery and the cancer spread as soon as they cut me open? What if I didn't go and it got worse?

I dabbed perfume on my wrists and behind my ears. I told Monica, "I'll take my dad's call now and have Mr. DuBois wait a few minutes." If Roosevelt brought me flowers, I bet they weren't dried up like someone had left them outside in the sun and forgotten to water them.

Every day something reminded me of Granville. He'd been quiet since my hospital visit. Wasn't sure if that was good. Perhaps he was preoccupied with finding employment or filing a lawsuit. Regardless of where he was, I had to steer him back where he belonged. With Loretta. Maybe I'd rehire him. At least then I'd know where he was forty hours a week.

I answered, "Hey, Papa. Before you say anything, we received a check from the city for one hundred thousand with the promise of another four by the end of the month. When the next payment arrives, we can exhale and cover a few expenses on the other contracts. This will allow us to wrap up the Westside project. Then we can invoice final payment to them. I know things are tighter than ever, but if the city starts paying us on time, we may not need to float Roosevelt's money."

The probability of Tyler Construction being able to balance its own budget was a long shot, but I was hopeful. Ten million from my husband-to-be could be reduced to zero, if I juggled the funds from other deals and sold my home and furnishings right after the honeymoon. We could meet payroll and my dad could take out a business loan with a low interest rate for the difference.

"That's good news, sweetheart, but it's best to have more of what we need than more of what we've got. Until we have money in the bank, you've got to stay focused on the initial plan. Ten million."

While I was working toward trying to do the right thing, Dad was trying to build his financial security on my man's back. I hope this pitfall taught him not to take on another huge project anytime soon.

"I appreciate the update, sweetheart, but money wasn't why I wanted to speak with you," he said.

My jaw dropped. "That's all you ever talk about with me every day."

"Well, not today. I'm calling to say I'm sorry for being such a jerk. Your mother told me I was insensitive about your heath situation and she's right. I mean, I guess I don't understand the seriousness of breast cancer because your mom had a mastectomy years ago and she's a cancer survivor. That's what we Tylers do — survive."

I was disappointed that my mother hadn't shared my family history. The good side was I'd have post-op alternatives. If I got new boobs, they could be bigger. Bigger wasn't always better, however. I liked the ones I had. What if I lost sensation in my nipples? Would I even have my own nipples?

Among my thoughts, Dad continued talking. "But I know if I had prostate cancer, I'd be devastated. I love your mother so much that losing some of her womanly attributes didn't matter, as long as I didn't lose her. I feel the same way about you, sweetheart."

A lump formed in my throat. "It's okay, Papa. I'll be fine." I hoped Roosevelt would love me unconditionally after I let him know.

I prayed he wasn't so attached to my breasts that he'd let me go if I had to sacrifice them. I didn't think he would, but what if he didn't see me the same?

"Madison, my behavior was unacceptable. I acknowledge that. Your mother wants to go with you to your doctor's appointment today, and no, it is not negotiable. Rosalee is picking you up from the office. And whatever you need this bullheaded dad of yours to do, sweetheart, let me know."

I needed him to back off my fiancé's inheritance, tell my mother not to come, and stop apologizing from his mouth. Nothing he'd offered me or said about me was heartfelt.

"I'm not handicapped. Tell Mama to meet me there. Papa, I gotta go. Roosevelt is waiting in the reception area."

"Speaking of Roosevelt, don't tell him about the big C or the bun in the oven. After your honeymoon we can send you away for a year or stage that you're missing until after you've had the baby and your surgery. If the kid isn't his, put it up for adoption. Keep your conditions in the family until after the wedding and wait until our company is stable. Let me work this out for you, sweetheart."

Papa still didn't get it. I was not abandoning my husband. What if I got morning sickness? Or my stomach started rounding early? On the one hand, my dad was apologizing for not being considerate. At the same time he was obsessed with my getting access to money that wasn't ours. Could I go to jail for embezzlement if the funds came from my husband's account? I'd have to ask our lawyer.

I opened my jacket and unbuttoned my

blouse. My stomach was still flat as a washboard. This would be one of the last times I'd have his warm lips on the breasts God gave me. I wondered if cancer was God's way of trying to make me suffer. People didn't die before their time, did they? I slid on top of my desk, raised my skirt midthigh, and then crossed my legs.

"Monica, send Mr. DuBois in."

Pressing the eraser side of a pencil to the side of my mouth, I tilted my head and pouted like the naughty girl that I was. My pussy tingled. Normally, she'd pucker, but I guess the meds had an effect on her too. I wasn't ready to give it up on the job. Seduction was on my mind. I wanted to give him something he'd think about the rest of the day. Or perhaps I should live in the moment and have wild, uninhibited intercourse now.

I envisioned unfastening his belt, sliding his zipper down, then easing his pants to his ankles. I'd take my time and admire the bulge in his boxers. Nibble on his dick, making it grow. Putting my hand inside his waistband, I'd move to his pubic hairs, squeezing his shaft and balls at the same time. Then I'd step out of my panties, shove him in my chair, and hoist my skirt over my smooth, creamy ass. Leaning forward, I'd spread my cheeks and give him a perfect view of Aphrodite. That was a nice, little fantasy until I saw who walked in.

"Thanks for agreeing to see —" Chaz stopped midsentence. His eyes feasted upon my hard, protruding nipples.

"Aw, hell no." I leapt to my feet, turned my back to him as I quickly covered my titties, then closed my jacket. I pulled down my skirt. "What are you doing here?" I asked, facing him. "I thought you were Roosevelt."

He laughed. "I certainly hope that's true," he said, inviting himself to the seat in front of my desk.

I sat in my chair, faced him, then put on my war paint — two imaginary black stripes, one under each eye. Game time. If Chaz came here to challenge me, I was ready to nail his ass to the goalpost.

"I'll get straight to the point." He handed me an envelope with my name on it.

I placed it aside. "You didn't have to write me a letter. I'm listening." I leaned back and folded my arms under my breasts.

"My dad did a little research on Tyler Construction. We know your company is going broke. Since money is what you need, my family is prepared to pay you a million dollars not to marry my brother. It's in the envelope."

*Really? Let's see. A million-dollar check or a multimillionaire husband? Hmm.*

"Sorry, Chaz. Besides the fact that your dad is wrong, you're wasting your time and mine. My love for Roosevelt is not for sale."

Chaz dug in his shirt pocket and placed a cashier's check in front of me.

"Two million," he said, laying payment in front of me, payable to Madison Tyler.

He was no fool. Neither was I.

I shook my head. I wondered if Loretta would squeal like a pig if he offered her that much to tell him my business. I didn't think so, but I wasn't sure.

"Three, four." Peeling off one more check, he said, "Five million, Madison. Last and final offer. Chicago will never know. It's all yours if you just walk away. Let's keep it real. You've fucked Blue Waters and Blue has told my brother that you're on his team. If you're setting my brother up to lose his job instead of getting paid, I'm going to make sure you pay."

I laughed. Now I knew he was fishing. Blue was beneath my standards in more ways than his height.

"Face it. Even if you didn't fuck him, I could pay Blue a fraction of what I'm offering you. If I convince my brother that you've cheated on him, he'll walk. If you walk, you can save his dignity and yours. Bottom line, you're a tramp and we don't want you to be a part of our family."

I rocked back and forth. "Not my problem."

"Loretta said this is your ninth engagement. So why haven't you made it to the altar? Is it because men find out the truth about you, then dump you?"

"What's your point, nigga?" I released a heavy sigh, wishing he'd stop wasting my time and raising my blood pressure.

Raising his brows, he nodded and smiled with closed lips, like he'd defeated me. He tapped the checks. "Consider this a win-win."

*Good ole girlfriend of mine. Loretta just can't keep my name out of her big mouth.*

"Let's see what you can do with your one, two, three, four, five. Hmm." I stood and placed the checks in his pocket. That's when I noticed his iPhone was in video record mode. I stared at the screen.

"You bastard. You can wipe your ass with your bribery or shove your checks up your mother's ass, one at a time. I don't care, Chaz. It doesn't matter. Madison Tyler is not for sale. Report that!"

Chaz was used to dating little girls like Loretta. He couldn't handle a real woman like me.

"You're right. Why did I think you'd do the right thing? It'll cost me a fraction of what I'm offering you to hire a private detective to find out what's really happening with Tyler Construction."

My family had a good history. The bad decision I'd made with Granville was buried, as far as I was concerned.

"Need a moment to think things over?"

"All I want you to do is get up, get out, and stay the hell away from me."

Chaz wasn't moving fast enough, so I opened the door for him.

"Have it your way. But when I prove you're a whore . . ."

"If you had proof, you wouldn't be here."

I started to slam the door, then stopped. He wasn't worth my getting upset. Men like Chaz were quick to degrade women. He probably had to make females feel inferior in order for him to appear superior. Had to please his parents. Needed to be their superhero. I bet he'd stick his dick in any female who would let him, then want her to chase and respect him.

He was clearly an all-about-me kind of guy. Call-me-later type of dude. *Do you love me? What do you like about me?* I could read right through him. But he didn't know shit about me.

I was no man's whore, and I had the rings to prove it.

# Chapter 31
## Loretta

I was tired of starting over.

Meet a man. Get to know him. Have sex. Realize I didn't know him that well. Liked him more than he liked me. Compromise my standards to accommodate his. Fall in love. Love transitioned to an *"I can't stand your ass"* resounding in my head whenever I saw his face.

Then followed my apologies: "I'm sorry. I didn't mean the bad things I said. I won't hack into your computer, check your e-mail, or search through your phone again. I thought you were cheating on me. Where were you last night? I didn't mean to cuss out your client. I thought you were fucking her. I trust you. Baby, come back."

It was late for lunch, early for dinner. Raynell was home from school, but I was fortunate her dad had agreed to pick her up. I didn't tell him about my date with

Chaz, but he'd figure it out when he saw me.

How could I trust a man if I was afraid of losing him?

I wasn't the only nice woman with psychotic tendencies and insecurities. After a while it didn't matter who was to blame, as long as he didn't leave me. I'd overlooked faults that I shouldn't have. Justified why the disrespect was acceptable to avoid being alone, being lonely, being single . . . again.

All of those things had happened. Sometimes within a year, often over several months, occasionally after a few weeks, once I became emotionally attached to a man I barely knew. Was any man keeping it one hundred? Was anyone meant to stay together for a lifetime? Granville was the exception. He'd overstayed his welcome. He was desperate. He was the only man who terrified me.

I wanted to try making it work with Chaz.

I had all the hair below my waist, under my arms, and the strays surrounding my eyebrows waxed. I'd taken time to massage my body with Vaseline and baby oil, toweled off the excess, and moisturized my face with sunscreen.

Dating brought many uncertainties. Compromise beyond common sense. Staring at my reflection in the bathroom mirror, I asked myself, *Does he truly like me? Does he honestly want me? Or am I just an outlet with the convenience of an outhouse? A place where he can release himself?*

Men often masked their true feelings just to get laid. I prayed he wasn't using me.

If a man was nonchalant, could he be caring? If he was evasive, did that peg him as a liar? Men had drained me by making me a detective. I didn't want to snoop; but if I didn't, how was I supposed to find out the truth?

I told myself, *This time things are going to be different.*

I'd believe whatever Chaz said. I'd compromise. I'd stay until I was sure he loved me more than I loved him. I would not invade his privacy. The deal breaker would come if I found myself settling. I refused to settle.

Slipping my red halter dress over my naked body, I admired the way my breasts and hips curved. My three-inch, open-toed heels made my shiny chocolate legs glow.

Fingering my hair, I smiled. I was naturally beautiful without the gloss I was about to smear on my lips. Maybe it was time for a new color. Black cherry was too dark. Pink didn't complement my complexion. I didn't have time to go through the shades I'd bought but never used. I reached for my usual.

My doorbell rang. That should be Raynard picking up Raynell, but it might be Chaz if he was early. I hurried downstairs to the foyer. Raynell was sitting on the sofa. Her head hung toward her lap. I sensed something wasn't right. I sat beside her. Whoever was outside could wait a few minutes.

"Baby, what's wrong?"

She stared up at me with pleading eyes. "Mommy, I love my daddy, but I don't like going over there every time you go out. Please don't make me go."

My heart pounded. "Is someone mistreating you? Or doing bad things to you?"

I was relieved when she shook her head, but I was sad to see tears streaming down her cheeks. If I gave in to my daughter, I might never have a man. She'd be fine.

"Next time Mommy goes out, we'll discuss it first. Okay?"

"Okay," she said, following me.

Opening the door, I damn near screamed.

"What in the hell are you doing at my house?"

"I came to find out why you had Madison fire me?" He stood there, dressed in his

346

usual denims, big belt buckle, cowboy hat, and boots.

"Raynell, go to your room until I come and get you." I watched her happily run away. She probably hoped she could stay there all night.

"Granville, our court date is tomorrow."

He cleared his scratchy throat. "I know. That's why I had to come today. I won't be in court tomorrow. You had no right interfering with my relationship with Madison. Now she's with another man. That's what you wanted, huh? Couldn't stand to see me happy with another woman."

My body tensed from the neck up. A gun would be nice right now. "Let it go. Madison never wanted you. It was a bet that everyone lost. Madison is happy and she's engaged to marry the most eligible bachelor in Houston."

"I lost my fucking job over a bet? You two have fucked with the wrong man." He wiped his wet nose and upper lip. "Oh." His forehead wrinkled. His eyebrows drew closer together, almost touching. "Hmm. She was serious about that dude? I thought she was kidding. When is the wedding?" he asked, acting as if he were invited.

"Please leave before I call the police."

"You need to convince Madison to give

me back my job. If I can't find work, I'll move in with you until I do," he said, shoving his thumbs inside his belt.

Glancing around Granville's shoulder, I saw Raynard cruising into my driveway. He parked behind Granville's ridiculously humongous truck.

"You might want to leave before there's trouble."

"An eye for an eye. I'll beat his ass. I'm not afraid of him. You think I won't." Granville tightened his fingers into a fist and walked toward Raynard.

I held my breath. "Lord, please help me." A fight would be all Raynard needed to prove why he should have full custody. Chaz parked behind Raynard's car.

I went inside, closed and then locked my door. I leaned my back against the wall and prayed again, *Lord, I need you now.* I heard one car start. Hopefully, that was Granville driving off. I couldn't tell the difference between the sound of the truck and the SUV.

Another engine roared, and then a third purred like a kitten. My heart pounded. I leaned against the wall and slid to the floor, covered my face and cried.

The doorbell rang. I dried my tears, held my breath, counted to three. Opening the door, I wanted to smile because I was happy to see him, but this wasn't a joyful moment.

"You've got a lot going on," Chaz said, walking in. "You look nice."

"Thanks, but I can't go. Raynard was supposed to take Raynell. Guess he changed his mind when he saw you." Fearing Granville was near, I scanned Madison's driveway. Her car was there; his wasn't.

Chaz went to my wet bar and poured himself a drink. "What's up with the guy with the truck? Maybe Madison isn't the one my family should be concerned about." He handed me a cocktail, then said, "Have a seat." He was behaving as though I was a guest in my own home.

We sat on the stools next to one another at my bar. "It's not as complicated as it appears. Bad timing more than anything."

"I can see you're dealing with family matters. I don't want to come between you and Raynard or Raynell. But if you're still dealing with that other dude, you need to let me know. Why don't you get your purse, take Raynell to Tisha's, and you can tell me over enchiladas at Escalante's what's really going on. Or we can skip the date and you can let me make love to you. You decide."

Picking up my drink, I didn't hesitate to lead the way upstairs. Chaz was right behind me. Raynell stepped out of her room.

Her face lit up. "Chaz!" She gave him a big hug, then let go. "You came to take my mommy away from me again today?"

His eyes shifted to mine. I hunched my shoulders. He picked up Raynell. I was uncomfortable, but I didn't say anything. I'd shielded my daughter from the men I'd dated. I didn't want her getting attached to a man who might not be around.

"I like your mom. I'd never take her away from you."

"So you like me too?"

I had to interrupt. "Raynell, that's enough."

Chaz smiled. "What do you say, if your mother agrees, we go to the movies. The three of us. And you get to choose what we see," he said, putting her down.

"Yes! The Dr. Seuss movie! Mommy, can we go? Please," Raynell pleaded.

"Go change your clothes."

"That's a yes?"

"That's a yes," I confirmed. When she closed her door, I looked at Chaz. "I sure hope you know what you're getting yourself into."

He backed me into my bedroom and pressed his lips to mine. He opened his mouth; I did the same. Our tongues danced in and out of each other's wetness. He squeezed my breast; then he held my face in his strong hands.

"Do you want me to be in your and Raynell's life?"

Staring into his eyes, I was speechless.

# CHAPTER 32
## MADISON

A month had gone by since I'd been diagnosed. If my mother hadn't insisted, it would've been over another month before my next appointment.

"Explain it to me again. This time like I'm a third grader," I said, sitting in the doctor's office with my mother.

The doctor began speaking and my ears became antennas as my mother held my hand. I rubbed my thigh.

"You're pregnant. Approximately four weeks," she said. "That means, in about eight months you'll have a baby."

The room was freezing, I think. My fingers felt like ice, but my mom's hand was warm. I held on more tightly, trying to draw in her heat. I stared into the doctor's mouth, as if that would make what was coming out clearer.

"Maybe. Maybe not. I can control whether I'm ready to have a child. Tell me about my breasts."

Maybe Dad's idea of going away wasn't so bad. If all went well, I could lie to Roosevelt and tell him the implants were my gift to him.

"You have cancer, Madison. In both breasts."

I hated hearing her tell me that. My mother leaned my head on her shoulder. I sat up straight. "Ma, don't. I have to deal with this." I whispered, "Okay, Doctor. What else?"

"You have stage two, level B. That means it may not be contained and it can potentially spread to other parts of your body. Cancer is treatable. The sooner we operate, the better your chances for survival."

*Boom, boom, boom. Survival, survival, survival . . .* echoed in my mind. I grabbed the sides of my head. Tears filled my eyes.

Holding on to my mother, I asked, "Ma, what stage and level were you?"

"I was stage one, level A."

"They caught your mother's earlier than we diagnosed yours. But it was a good thing you came in," the doctor said, "or we may not have known until it was too late."

Stage one? Level A. "Then why did you have to have a mastectomy, Ma?"

"I didn't have to. I wanted to. I didn't

want to have a second or possibly a third surgery."

"Did you do chemo?" I asked her.

"I did radiation and chemo, sweetheart. My cancer is gone. I —"

I yelled, "This doesn't make any sense!" I paced the small area between my mother and the doctor.

The doctor said, "I agree. But no matter how senseless it is, it's real. I'm going to set up the next appointments for you. First your MRI, then we'll meet with a surgeon, medical oncologist, and a radiation oncologist. We'll explain in detail what will be done before, during, and after your surgery."

I hated hearing her say "your surgery." The word "your" made it personal. "The" would've been better. I guess it was my turn to be Chicken Little. My sky was falling.

*I'm going to die. I know it.*

"You can do like I did, honey, and have your breasts removed."

"No, Ma. For you, it was breast, singular. For me, it's breasts, with an *s*. There's a difference."

"There are great post-op reconstructive options for you, Madison, that your mother didn't have."

I sat on the edge of my seat. "Don't you mean post-op reconstructive surgeries?

354

More surgeries. Exactly how many surgeries are we talking about here?" My eyes watered; mucus rolled out of my nose.

The doctor gave me a box of tissues. I took one and handed the box to my mother. I felt I'd need many more before we were done.

"We can start with a lumpectomy. But if we don't get it all the first time, you'll have to have a second surgery. And there's a possibility your margins may still not be clear. If we have to do a third, I'd recommend you have a double mastectomy."

She said that like a bartender suggesting a double, which was exactly what I needed right now — a strong drink.

"Why did this happen to me? Why?" I grabbed my breasts and pressed them close to my body. I wanted to reach inside my purse and take all the painkillers I had left. "Can you prescribe Tylenol 4 with codeine for me?"

The doctor didn't hesitate. "No. I don't recommend you take anything with codeine while you're pregnant."

What was her problem? It was so easy to have doctors write prescriptions that I was shocked to hear her answer. "If I have the surgeries, you'll have to give me something for pain before, during, and after *the* surgery. So why can't you give me something now?"

"Are you experiencing rectal discomfort?"

I yelled, "Yes, my ass and my head hurt."

"Fine, Madison. I'll call in an order for thirty Tylenol 3, not 4. Do not take more than what's prescribed."

Frowning, my mother asked, "What's this about your rectal discomfort, Madison? Is there something you're not telling me?"

"It's nothing, Ma. I'll tell you later."

The Tylenol 3 would do for now. I'd have to take four 30 milligrams instead of two 60s. I'd call my family doctor and ask him to phone in an order for what I wanted. If that didn't work, I could ask Loretta to supply my needs.

"So when are you available for your next appointment? There's an opening in two days."

My mother raised her blouse, unfastened her bra, and removed a cushion-shaped cup. "Madison, look at my breast."

My stomach churned so tightly that I bent over. I heaved but didn't throw up. "Ma, cover up. This is not the time."

What in the hell was she thinking? She hadn't shown me it during all these years. I did not want or need to see a scar where her titty once was.

"Two days is too soon. How about six weeks from now? I want to get married first."

"Does your husband know?"

Was the doctor a counselor now? That wasn't her business.

"Let me deal with my family. The wedding will take place next month. I'll come in after my honeymoon."

"It's your decision, but it's not a good one." The doctor searched her computer. "I have an opening exactly six weeks from today."

"I'll take that," I said to get her off my back. "Send me a reminder. Ma, let's go."

My mom walked; I marched, stomping each step to the garage. I escorted my mother to her car. I knew what she was thinking, but I was glad she didn't pressure me to have the surgery sooner.

We hugged for about three minutes. In that moment I'd decided to have an abortion after my honeymoon and before my surgery. There was no way I could mentally manage both or take a chance on having Granville's baby.

"I love you, Ma. I'll call you later," I said, closing her door.

I got in my red convertible and let the top down. That song by Martina McBride came on again. Bad timing. I didn't want to be more depressed, if that were possible.

I had to cheer up. Driving on Interstate 610, I was headed to meet with my wedding planner. Suddenly I was blinded. My vision was impaired. I could hardly see the road ahead through my flooding tears.

"Why me?" I cried out, exiting the freeway as Martina sang. I yelled at the tune blaring through my radio, "Shut up! I'm thirty-five and I don't want to wear baggy shirts or have fake breasts!" I parked at a meter on Westheimer. Every tear in my body was in line waiting its turn to fall into my lap.

Leaning on the steering wheel, I cried out, "Why me?"

I lowered my visor. Stared at my face in the mirror. My flawless skin was amazingly beautiful. So gorgeous. One day I was queen of everything. I touched my cheeks. "Who's going to love me after all this is done?" I punched the visor to the roof.

Maybe I should call off the wedding, give back the ring, and focus on my health. My cell phone chimed. A text message registered from Roosevelt: Meet me at the news station in an hour. They want to officially announce our engagement.

# CHAPTER 33
## GRANVILLE

Sitting in my living room all day waiting for Madison to come home made me hate that bitch. I wish she would've never found the GPS I put on her phone. Maybe I could strap a tracking device on her car. I was going crazy not knowing where she was every minute of my day.

"Bitches," I yelled, then punched the air in front of my face. I wasn't angry enough to slam my laptop, throw my iPhone, or knock over a bottle of beer. That would be a waste of my money.

I valued my mama's opinion. She was right. What was wrong with women these days? Loretta's ass would rather be alone than to have me as her man. For all I knew, she could've been cheating on me the entire time we were together. I'd seen the same dude at her place twice. He was probably an ex she'd never stopped opening her legs for. So what if he fucked her? I'd torn that pussy up too.

Loretta didn't know how to treat a good man like me. Madison used me for my dick. She already had a man she was engaged to when she fucked me? What kind of game or train were they trying to run on me? Had I heard her right? They had a bet. What kind? Wasn't I supposed to be the prize?

Loretta probably told Madison, "Girl, he's got a ri-dick-ulous dick. You've got to ride that bull."

Whores! All women were whores! The scandalous tricks didn't care about sharing good dicks like mine. I was a piece of meat to them. Had them laughing and swapping stories about how I grabbed my dick and put this on 'em.

That sending me to a sex therapist shit was Loretta's way of breaking me down. Making me believe something was wrong with my shit, when it was her stank-ass cunt that was bad. She couldn't make me cum. It wasn't the other way around. Madison came. She used me too. A bet? I'ma fix both of them.

Maybe I was being inconsiderate. Perhaps Madison was still in pain, but I was the one heartbroken. My chest was fucked up with a tattoo I wasn't proud of. I grabbed beer number six from the fridge and sat on the sofa and stared at my computer.

A woody appeared from nowhere and stood tall through the opening in my boxers. I wasn't thinking about cumming, but I hadn't had sex since my night with Madison. Why was I being faithful to her, when she was with another man? How long was I supposed to wait?

The reporter announced that the mayor was up next on the five o'clock news. My dick got harder. I had to do something before it drained too much blood from my body.

I checked my address book.

*Nah, Lisa isn't answering my calls. Brenda, Tammy, Rolanda, and Kim have protective orders against me.*

I got to the *P*'s and stopped at Precious. She'd given me her number at Grooves. I decided to hit her up.

I was glad she'd answered.

"Hello?"

I cleared my throat. "Hey, Precious. This is your secret admirer. I'm your lover man." Silently I laughed. I cracked myself up.

Sounded like the call dropped, but I didn't here that interrupted tone. Checking my screen, we weren't connected. I dialed her back.

"Who is this?" she asked without saying

"Hello."

"Did you hang up on me?"

"You've got two seconds before I do it again."

What was up with the attitude? That's why females were single. She didn't have to hang up on me. If my dick wasn't about to explode, I'd hang up on that bitch.

"It's Granville, Precious. We met at Grooves. I gave" — I wanted to say "your stank ass," but didn't — "you a ride home. You gave me your number."

"And you're just now calling me? That was a month ago. You must be scrolling through your numbers to see who's willing to kick it with you!"

"Uh, no. Women hit on me all the time. I wanted to call you sooner, but my mother wasn't feeling well." That was more truth than a lie because Moms was always claiming she wasn't doing well. Thinking of her, I needed to visit my mother soon. I hadn't gone to Port Arthur since I'd been fired.

"Oh, I'm sorry to hear that. Is she better?" Precious asked.

She seemed caring. Maybe Precious was the woman for me. There had to be one out there, somewhere.

"Would you like to go with me to visit her this weekend?"

"That's weird," she said.

"Why?" (I wanted to say, "Why, bitch? Because a man can't invite you to meet his mother before he fucks you?") Instead, I told her, "You don't care about my mother."

"No. I didn't mean it like that. I don't know her and I don't know you. Not really."

"Well, let's work on changing that. I'll order pizza. I already have beer. You can come over and we can watch a movie and get to know one another. If things go well, I'll take you to Port Arthur this weekend. You got a ride here?"

"I do," she said. "I'll get my girlfriend to drop me off, but you'll have to bring me back."

"I can do that," I said, although I didn't want to. If I'd told her "no," I'd have to find somebody else, and I didn't feel like doing that since she was willing.

It didn't matter if she was coming out of curiosity or if she had nothing better to do. I gave her my address. When she got here, I was busting a few nuts inside her before she left. Once she saw my big dick, like all the rest, she'd be dick-no-tized. She wouldn't be able to resist.

We exchanged small talk for a few more minutes; then I said, "Text me when you're on your way." Most women weren't as up righteous as they pretended to be. If men didn't label women as whores, they'd be worse than us.

The mayor was just coming on. I'd applied online for a few jobs with the city. "Gimme some good news," I said, clapping and then rubbing my hands together.

I'd learned a lot about technology by mistake playing on my laptop while unemployed. Setting up a Facebook and Twitter page was a disappointment. I hadn't accepted any friends or followers. My only requests were for Madison to be my friend and let me follow her. All those girls who sent me requests didn't mean anything to me. I was old-fashioned and preferred meeting women in person. My satellite viewer was in a small window at the bottom of my screen so I could keep an eye on my woman whenever she got home.

I ordered an extra-large meat lovers' pizza, then turned up the volume on my television. I was all ears waiting to hear the mayor say, "I'm glad to announce we don't have to lay off a single city employee and we've created new jobs."

I didn't need that many hiring opportunities. One offer would do if I got selected. I'd do anything for a paycheck. Wash windows. Collect trash. Scrub toilets.

Staring at the screen, I wondered how a white woman got into office. I didn't vote for her. I'd never support a woman to run my city. They were too cold; and not to mention when it was that time of the month, they were mean for no reason.

"Regretfully, we have to hand out pink slips to over a thousand employees. This doesn't mean everyone will get laid off. But we do have to put city employees on notice. . . ."

*Well, there goes my chance of getting hired by them. Better . . .*

Suddenly I had a clever idea. I logged on to a site and created a free e-mail account under the mayor's name, inserted an underscore, then added MayorofHouston. I was taking a risk, but it was worth it if this worked.

My first message was Greetings Madison Tyler, I want to come to your wedding.

No, I backspaced to right before Madison's name. I had to be more convincing. I listened to the way the mayor was speaking; then I asked myself, *How would she invite herself to Madison's wedding?*

It took me a half hour to get it right, but I was convinced Madison would respond with the details I needed to be her invited guest. At the end of the e-mail, I added, As my personal gift to you, I'd like to cover the cost of your limo expense. Please send me the name of the company and I'll contact them directly.

I'd contact them, all right. For a chauffeur's position. I made a mental note to see if I needed a special license.

I laughed hard. *Boy, you're a genius!*

Heading to the bathroom, I got another brew, set it next to my toothpaste, then showered. I was so happy I shouted, " 'I don't turn it down! Hell yeah!' " Didn't take long to wash my body. Most of the attention was on my johnson. Even when he hung, he was long and pretty. I slapped my meat, brushed my teeth, grabbed my beer, and headed back to the living room.

What I saw made me stop in the doorway. *That bitch. Now she is rubbing it in my face.*

The news reporter was interviewing Madison and Chicago.

"So congratulations are in order. And how did this lucky lady snag the most eligible bachelor in town?" the reporter asked.

Chicago smiled. "Look at her. She's beautiful. Amazing. Smart. Make that brilliant. I'm the lucky one," he said.

Talking as though Chicago could hear me, I said, "You're damn right you're lucky. Lucky I haven't beat your ass for screwing my woman."

"So when is the big day and where is the wedding going to be?"

I sat on the sofa in front of my computer. Put my fingers over the keyboard. I wasn't the fastest two-fingered typist, but I was ready to take notes.

Chicago opened his mouth. Madison touched his thigh. "Our wedding and reception are invitation only."

"Of course you're invited," Chicago told the reporter.

She smiled, then said, "Congratulations on making the play-offs."

"Thanks, we're already preparing our strategy for next season. Got a huge announcement coming up soon."

"Well, I hope you'll come back and give us an exclusive."

Madison's eyes shifted to the reporter, then to Chicago. He didn't respond.

"One last question," the reporter said. "Since this will be a first marriage for both of you, any plans on starting a family soon?"

I watched him thrust his chest forward. Chicago never smiled wider. "I'll let my fiancée answer that."

Madison batted her big, beautiful eyes at him. "Well, honey, I was going to wait to tell you, but" — she paused, then placed his hand on her stomach — "we're already pregnant."

Chicago covered my woman's lips with his mouth.

"That's my baby! That's my woman! He's not going to take my future wife and my baby away from me. I'll kill him!" I yelled at the TV.

*Knock. Knock. Knock.*

*Damn, I forgot I invited that girl over.* I put on a pair of sweats and a T-shirt, then opened the door.

"Hi, I'm Precious."

I wondered if she'd done all that for me. She had on a black lace top that clung to what had to be double E's. Her lips were shiny. Hair was straight, with a bang like that Nicki Minaj chick. She smelled fruity. The skirt was short and tight around her wide hips and the heels were so high that I was amazed she could walk in them.

When she came in and I saw her big ass, instantly I got hard wood.

"You look great. Want a beer?" I had plans to get her drunk right away. "Make yourself comfortable."

"Sure." She sat on the sofa.

*Knock. Knock.*

I scraped a twenty and three singles off the dresser in my bedroom, then opened the door. Lifting the top on the box, I handed the delivery guy the cash. Had to make sure my order was right first. I set the box on the kitchen table and grabbed two beers.

Precious laughed. "I need me a computer like this. Are you some type of private detective? You've got someone under surveillance? Whose house is this?"

"Nosy bitch." I set the beers on the coffee table, closed my laptop, picked it up, and took it to my bedroom.

"What did you call me?"

Narrowing my eyes at her, I tightened my lips, then said, "You don't live here. Why would you touch my computer? That's like me searching your purse without your permission."

"Dang, it's not that serious." She picked up a beer and handed me the other one. "Forgive me?"

"Yeah, it's cool." I was disgusted with the news. I switched to my DVD player. "What do you want to watch? *Why Did I Get Married Too, Safe House,* Kevin Hart, or *The Temptations?*"

"That's all you got?" she asked, crossing her legs.

"No, that's not all I've got." I had a big dick ready to stick inside her. "I was trying to give you a variety. Why don't you tell me what you'd like to see, and then I'll see if I have it?"

"Man, you are on one. Relax. Let's watch Kevin. I need to laugh at your pain, and you need to loosen up."

She was right. I did need to unwind. Thirty minutes into the movie, I felt better. I fetched another round of beers, waited another thirty, then got round three. Precious was holding her liquor well, until I got us a fourth. When the movie went off, love songs started playing from her phone.

"How did you do that? Is that thing an iPod or a cell phone?"

"Both. But I'm listening to Pandora."

"Pan who? Who's that?"

"It's an app, silly. You download it to your phone. Want me to show . . ." She stopped. "Never mind. I'm not touching your phone. Just go to your apps when you have time, search for Pandora, then install it."

"She got country music? That's my favorite."

"She's got whatever you want," Precious said, wrapping her lips around the head of that bottle like she knew what she was doing.

"Anybody ever tell you you're beautiful?" I said, cupping her breast.

"Let's not talk." She grabbed my dick. "You don't have to charm me. We both know what we want." She eased her hand inside the elastic band of my sweats. "Damn, is this thing real?"

She'd find out in a few minutes. I slid my hand up her thighs, all the way to her naked, hairy pussy. "Yes, I love pussy hair. Let me taste you."

I didn't wait for a response. I pushed her back on the couch, shoved her skirt over her hips, her blouse over her tits. "Wow! I've got to fuck these!" Her breasts spread east and west. I pushed them together; sucked her left, then right nipples. They were big too, like those thimbles Moms used to put on her fingers while sewing. Precious had so much going on, I didn't know where to start. I had one hand full of titty; the other filled with ass. Burying my face in her bush, I grunted.

"Slow down," she said. "We've got all night."

That was a lie. I kept licking and sucking her juicy pussy into my hungry mouth. I gripped my dick, separated her legs, and penetrated her raw. She didn't say to stop and I didn't want to, so I thrust my dick deep inside her.

My eyes rolled toward the back of my

head. There was nothing better than the feel of hot pussy without a condom. I pulled back and held still, to fight cumming too soon. A sound came out of her that I'd never heard before. It was a grunting sigh that ended with so much bass that if I weren't inside her, I'd swear she was a man.

"You on birth control?" I asked.

"Fuck me harder," she said. "Go deep again." Her hips started rising.

First I had to slow down. Now she wanted me to go harder and deeper, which meant I'd have to go faster.

"Are you on birth control?" I already had one baby on the way. Didn't need two.

"Yes, now shut up and fuck me."

Once she confirmed what I wanted to hear, I tried to push my dick and balls inside of her stomach. She dug her nails into my ass. I didn't care. We fucked like two dogs in heat for an hour straight. I came inside her twice, then took her home. On my way back I drove to Madison's house. I parked in her driveway, turned off my engine, and waited.

For what? I had to confess to my woman that I had had an affair too. And I had to let her know I'd be there for our baby.

# CHAPTER 34
## MADISON
---

Roosevelt was asleep. I was wide-awake.

I hadn't slept much last night. My life was a lie. If I kept refusing to tell him the truth, our relationship would fail. Staring toward the ceiling, I couldn't see it. The room was dark. I felt my fiancé's warm body next to mine. He placed his hand on my stomach.

"Good morning to both of you."

"We thought you were sleeping," I told him, covering my hand over his.

"I was. But I'm up now." He kissed me. "You have made me the happiest man in the world," he said, turning on the light. He pressed his lips to my navel. "Hello in there. Daddy can't wait to see you. You know our baby is going to be spoiled. He or she will be the first grandchild on both sides."

*Yeah, and what a mess I will have created if it isn't his.*

My folks knew, but his parents would be disappointed. Actually, his mom might be relieved to finally say, "I told you not to marry *that* girl."

"Let's not pretend your mother is okay with this."

"She'll have to be. Your being pregnant will change the way she feels about you. I'm glad we didn't have to plan a private gathering to let our people know. Everyone knows," he said, smiling widely. "Are you going to breast-feed both of us?" he asked, cupping his mouth over my nipple. "I hope I don't get jealous. Well, that must be why God gave women two breasts. One for the baby, and one for the husband."

I hoped he was right about his mom. "I love you so much." I wanted to cry knowing I'd never be able to nurse the child inside me. What if I gave the baby cancer? Was that possible?

"Twins. I want you to be pregnant with two. That way you'll only have to be in labor once and they can grow up together." His eyes were bright. He straddled me. Sat on his thighs. "I want to make love to you."

Anything to take my mind off what was happening inside my body. I didn't deny him. He leaned over me, braced himself with one hand. He rubbed his swollen head on my clit. Instantly my pussy juices flowed. I roamed my fingers up and down his chest, shoulders, neck, and back. Roosevelt DuBois was my man.

He eased in the head, then pulled out.

I asked him, "What's wrong, baby?"

"Nothing. This is the first time I'm penetrating you, knowing you're carrying our child. Is it okay?"

"Of course it's okay."

If I were lucky, I'd have a miscarriage. As much as I wanted to have an abortion, I'd decided against it, for now.

Roosevelt's slow, deep strokes made my entire body feel amazing. I closed my eyes. Allowed myself to appreciate all of him. With each throb of my pussy, I floated into a space, an abyss, where I wished I could stay forever.

"Damn, is it me or are you quivering?"

"You are making me dance all over."

"I love the way you said that. Why am I so lucky?"

I didn't answer. If he knew the truth, he'd put me out.

"You ready to cum with me?" he asked, then leaned forward and kissed me.

Tilting my pelvis upward, I held him close, then whispered, "Yes." I wish there were a way to make sure his sperm had fertilized my egg, but the conception couldn't be undone.

His dick spasms throbbed; my pussy tightened, then released. "Oh, my God, baby." My back arched. His did too. For the next couple of minutes, neither of us moved. It was like we were stuck in paradise.

I waited for him to pull out. He rolled over, then snuggled next to me. "Our relationship is too good to be true. It scares me at times how much I love you."

Fighting back tears, I said, "I love you too. I have to stop by my house before going to the office, so I need to get up."

"I need to get up too. I know it's going to take you a moment, so I'll use the guest bathroom."

The first thing I had to do was go to the kitchen, get a glass of water, and swallow two painkillers. That had become how I started and ended each day. I filled his tub with water and bath salts, then soaked for fifteen minutes. I cried the entire time. I brushed my teeth, repeatedly splashed cold water on my face. I put on a black-and-white checkered skirt, with a pink blouse and pink platforms.

"You have time for lunch today?" he asked.

"I'm having a late lunch with Tisha and Loretta at Spencer's at three. Loretta has —"

"Loretta has what?"

*Damn, can't I get her name out of my mouth without my man cutting me off?*

"Although we have a planner, Loretta has to tell me her ideas for our wedding." I hated lying, but I couldn't let him know she had a hearing to get a protective order against the man I might be pregnant for.

"Oh, okay. That's good. I'll see you tonight. I'll come over to your place so we can finish what we started this morning. Have the Jacuzzi ready."

I planted a sloppy, wet kiss on my man. He didn't know it, but we'd be in the oversized tub in my bathroom, with the drapes fully drawn. Granville had enough porn footage of Roosevelt and me. Hopefully, he wouldn't send that too.

"Bye, babe." I could refresh my lipstick later. I got into my car, let the top down, and exhaled. When I pulled into my driveway, I couldn't believe Granville's truck was there.

I called Loretta. Her phone rang several times.

Finally she answered. "Hey, Madison. I stepped out of the courtroom to take your call. Are you going to make it to my hearing?"

"Is Granville there?"

"Not yet. I don't think he's coming."

"You're damn right he's not coming! His truck is parked in my goddamn driveway!"

"Yeah, I noticed that when I left."

"And you didn't call or text me!"

"So much has happened with us. Things between Chaz and me are good. I was trying to stay out of your business and tend to my man. Tisha is here. You should come too. I might need you to be a witness for me."

*Is she serious? Her man? She wishes. A witness for her? Wow.*

"I'll see you at three o'clock at Spencer's." I ended the call, walked up to Granville's truck. *What if Roosevelt had come over with me?* I should've called the police, but I couldn't afford negative press before the wedding.

*Bam! Bam! Bam!* I pounded his window with my palm. He didn't respond. I stared inside. No one was there. My heart thumped.

I entered my house, left the door ajar, and kept my keys in my hand. I removed my shoes, tiptoed through the living and dining rooms. I didn't see him. I searched my kitchen, picked up a butcher's knife, wishing I had a gun, instead. I did a complete downstairs tour twice. Nothing. I went upstairs, checked the bedrooms. Where was he?

*Slam.*

I jumped. Turned around. No one was in sight. The sound had come from the living room. Slowly I traveled one step at a time, pausing in between to see if I could spot him. I was prepared to run in either direction. Halfway I noticed the front door was closed.

I cried uncontrollably. "Where in the fuck are you?" I yelled. "Get the hell out of my house! Leave me alone, you bastard!"

No response echoed back. Gripping the knife more tightly, I held it above my head and slid my patio door open. Dropping my arm, I stared in shock.

"Get out! Get out! Get out!"

Granville stood up in my Jacuzzi, totally naked. "Hi, dear. Welcome home."

I swear, if I had a gun, I'd shoot him.

He got out, wrapping a towel around his waist. "If I had a job, I'd be at work. If I lose my apartment, I'll have to move in with you and our baby. That's not a bad idea. We should be living together."

*Aw, hell no.* "This is not your baby. Get out of my house!" I threw his clothes at him. They fell at his feet.

"Does this mean I'm rehired or retired?"

*More like incapable of processing rejection.*
"I'll think about it. Just get the hell out!" I was willing to say whatever for him to leave.

"Okay, dear. Calm down. Don't cut me. Don't stress our baby out. And don't forget I still have that videotape of us making love," he said, raising his brows. "If you don't call off your wedding, I'll *bet* you ten million dollars that I'll send a copy to that news station."

Was he insinuating what I thought? No, Loretta didn't. When did she talk with him? I couldn't wait to see her.

He did still have the video. Had probably made several copies. All I could do was hope he wasn't serious. The tape of Roosevelt and me was in his possession too, but that wouldn't help him if it got out. He picked up his sweats and T-shirt, put them on, then dipped his left shoulder as he left. He didn't go through my house. He went around the side. I was having a better gate installed today.

Since Loretta's house was less than one hundred feet from mine, I prayed the judge approved her protective order. She might have to file one against me if she kept fucking up. Why would she tell him we made a bet? Fluid gushed to my throat. I ran to the bathroom. I had to stop taking the meds on

380

an empty stomach. I heaved bile until there was nothing left but air.

Granville had made me so sick that I jammed my finger in my mouth, wishing I could vomit and flush the baby in my womb down the toilet. I announced my pregnancy on television because I knew it would bring Chicago closer to me. Granville hearing the news was not on my mind. If I had thought he'd be watching, I wouldn't have mentioned it.

# CHAPTER 35
## MADISON

What was it going to take to get rid of Granville Washington permanently?

I wasn't from the streets. Couldn't call in any hit favors. Didn't have any brothers. But if I had any of those options, I wouldn't hesitate. For real, he was soaking in my Jacuzzi? He'd gone too damn far!

"What can you do to maximize my home security without turning my house into a prison?" I asked the owner of Invisible Bars. This was a company that had lots of billboards across town. They advertised that they consulted with ex-convicts who'd served time for breaking, entering, and robbing homeowners. I never thought I'd need them, and I hoped they were as great as their ads claimed. I wanted to employ the criminal minds, but not the criminals. The Web site stated that the owner had served as an expert witness on several high-profile cases. His bio stated he knew what systems worked and which ones didn't.

The owner said, "Crooks are equally dumb as they are intelligent. Otherwise, they'd never get caught. The best way to catch a thief is to make access *appear* easy."

I didn't want to waste time talking to any of Invisible Bars' workers. Not that the employees didn't know their jobs, but being the CEO of my family's firm demanded that I communicate with my equal. Any person who had to call someone else before making a major decision was not worthy of my time or money.

The guy with a hot stripper body was the CEO? He surveyed my residence four times, then said, "Your place is easily accessible. I recommend you install sensors around the perimeter and on each door and window. Basically, every point of entry needs securing. Whenever the alarm is activated, if anyone or anything breaks the invisible barrier, you'll receive notification via your iPhone. At the same time we will be notified at our central call station and we'll notify the police right away. Our system helps catch most robbers because they won't hear anything. We can add a layer of security by placing hidden cameras inside decorative domes that blend with gutters, downspouts, siding, flowers in your garden, and fixtures in and outside your home. I also recommend bright motion-sensor lights."

*Wow, he is good.* I didn't like that part about them being able to see what was going on inside my home, but what if Granville was in my house while I was inside too?

"So far, I like what you've said. But can you block satellite viewers from spying on me when I'm outside?"

"Absolutely. And you'll love that we can sync everything to your cell through our free application designed by your soon-to-be brother-in-law, Chaz DuBois. You can be in Italy and see what's happening right here." He pointed toward the ground. "And we can scramble satellite signals so no one can even get a snapshot of your house. If you sign a contract with us today, I'll throw in a free toxic chemical and radon gas testing, just for you."

*Just for me? Yeah, right. What he seems to be is too good to be true.*

We stood in front of my house. He appeared forty-five, give or take two years. He had toasted tan skin — evident that he'd spent time in the sun somewhere. Probably vacationing in Brazil or in the Dominican Republic with lots of gorgeous women catering to his needs.

I wasn't lusting or hating. I actually admired the ripples of his washboard stomach through his black wife-beater shirt. The bulging biceps were exposed and his thunder thighs showed through his fitted black slacks; it made me want to touch him all over to see if he was real.

Generally, a man that fine had spent years in an institution working out every day to maintain his sanity and protect his ass. Maybe in the pen was where he'd created the idea for his company and built his image. I sure hoped I wasn't making another mistake and would come home one day to an empty house. With lots of time to think and read, most inmates could overwhelm and outsmart most women.

Men who had been oppressed knew all the right things to say and the exact time to strike in order to capitalize on a female. That's how inmates doing life got a wife. He'd find out what she liked or needed, then capitalize on her weaknesses. Make her put money on his books and dare her to make a move without his permission.

"Have you ever been to jail?" I had to know. If he said yes, I was hiring someone else.

He stopped looking at the roof and stared at me. He lowered his iPad to his side.

"Why? Every black man with a bodybuilder's physique has to be on probation or behind bars? If what you mean is have I served time, the answer is 'No.' Look, lady, this is strictly business. I'm the best at what I do, but I'm not hard up for money. I've grossed a solid five million this year. If you've changed your mind, all you have to do is say so and I'm gone. You don't have to judge me. I'm here to help you."

I nodded. "You're right. That was rude."

"No, *you* are rude," he said, shaking his head. "You won't find another company to do for you what I just suggested. They don't know how."

*Damn. What is his problem? I'm the client, not the enemy.*

As if he'd read my thoughts, he said, "Have a good day"; then he turned and walked away.

A vision of Granville lounging in my hot tub came to view. I couldn't allow that to happen again. "Wait! Don't go." I gave him my business card with my e-mail at Tyler Construction. "I'm really interested in what you have. How much will everything cost?"

The sexy way I'd said that didn't come out right. I wasn't flirting. It was my Southern charm, which at times I couldn't turn off.

He sat in his truck, tapped on his iPad, then said, "I don't give verbal quotes. I just e-mailed you a breakdown. Take your time and look it over. I can have a crew here as early as tomorrow. It'll take two men two days to complete everything."

"Thanks."

"No problem." He got out of the car and extended his card and his hand. "If you have any questions, call me on my cell. I'm available to you, twenty-four/seven."

Okay, I had given him the wrong impression. Now he was flirting. My policy was "If I pay you, I'm not fucking you. If I fuck you, I'm not paying." Thanks to Loretta, my life was complicated enough. I didn't need his fine-ass problems, but his attention was flattering.

I wish he could've had my home wired before he drove off. I closed my door. Opening his e-mail, I saw the package price wasn't bad and well worth my peace of mind. A 50 percent deposit was required. I entered my American Express card number, expiration, security code, and replied, Schedule me asap.

Until the work was done, I'd stay at Roosevelt's. Just like that, Granville had cost me $27,000.

A shower and wardrobe change into a

long-sleeved banana-colored dress, which stopped above my knees, was sufficient for a late lunch with the girls. I stepped into my lavender sling-backs, picked up my purse, and headed to Spencer's on Lamar.

I approached the hostess. "Yes, reservation for three for Madison Tyler."

"Yes, Ms. Tyler. Your guests are already seated. Right this way."

I followed her to the table, where Loretta and Tisha had gotten started without me. The champagne was already flowing.

"Congratulations on your engagement and new addition to the family. The owner is taking care of your tab," the hostess said, pulling out my chair.

With the exception of three other women at a nearby table, the restaurant was empty. I started to request the hostess reseat us away from them so they wouldn't overhear our conversation. "You guys want to move?"

Loretta said, "I'm good."

Tisha agreed, "Me too."

I checked out the other ladies again. They seemed sophisticated enough for me not to classify them as eavesdroppers, but nowadays it was hard to tell. I politely thanked the hostess and sat between my friends.

I greeted my girls. "I'm what you call a friend with benefits, and it's only going to get better. Y'all lives would be boring without me."

"More like uneventful," Loretta countered.

"So how did court go today?" I asked, smiling at her when I honestly wanted to snatch her by the hair, tell her about my day, and put my bun in *her* oven.

Loretta dug into her purse, then waved a piece of paper. "I've got it!" She tipped her flute to Tisha's.

I filled my own glass and took a sip. I felt out of the group. Like they'd moved on without me. It wasn't like Loretta didn't invite me to court.

*Oh, well, I have my own issues to deal with.*

"Do you know who's the father of your child?" Tisha asked what I expected Loretta to question.

"Yeah, we heard you announce it on the news. You should've told us first," Loretta commented. "You know, Madison, if you're not sure, get rid of it. We can help you stage a miscarriage. Chicago will believe us, and he'll love you more. If it turns out to be Granville's baby, you'll have made the biggest mistake of your life."

I held the power to let an innocent child live or die. It wasn't the baby's fault. It was

Loretta's. And mine. I chuckled in a sarcastic way.

"Too late for that. Instead of being at court with you, he was at my house in my Jacuzzi because somebody" — I stared at her ass — "told him we had a bet, and when I asked what he was doing at my place, all he had to say for himself was 'Okay, dear.' Because of him I'm spending twenty-seven grand to have my entire house wired by Invisible Bars."

Loretta laughed. "He does that 'okay, dear' and 'yes, dear' thing with you too? Well, between your home security, my protective order, and my license to carry a concealed weapon" — this time she fanned another sheet of paper, patted her purse, and continued — "stick with me. I think we're covered. On a different note, what I need to know is the truth. Did you persuade Raynard to file for full custody?"

"Has he?" I asked.

She nodded.

"I'm sorry to hear that, but trust me I'm not involved." That was the truth. I loved Raynell, and didn't want Gloria and Raynard to have her all the time, knowing that would break Loretta's heart.

"How did we get here?" Tisha asked. "All our lives are screwed up. Mine isn't as dramatic as y'all's, but, Madison, you were right. I never should've married Darryl's broke behind."

Since we were on a roll, I wanted to tell them about my cancer, but I didn't. I simply wasn't ready.

"My wedding planner will contact both of you for a fitting. You don't have to do anything else except show up at the church an hour early. She'll bring your dresses, shoes, and accessories. The makeup artist and hairstylist will take care of the rest."

The waitress appeared. "I didn't want to interrupt, but can I get you ladies anything?"

We ordered appetizers and continued talking.

Tisha said, "Loretta, now that another man is showing you interest, Raynard is jealous. I bet if you were by yourself, he wouldn't care about custody."

"And don't overlook the fact that he feels he can hit that anytime he gets ready," I added, scrolling through my e-mail on my iPhone. "Oh, my gosh!" I bounced in my seat. "You guys won't believe who I just received a message from."

"Don't tell," Tisha said. "Let me guess. Granville?"

I rolled my eyes at her. "The mayor wants an invite to my wedding, and she wants to pay for my limousine service. I hope she knows I have three."

One was for the bridesmaids and groomsmen. Another was for our parents. The third was for Roosevelt and me.

I was so excited. I was in the innermost elite circle of Houston, but I just realized it!

"She said send her the company's information and she'll take care of the rest. Isn't that great!"

"Miss, you can't record other people's conversation. It's a violation of their privacy."

We all stared in the direction of the waitress.

"It's my phone, and who's to say I'm recording them," one of the women responded.

"Aw, hell no!" I got out of my seat and approached her. "Are you recording us?"

"I don't know. You tell me," she said, waving her iPhone. "Is Chicago the father? Or is it Granville?"

Tisha picked up the champagne bottle on our table, stood beside me, snatched the woman's phone, and proceeded to beat the phone like it had stolen something. The other two women backed away. I was partially relieved.

The woman screamed, "What the hell are

you doing!" Then she picked up a steak knife.

Loretta eased her hand into her purse. "Miss, you don't want to make me use this. I'm not asking. I'm telling you. Put the knife down."

# CHAPTER 36
## CHICAGO

The closer I got to the altar, balancing the ongoing battle between my fiancée and my mother had become a fight I didn't want to referee. Why couldn't the two women I loved get along?

"Look, she doesn't have to stay long, but I can't disrespect my mother's wishes. If she wants to talk to us, that's exactly what we're going to do."

I prayed Mom or Chaz hadn't seen the video of that dude fucking Madison. The harder I tried to get that image out of my mind, the more I had to meditate to keep from arguing with Madison. We both had history before we'd met. I just hoped that incident really wasn't during our relationship. I didn't ask Chaz to find out where the link originated. If he saw the footage, that would give him one more reason to hate Madison.

"I don't want her coming to your house.

Why can't we go to hers? That way we can leave when we get ready."

"You mean when *you* get ready. She wants to come here, so she's coming here. End of discussion."

This was the first time my mother was outspoken about a woman I was with. It was also the first time I was serious about saying, "I do." I wasn't a mama's boy. I was ready. None of my exes made me second-guess my decision. None. And my mom wouldn't either.

"Then let's see if the formal dining room is available and meet her there. I don't want her in here. She makes me sick."

"What's gotten into you? Is the baby turning you into some woman I don't know? Since when did my mother start making you sick?"

I'd never leave Madison, but I honestly didn't like the person she was becoming. She'd gotten more verbal about everything, especially her dislike for my mother.

"Being pregnant does not give you a pass to be rude or disrespectful to any of my family members, especially my mother. If you don't want her here, you can leave right now."

"I'm sorry, baby. You're right. Let her come. I'll stay in the bedroom. I'm not feeling well."

All of a sudden she wasn't well? I watched her get a bottle of water, open a bottle of pills, shake two in her hand, then swallow them.

"What's that you're taking?"

"It's aspirin. I have a headache. I'm going to go lie down."

"And you're going to get up when my mother gets here. That's not negotiable."

"Okay, I will," she said, closing the bedroom door.

I sat on the sofa, turned on the basketball game to watch Miami play Boston. My cell rang. I looked at the caller ID. What did he want?

I answered, "What's up, Blue?"

"I saw the news. Congratulations on your baby, man."

"Thanks. What can I do for you?" I didn't want to do small talk with him or any other person I labeled as slimy.

"Just calling to check on Madison. I heard —"

"Madison? My Madison?"

"Yeah, man. I heard —"

"Save it. I don't let outsiders wedge their way into my personal life. The wedding is invitation only, and no, you're not invited. Good-bye," I said, ending the call. What could he have heard that I didn't already know about my woman?

The knock at the door was a welcome distraction from the dialogue in my head. It couldn't have been Mom this early, and I wasn't expecting anyone else. I peeped through the hole. It was Chaz and Loretta. I stared a few extra seconds at Loretta. I missed praying with her.

Opening the door, I said, "Well, to what do I owe the pleasure?"

"Stop acting like you're surprised to see me," my brother said.

"No, not you. But I am happy to see the two of you are still hanging out. Come in. Mom is on her way. I might need your support, man. I have no idea what she wants to discuss. Do you?"

"Yes, you do." Chaz went straight to the pots and pans in the kitchen. "We're definitely staying." He picked up a fork. Ate two shrimps. "Damn, baby, try this," he said, feeding Loretta.

"Oh, this is so good. All of a sudden I'm ready to pig out. Madison cooked?"

Chaz and I laughed.

"You spoil her too much, man. A woman is supposed to cook for her man. It's a good thing you can afford a chef. This spread is undeniable." He placed two glasses on the bar.

"Make me one, too, while you're at it," I said.

I opened my arms to Loretta. She wrapped hers behind my back. I whispered, "Good to see you." She didn't respond with words. I could feel in her hug that she missed me too.

"Man, let go," Chaz said. "Loretta, make yourself comfortable."

She stared at my painting in the foyer. "You really do have one too."

"I miss praying with you, Loretta." I wasn't sure how that came out, but it was the truth.

She nodded. "Me too."

"Hey, stop pushing up on my girl, man," Chaz playfully said, handing both of us a cranberry and vodka. "Where's Madison?"

"She's resting."

"Oh yeah. That's right. She's with child. That's probably why Mom is coming over," Chaz said, sitting on the sofa next to Loretta.

My cell rang. I answered, "Yeah, let her up." I paused, then said, "How many?"

The doorman said, "Three."

"Okay, if they're with my mother, it's cool." I opened my door so they wouldn't have to knock.

"Who's she with?" Chaz asked.

"I have no idea. I hope she didn't bring any of her church members to counsel me about my engagement or our premarital pregnancy." I tapped on the bedroom door. "Madison, sweetheart. My mother is here." I'd give her a few minutes to get herself together; but like it or not, she was joining us.

Mom entered with Dad and my grandfather. "Well, isn't this a mini family reunion. I didn't know all of you were coming. Madison will be out momentarily."

My grandfather said, "Hello, everyone. Son, we're forced to come, but we're on your side."

Chaz gave everyone a hug and our mom a kiss. Loretta responded by simply saying, "Hello."

Mom didn't hesitate. "We don't need her, Chicago, but I am glad that Chaz is here. Hello, Loretta," my mother said in an extremely proper tone that indicated she wasn't particularly fond of Loretta.

I wondered if that was because Loretta was Madison's friend. Or had Loretta done something to piss my mother off? I asked, "Are you okay with Loretta being here?"

"Well, there are only six seats at the dinner table," Mother said, sitting next to my dad.

Loretta stood. "Oh, we can go."

"I want my family to stay," Mother insisted.

"Then I can wait downstairs in the rec room," Loretta said, handing Chaz her drink.

"Keep it," Chaz said. "Sit down on the sofa. Ma, if she goes, I go. This is Chicago's meeting. Not mine."

Mom pretended she hadn't heard Chaz. "Madison can go downstairs with Loretta. What I have to say won't take long."

"Here I am," Madison said. "Oh, hey, Loretta, Chaz. I didn't know all of you were going to be here."

"Hey, baby. Neither did I. Have a seat at the table."

Madison rolled her eyes at me. Mom smacked her lips. I pulled out the chair diagonally across from my mother and waited for my fiancée to sit. I sat next to Madison, facing Mom.

"I just lost my appetite. Chaz, come. Have a seat, son."

Chaz sat in the remaining available chair at the head, facing our grandfather. "Let's do this."

Mom said, "Yes, let's. I'll get straight to

400

the point. I had our family lawyer draw up a power of attorney. All I need you to do, Chicago, is sign it. That way your father and I can protect you. And I can be on my way."

I was certain Mom didn't have anything pressing. But with her terrible attitude, I wanted her gone.

I held Madison's hand. "Protect me? From what? My wife?"

"She's not your wife yet. We don't even know if she got pregnant on purpose, or if that's your baby. I don't trust her. She's moving too —"

Loretta interrupted, "With all due —"

Mom cut her off. "Respect? Really, Loretta. You're not much better. Sit down over there and stay out of my family's business."

"We're out," Chaz said. "Chicago might sit there and let you disrespect Madison, but I'm not having it with my woman. Let's go, Loretta."

*His woman?* I watched Chaz kiss Mom on the cheek, pat Dad and Grandpa on their backs, then escort Loretta to the door.

"Ma, you're doing the right thing. But the way you're going about this is dehumanizing. We'll be down the hall at my place. Ma, don't bring this foolishness to my house."

Madison went into the bedroom and

closed the door. At this point I was not going to stress her out. Chaz was right. I stood. Stared at my mother. "Ma, I'm not signing it. If that's all you came here for, you can see yourself out."

Dad spoke for the first time. "Son, don't talk to your mother that way. She's looking out for your best interest."

"Mine or hers. Dad, did you sign a power of attorney or a prenuptial before you married Mom?"

He shook his head. "No, son. But things are different now."

I looked at my grandfather, who was nodding. "Grandpa?"

"Huh, what?" He picked up his fork. "Where's the food?"

"Grandpa, did you sign a power of attorney or prenuptial before you got married?"

"I'll sign whatever you'd like if it has cherry-flavored Jell-O."

We all needed to laugh. Mom was straight-faced.

"Helen, let me see why you're denying us dinner. Hand me that power of attorney," Grandpa insisted.

Mom passed it to Dad. He gave it to my grandfather.

"First off, why is your name the only one

on here? You're trying to control my grandson's financials. If it's money that you're worried about, Helen, we've got plenty of it. Chicago, if you love that girl, marry her without this."

I watched my grandfather rip the document in half. That was a defining moment for me. Madison had never made our relationship about money. Nor had she given me a reason not to trust her.

"Thanks, Grandpa. I needed that."

Mother's jaws were tight. "What you need is a head on your shoulders. Don't say I didn't warn you." She stood. "Martin. Wally. Let's go."

Grandpa scooted his chair closer to the table. "Y'all go. I'm going to eat and watch the game with my grandson."

Dad said, "I'm staying too. Helen, you can go. Chicago will bring us home."

Mom picked up her purse. She slowly walked toward the door.

"Helen."

Mom stopped and answered, "Yes, Martin."

"Stop and tell Chaz to bring that girl back over. If we gon' be family, we might as well break bread together. I'll be sure to bring you a plate. See you when I get home."

# CHAPTER 37
## LORETTA

This day did not come soon enough, but I was glad it was here.

Any opportunity to put negativity behind me and start new was refreshing. Now that I was on the receiving end of Mrs. DuBois's insults, I understood why Madison wasn't nice to her. Helen was afraid of losing both of her sons to women she felt weren't worthy. Did she honestly think her comments would run me off? I was hoping to be next in line at the altar.

"You look so beautiful, Mama," Raynell said. She slid her hand along my dress. The stylist had decorated my daughter's hair with Shirley Temple curls and baby's breath. I let her wear a little light pink gloss and a hint of blush.

"You too, princess." I faced her toward the mirror and stood behind her.

"The wedding should be yours and Daddy's."

Why did she have to bring up Raynard? I smiled, not wanting to explain to her that I was in love with Chaz or Mr. C., as she called him.

From the bouquets of white lilies and magnolias to the pearls around our necks, I had to give it to Madison. She'd planned the most elegant wedding.

"Madison should've been here by now," Tisha said.

Caught up in the moment and my own wedding fantasy, I'd lost track of time. Glancing at my phone, I said, "You're right. She's never late." I dialed her number.

"We're leaving now. I'll be there in fifteen minutes."

"Madison."

"Loretta, I've gotta go."

"I love you," I said, thinking about Romans 13:10: *Love does no wrong to a neighbor; therefore love* is *the fulfillment of the law.*

There was silence. Then she said, "I love you too."

After today I'd be the only one without a husband, but I was thankful I finally had a man. Maybe Chaz would propose to me at Madison's reception.

Tisha peeped out of the dressing room's window. "Raynard just drove up."

"Daddy! Daddy! Can I show him my

dress?" Raynell said.

"No, honey. We don't want the guests to see you before you scatter the flowers. You have to make your grand entrance."

"Just like we practiced?"

"Exactly like we practiced. You can ride with your dad to the reception if you'd like."

She smiled and nodded. "I'd like."

Being a mother, I'd backed off on my snide remarks about the paternity of Madison's baby, and she'd become supportive of my having to fight with Raynard for custody of Raynell. Tisha locked eyes with me. I read her thoughts, which were also mine. Why had Madison invited Raynard to her wedding? I wasn't giving up Chaz to appease Raynard, and I'd fight with all the strength in my body to keep my daughter.

"What's taking Madison so long? It's fifteen minutes past the fifteen."

Checking my phone, Tisha was right. I told the planner, "Go to Madison's house and bring her here."

She raced out the door like she should've thought of that herself. If Madison was still at home, it might take another thirty before the wedding started.

"Have you heard from . . . ?" Tisha asked, then circled her finger around her ear.

We had to talk in code around Raynell.

I said, "Not since I got my PO."

"Do you think he'll show up today?"

I opened my purse and showed Tisha my handgun. "Just in case."

Tisha nodded. "Good decision."

# Chapter 38
## Chicago

Today was the last day I'd officially be a single man.

I thought I'd be nervous when we selected our wedding bands. I wasn't. I expected to feel guilty this morning after my Wet-N-Wild bachelor party, which one of the players hosted at his mansion in Katy, Texas. I did not.

Madison didn't complain or demand to be there. I was shocked. She knew the running back had arranged to have exotic performers flown in from Rio. I was told the girls did everything, and that was no lie. What happened at my bash was smashed.

There was a woman on my lap the entire night. It was hard not to do any of them. I was so drunk, if I confessed to my soon-to-be wife, all I'd say was "I don't remember," and that was the truth. Half the team, plus the coaches, with the exception of Blue, gave me the best sendoff a man could dream of. I loved that Madison hadn't called me once in the last twenty-four hours.

"Who's out there?" I asked Chaz.

He looked distinguished. Madison had my people looking better than I'd imagined. It all worked: from the tailor-made tuxedos, to the barber, to the woman who'd put a touch of makeup on all the men to make us what she called, "Photo and camera ready."

"Man, looks like everyone is here, except Madison. We were supposed to start an hour ago."

"Seems like I waited forever for your grandmother to show up. This is Madison's special day," Grandpa said, "she wants to look flawless. If she's not here in another hour, then I'd worry."

We sat in our dressing room down the hall from Loretta. I wish I could pray with her in private. Madison was cooperative with my having a party, even though she didn't want one. But my kneeling beside her best friend right before taking her hand in marriage might make her say, "I do not," instead of "I do." That was one chance I couldn't take with our baby inside her.

"So you gon' pop the question to your girl at our reception?" I asked my brother.

"Let's just get you down the aisle. She might be the one, but don't worry about me," he said.

Dad commented, "I know that look. He's next."

We were blessed. Judge Vanessa Gilmore was performing our ceremony. Madison told me that the mayor had covered the limousine expense. Mr. and Mrs. Tyler paid for everything else. My parents didn't have to spend a penny, not even for their clothes. Madison made sure that was taken care of too.

Mother stuck her head in. "I hope she doesn't make it, but if she's not here in twenty minutes, I won't be here either."

Dad walked to the door. "Not today, Helen. Don't do this to our son. She'll be here and you will too. Now go sit down and wait like everybody else."

# Chapter 39
## Granville

I was so excited that I almost peed in my pants.

"Thanks for helping me out on this, Precious."

"So you're sure she doesn't know about her husband's request? And he's okay with this bondage thing to his wife on their wedding day?"

"That's what he said. I'm just doing my job."

This woman was so gullible; if I didn't like her, I'd call her a dumb bitch to her face. I told her I used to play pro football and she believed me! I was joking; but when I saw how excited she was, I gave her stats. Obviously, she didn't know shit about sports. She didn't question if I was telling the truth or research my background. Madison and Loretta would've googled me on the spot.

"It's cool that you haven't seen your

cousin since she was a little girl, but what if she hates us for doing this? I don't even know her, and I'm going to tie her up? I'm happy we're driving her to her wedding, but I have to say this is the weirdest bondage fetish I've heard of. But I'll do anything for you."

"That's why I love you, dear. Give me a kiss."

*Ignorant trick.*

Precious opened her mouth and I let my saliva drain down her throat. "That's the best kiss ever," I told my woman.

Finally I'd met a person who appreciated me. But she wasn't Madison, and Precious wasn't carrying my baby.

I'd offered her five hundred dollars to help me out, but she'd refused. Said, "I'll help because you have a big heart."

"If this goes well, I'm taking you to Hawaii. You ever been there?" I asked her.

"Hey, the door just opened."

There was no way Madison was getting into the limousine if she saw me. I flopped on the seat. Precious looked sexy in her tight white shirt, black jacket, and black pants. The chauffeur hat and dark sunglasses gave her an undercover stripper look.

I whispered in my sexy, scratchy voice, "I got hard wood."

"Well, I'll have to do something about that after we drop her off. Be quiet. Here she comes."

"Don't forget what I told you."

"I know. Smile. Open the door. Congratulate her. Help her with her dress. Then close the door. Now shut up," Precious said, getting out on the driver's side.

I couldn't see Madison or hear what she was saying. I bet she was wearing nothing under whatever she had on. The big surprise was that she was getting married today.

*To me.*

# CHAPTER 40
## MADISON

"Hurry, please. I'm late enough."

The photographer took photos of me getting into the limo.

The chauffeur stared at me like she'd never seen a woman in a wedding dress.

"You are so pretty," she said.

I'd just taken two painkillers and I was feeling good. I did not have time for complimentary delays. I'd sat inside debating on whether or not to cancel. I realized I could find another fiancé, but not another Roosevelt.

His mother would rejoice, while he'd cry if I was a "no-show." I refused to give Helen, that evil witch, the satisfaction. She wouldn't care. Her family wouldn't lose any money. The main reason I was going through with it was to please my father and not to embarrass my man.

"Wait. Can you lower the divider, open the sunroof, let me get into the front, and take a few last snaps of the bride from inside?" he asked the driver.

Her eyes shifted toward the ground. "Um," she hesitated, then looked at the photographer. "It's against company policy to allow anyone to get into the front. Sorry."

Objecting, the photographer said, "I always get that angle. It's one of my signature shots."

"Time is money, but you probably wouldn't know anything about that. Listen, I've got to go. But you are going to let him take this picture. Call your boss. Get permission. If I have to have my husband call your supervisor, you'll be fired. Now close the door," I ordered.

*Women are always hating on me.*

"Why don't you get in the back and sit at the opposite end," she suggested.

"You do have some sense," I said, then told the photographer, "Hurry up."

I raised my gown to my hips, crossed my legs. Reclining a little, I thrust my breasts forward. I'd chosen a strapless gown with the longest train I could find. The cleavage was a tad more than I should've exposed; but if I had to part with my twins, I wanted lots of memories. I even had the photographer capture a nude spread.

He'd gotten up close and personal with

my inner and outer lips, my boobs, and my butt. I was in a bubble bath, the shower, my bed, and my garden. With my new security system, I wasn't worried about Granville.

The pictures the photographer had taken hours ago were my priceless centerfold moment and my gift to my husband. What man didn't want sexy, naked photos of his wife? The problem with most brides was they were too conservative. Some hadn't seen their pussies in a mirror, let alone in a picture.

"Thanks, I'll see you at the church," I told the photographer. When he got out, the driver closed the door.

I phoned Loretta.

"Madison, where are you?"

"I know. I just got into the limo. I'll be there in fifteen minutes. For real, this time. Thank you for being a — make that *my* friend. I love you," I said, ending the call.

I was getting married in a church. How about that? Glancing around, I didn't see any alcohol. "Excuse me," I called out. "Where's the champagne?" I knew the mayor didn't take it off the bill. I'd ordered twelve bottles, four for each limo.

The divider lowered. The woman who closed my door climbed into the back with me. The divider shut. She slapped me and I punched her ass in the nose.

"What the fuck is wrong with you? Who's driving the limo?" I grabbed her hair and banged her head into the door.

That muscular bitch struck back, knocking me flat on the seat. She unraveled a bath towel. When I saw what was inside, I knew some serious shit was about to happen. She locked cuffs around my ankles and pushed me back onto the seat. I kneed her in the forehead twice.

I had to keep her from getting to my hands. She grabbed my dress at the hips, slid my body toward hers, then flipped me over. She handcuffed my wrists behind my back, then sat me straight up. I lifted my feet and kicked her between the legs. She doubled over, then slapped me again.

Did that trick from the restaurant send her? I had a few people who didn't like me, but I did not have any enemies. The car started going faster. I stared out the window. We were on the freeway. Headed where? I had no idea. The route from my house to the church was on the street.

"Okay, what is this about?" I asked her, trying to reason. "If it's money you want, I'll give it to you, but please take me to my wedding. I have people waiting."

The divider lowered. "Hi, dear."

What the hell! "You fucking bastard!"

Granville laughed. I hated the sound of his nasty-ass voice.

"Gag and blindfold her, Precious."

Shoving a scarf into my mouth, she tied it tightly, then asked, "You want me to come up there?"

"No, dear. Stay back there," he said. The divider closed.

That idiot was dangerous and thought this was a damn joke. Rocking back and forth, I tried to come up with an exit strategy. The woman sat staring at my breasts. She moved next to me. Touched me. If I could curse her out, I would.

She folded my dress above my hips, pulled me forward, and spread my thighs. The ankle cuffs dug into my flesh. I started crying.

Precious kissed my clit, then said, "It's okay. This won't hurt." Her tongue flicked fast. "You taste amazing. I see why your husband wanted us to put you in bondage."

I gasped. My what? Wanted what? I guessed with her own agenda she'd forgotten to blindfold me. I prayed she didn't do it. At least now I could see the large green signs through the dark-tinted windows. We were on Interstate 10, heading east.

Lowering my top, she exposed my breasts,

then sucked my nipples. "Damn. Oh yeah," she moaned. "You are so soft and sweet. This is amazing. What do you use?"

The limo must've been doing a hundred. My head started spinning. Was he going to violate me when she was done? I stared at my phone on the floor beside her. It was Loretta.

She shook her head. Went between my legs again. Tasted me again. She started playing with her pussy while eating mine. Tightening my thighs, I tried to break her neck. Soon as I got out of these handcuffs, she had an ass whupping coming. I was not aroused. I was not into women. I was so angry that I wanted to beat Precious's ass and file rape charges against her.

She struggled to break free. The divider lowered. Granville yelled, "What are you doing to my woman? Get your ass up. Touch her again and I will beat you. Madison, you okay, dear?"

My chest became tight. That was the only reason I'd let her out of the knee lock. I was not going to die before I got married. Inhaling the scarf that she'd tied around my mouth, the material temporarily blocked my airway. I exhaled, then mumbled as best as I could. "I can't breathe."

The limo swerved. Horns blared.

"I thought I was your woman," Precious said to Granville.

"You're not classy enough to be my woman. Now get up here with me, bitch."

The limo swerved again. Just when tears filled my eyes, I heard sirens. I prayed it wasn't an ambulance coming upon us. Silently I said, *Lord, please rescue me from these assholes.*

The limo decreased speed. Granville said, "I love you, dear."

*Who in the hell is he referring to now? I hate him!*

"Precious, wait. Don't come up here. The cops are on my tail. Put Madison on the floor. Get down there with her. Stay down there and keep her quiet. No mumbling, dear." He closed the divider.

The limo came to a complete stop. Cars zoomed by. I had to find a way to alert the cops I had been kidnapped.

My cell rang. I saw it was Loretta calling again. Precious picked up my phone and quickly silenced it. In that moment I wondered what Loretta had dealt with when Granville had taken her all the way to Port Arthur. I'd acted like it was no big deal, but now I understood how she must've felt. I owed my friend a huge apology.

Things were quiet for too long. I shrugged

my head toward the window.

"Shut up," she whispered. "You heard what Granville told me."

*Really? Is she serious?*

We sat there for ten more minutes. Finally she opened the door.

"Granville is gone."

*No kidding.*

"I'm sorry. I've got to drop you off at your wedding and go to the police station to check on my boo."

# Chapter 41
## Granville

"I don't know why you brought me here."

The police had me in a small room. What was this cop's problem? I was sure he was breaking the law. I was no criminal.

"You were arrested for reckless endangerment. The way you were swerving, you could've caused a major accident. Even killed someone or yourself perhaps."

I would kill myself if Madison was getting married while I was dealing with bullshit. I'd passed his stupid sobriety test. I wanted to say, "What's your fucking problem, dude? You're violating my fucking rights. Charge me with something or let me go."

I was no fool, so I said, "I told you. I reached for my cell phone. My foot hit the gas. Yes, I did swerve a little, but I didn't do it intentionally. Give me a speeding ticket and let me go. I have to be at a wedding."

My being 285 pounds, six-six, and dark black, I had to try not to appear intimidating. The scratchiness in my voice didn't help, so I gave it a rest.

He stared at me. I kept my mouth shut.

"A wedding?" the officer asked. "Were you transporting any passengers?"

I shook my head. I wanted to tell the truth and say, "Yes," hoping he'd take me back to the limo. If he hadn't taken my cell, I could find out from Precious what was going on with Madison.

He stood. "I need to run a more thorough background check. Sit tight."

At least he hadn't officially thrown me in the slammer. There was still a chance I could make the wedding.

# CHAPTER 42
# MADISON

The limo stopped in front of the church.

The engine was still going when Precious opened my door. She climbed in, helped me out. I expected her to uncuff me and remove the gag. She didn't.

Placing a small key in my hand, she said, "You'd better pray my man doesn't lose his job behind our trying to help your husband fulfill his morbid fantasy. If he does, you'll have to deal with me."

Was it possible for her to be more ignorant than Granville? How long had they known one another? They definitely deserved each other.

I bunny hopped from the curb to the bottom step. Loretta came out of the church. I was happy and relieved to see her.

"What happened to you?" she asked, removing the scarf.

I gasped for air. I opened my mouth, but no words came out. Only tears poured down my cheeks.

Removing the cuffs from my ankles, then my wrists, she said, "It's okay, honey. Let's get you inside before someone sees you. Do you want to reschedule the wedding?"

I shook my head.

She helped me up the stairs and rushed me into the dressing room. "Then let's get you cleaned up."

"Mommy, what happened to my god-mommy?" Raynell asked. Her lips started quivering.

"Tisha, take Raynell out of here, please. Let Judge Gilmore and Chicago know we'll be ready to start in twenty minutes," Loretta said, motioning for the hairstylist and makeup artists. "Make her more beautiful," she told them.

My wedding planner asked, "What happened, Madison? I went to your house and you weren't there."

Loretta answered, "No questions. Let's get Madison out of her dress. I need you to clean it up as best as you can. Trim the train to cut away those blood spots. Find some tape and make it look neat. The train is so long, no one will notice. Hurry. We've got a wedding to start."

I didn't have to tell my best friend who was responsible for my delay. She knew. Loretta hugged me and we both cried.

Drying my tears, she said, "Smile. We need to practice that million-dollar smile. This is your day. Don't let anyone steal your joy. And don't let Chicago see you sad. And stop crying. Save those tears for rejoicing after Judge Gilmore says, 'You may kiss your bride.' "

I whispered, "I don't know how much more I can take."

"God will never give you more than you can bear," she said, tapping my edges. "Now, that's better. We can't have a single hair out of place. You look amazing."

She helped me get back into my dress. Loretta may have been making up for all she'd done to me. Or protecting her relationship with Chaz. If I walked away from Roosevelt, she might have feared Chaz would leave her. Tisha had regrets about marrying Darryl. I didn't want to feel that way when I became Mrs. DuBois.

"Thanks." I stepped in front of the mirror and gasped. I felt like Humpty Dumpty, but I was fortunate. All the women in the dressing room had helped put me back together again.

I was perfect on the outside and fragile on the inside. My meds could help me keep it together, but they were at home. I'd have to make it through the wedding without them, but I would have our . . . I'd almost forgotten.

I told my planner, "Get us three limos from a different company." I had no idea how that idiot showed up as my driver, but I wanted no part of doing business with that company again in my life.

"Consider it done. Anything else?"

"No," I said.

Granville was where he belonged, behind bars. Hopefully, he'd stay there. What if Precious bailed him out?

*Not my problem. . . . Actually, it was.*

I motioned to my planner. "Wait. Add armed security for the reception."

Loretta shook her head. "You don't need to do that."

There wasn't enough time to give her the details of what Granville and Precious had done to me. I stared into her eyes. "Are you sure?"

She reassured me, "I got you into this. One way or another, I'm going to make this go away."

# CHAPTER 43
## LORETTA

The wedding was breathtaking.

Watching Madison step down the aisle, pausing in between, I was anxious to see her face. The white veil covered her expression. The dress was absolutely flawless. No one, not even I, could tell it was altered minutes ago.

I probably cried more than anyone at the ceremony. We'd cleaned my best friend up well. I didn't know how she stood tall beside Chicago with such poise and grace after all that had happened, but she did.

They faced one another. For a split second my eyes met with Chicago's. There was a strange feeling in my heart. It was a spiritual connection that felt right and at the same time forbidden.

How could that be? He was not marrying me.

I glanced at Chaz to see if he'd noticed. He winked and I was instantly relieved. I was glad Madison's back was to me because she would've never missed my exchange with her fiancé.

Women didn't miss much when it came to other women preying on their men. In many cases women also made assumptions that were inaccurate. Attitude usually came from females who were insecure. Those were the ones who thought every woman did not want but rather *wanted to fuck* their guy.

Judge Vanessa Gilmore was impeccably robed. Her brown-sugar complexion was radiant. Full lips were matted with a shimmering cinnamon. The tapered short haircut complemented her high cheekbones. I was proud to see a woman judge standing before us. I wondered how she'd met Chicago. Was she a longtime friend of the family? Did she hold season tickets?

She started speaking; and if a pin had dropped, everyone would've heard it. Her voice was strong yet eloquent.

"If anyone has any reason why this couple should not be joined in holy matrimony, speak now or forever hold your peace."

My handgun was hidden inside my floral bouquet. I prayed, *Lord, let Helen keep her mouth shut, and please don't let Granville be in or near this church.*

Judge Gilmore said, "By the power vested in me, I now pronounce you husband and wife."

A resounding exhalation of relief came from the guests. I had to empty my lungs too. It was a good thing that Madison moved up the wedding date. With so many things happening, I don't think any of us would be here to witness their union if she'd waited.

Chicago's lips locked with Madison's and my heart skipped a beat. I'd never seen them kiss. The passion in the movement of his mouth excited me. I concluded great lovers ran in their family. My Chaz was a complete package too.

Thinking of him made me look over my shoulder right as Madison and Chicago faced their audience to exit. Raynard was staring at me. How long? Why was he in the third row? Why was he here? Had he seen the way I looked at Chicago?

I didn't like hating anyone, but Raynard was in a group by himself. Our daughter was strikingly beautiful. She was so happy that she skipped as she held Chaz's hand. I wrapped my hand around hers. Raynard's eyes narrowed; his lips tightened. He shook his head. He slid his flat hand across his throat.

This wasn't my wedding, but it was my moment. Raynard's jealousy was not going to spoil the day. I glanced at Chaz and smiled. I was genuinely happy and in love.

# CHAPTER 44
## CHICAGO

"Aw, yeah!"

Madison's delay was worth the wait. My baby — make that my wife — was the sexiest woman on earth. She was the only one for me. But I'd be lying to myself if I said I didn't feel something magnetic when I looked into Loretta's eyes while standing at the altar.

Soon as the limo door closed, I said, "Let me hit it one time."

"Not now," Madison said, pushing me away.

"Yes, baby. This is a once-in-a-lifetime opportunity. This is our wedding day."

My dick was so hard that I unzipped my pants. Madison knelt between my legs. I admired how she licked my shaft like it was ice cream in a cone.

"Ah, yes. Do that shit, Mrs. DuBois."

She took most of me in and started massaging my head with the back of her tongue.

"Tonight I want you to lick my asshole again. That was incredible." I closed my eyes and re-created that sensation in my mind. Didn't take long for me to explode. My wife swallowed every seed.

The driver parked in front of Madison's house. We'd stopped for a wardrobe change . . . and I had to have another quickie. Oral was good, but I had to get deep inside her. We showered together. I swept her off her feet, carried her wet body to the bed, then laid her down.

"Again, Roosevelt? We have guests waiting."

"Let them wait for me this time," I said, penetrating my wife.

I entered her slowly. She moaned my name. I grunted hers. Married pussy was the bomb! Aphrodite legally had my name and I acted a fool.

"Whose pussy is this?"

Madison whispered, "Roosevelt DuBois owns this pussy."

That was what I loved. My woman knew all the right things to say and exactly how to seduce me with the tone of her voice.

"You ready?" I asked, not wanting to take too long before showing up at the reception. We were already three hours behind schedule and had to pay the hotel and DJ

433

extra. Money was not my concern. I didn't want to cum without her.

"Oh yes," she exhaled.

My cum came in waves. "I'm hitting this again tonight."

"Whenever you'd like," she said. "I'll never deny you the pleasure of my body."

We showered again. Madison put on a sleeveless white fitted dress, which stopped above her knees, and a pair of slip-on rhinestone clear heels. She'd selected a white suit, with a white V-necked shirt, for me. I would've never chosen that combo for myself, but I had to admit that I was looking suave in it. I wanted to fuck her again, but we had to leave.

The limo ride to the hotel was blissful. I proudly escorted my wife inside. Montell Jordan's "This Is How We Do It" had just come on. I broke it down to the ground, playa-style, for my wife. She was the only one for me.

"Babe, can you wait until we have the first dance?" Madison asked.

Women wanted traditional stuff. I was ready to enjoy myself. Married life was agreeing with me, in my heart and in my soul.

The DJ started playing "Songbird" by Kenny G. I held my woman close. She leaned her head on my shoulder. The lights made the pool sparkle like diamonds. Guests lounged on chairs and gazed up at the sky while we danced. My parents were nowhere in sight. That was okay. Mom was a trooper for staying three hours for Madison to arrive at the church. Chaz stood behind Loretta as they watched us.

Soon as the song ended, I shouted, "Let's get this party started!"

"Baby, I can tell you're going to get wasted. Let's do the toast now. That way you can party all night long."

I got the mic from the DJ. "Okay, the missus has spoken again. We are going to the toast now. Then we can tear the roof off this mutha."

Technically, there was no roof over the pool, and the poolside bar was busy. The champagne fountain was flowing. Once again my wife had done the damn thing.

I had plans on skinny-dipping in that pool and making love to Madison before the night was over.

# CHAPTER 45
## LORETTA

He was ruining my night. It was time for the toast and time for Raynard to leave.

He wasn't socializing with anyone. He stood by, with Raynell in his arms. That was fine, except he kept staring Chaz down, like he had a problem with my man. I was prepared to fight for custody, but I avoided a confrontation. A shouting match was what he wanted. An opportunity for him to publicly humiliate me and call me a whore or a slut wasn't happening. I was not going to let him dictate whom I slept with.

Madison announced, "We need everyone up here on the staircase."

"Come on, baby," Chaz said. "Let me escort my woman. I see the way your baby's daddy keeps checking us out. He missed out. You're mine now."

Chaz held my hand until I stood on my designated step. "Thanks," I said, giving him a quick kiss. I didn't want the makeup artist to see that or she'd have to touch up both of us. I couldn't wait to see all the pictures of Chaz and me together.

"You're not going to need your purse for the toast. I'll give it to the planner." He took my bag.

Taking it back, I told him, "It'll be okay. I got it."

"Okay, my bad. Never touch a woman's purse. I get it," he said. Making his way to the opposite side, he climbed the arch and stood next to Chicago.

Madison had outdone herself again. The white stairs arched over the center of the swimming pool like a rainbow. I wasn't too comfortable with only one rail behind us, but she was right. If she'd requested a rail in the front, the photos wouldn't be magnificent. Tisha and I stood to the left of Madison. The men were to the right of Chicago.

Chaz tapped his glass three times, then said, "May I have everyone's attention. It is my honor and privilege to do the toast. I couldn't have asked for a better big brother. He's always been there for me since the day I was born."

I'd almost forgotten that Chicago was thirty-two and Chaz was a year younger. Their parents had done well. They raised two handsome, successful, wealthy boys who didn't treat people like they were both above them.

Chaz continued, "I have followed in his footsteps all my life. If Chicago got straight A's, he inspired me to get all A's. When he went to college, I went too. The only thing I didn't do was play sports. I wasn't as brave as my brother. I did not see the satisfaction of having guys three times my size knock me on my ass every time I got up. I guess that's why my brother still holds the record for the most yards running."

We all laughed. I loved Chaz's sense of humor. I wished I could've seen the expression on Chicago's face. We'd been instructed to face the audience the entire time so the pictures would be perfect.

"Well, when my brother told me he was getting married, I didn't believe him. I mean, he's the youngest executive vice president and general manager in the entire league. Some of you might not know he's on the GM Advisory Committee. He gives advice to operations on the integrity of the game, how to expand technology, and ways to improve the game."

Wow, I was more impressed. I had no idea, but I wasn't surprised that Chicago was doing so much behind the scenes. Still, he made time for Madison. Plus, he attended church service whenever he was home.

"I've never seen him happier," Chaz said. "Madison, you are an awesome woman. We got off to a rough start, but you proved me wrong. You and your family paid for the entire wedding and didn't ask us for a dime. I owe you an —"

"I'd like to finish the toast."

"Aw, hell no!" Wanting to throw up, I clutched my purse to my stomach.

"Hi, dear," Granville said. "I hope you haven't signed that marriage certificate, because I have ours right here." He waved a piece of paper.

Chicago said, "That's the dude in the video. You lied to me, Madison? All I asked was for you not to lie to me."

"No, baby, that's not true. I wouldn't do that," she cried out. "I should've warned you that he's crazy."

"Loretta, that's the guy who was at your house," Chaz commented. "What in the fuck is going on?"

I opened my mouth, when I should've opened my purse. Nothing came out of either. I was speechless.

Granville pointed a gun at Madison. "Let's go, dear."

Guests screamed and started stampeding into the hotel. I was glad Chicago's parents

439

weren't there, and happier that Madison's parents and mine had made it out, but where was the mayor? I hadn't seen her at the wedding or the reception.

Chicago pushed Madison. She slipped and fell into the pool below. Her landing created a huge splash. Tisha brushed by me and raced down the stairs. I thought she was going to help Madison, but Tisha ran into the hotel.

Granville pointed his gun in the air. "You trying to kill my woman and my baby! You crazy? You trying to kill my woman? I will kill you! I'll kill you!" Granville said, lowering his arm. He aimed at Chicago.

I prayed, *Lord, please don't let him do it.*

*Pow!* Granville fired above his head and I almost died.

I couldn't see Madison. I hadn't seen her get out of the pool. Was she under the stairs beneath me? Was she at the bottom? Did she hit her head?

*Lord, Jesus, save us.*

Slowly I slid my hand inside my bag. I wanted to shoot Granville; but when I saw Raynard shielding Raynell's body behind the bar, I had to think about my family. Why didn't he get our daughter out of here? If I hadn't seen them, I would've pulled the trigger. I closed my purse and cried.

440

"Loretta, come down from there!" my dad said. I thought he was gone.

"Get Raynell and leave!" My father had nothing to do with this. "Get my baby out of here!"

If Raynard wanted to risk his life, fine. But he wasn't trying to save mine, so I knew it was personal. He was somehow going to use this against me to get custody of Raynell. I could only fight one battle at a time. I was relieved when my dad got my daughter to safety.

*Pow!* Granville fired again. This time directly at Chicago.

Chaz grabbed Chicago. "Jump!" They both plunged into the pool, feetfirst.

I was relieved they'd escaped the bullets.

*Pow! Pow! Pow!* Granville fired into the pool.

All I saw was blood floating in the water. I needed to do something. I was frightened. I stood there watching the people I love drown and prayed I wasn't his next victim. I wanted to jump, run, or slide down the stairs. I wanted to do anything, except stand by, but my legs wouldn't move.

Granville put the gun to his head.

*Do it. Do it. Pull the trigger.* He deserved to die.

"Do it!" I yelled.

441

The police rushed in and slammed him to the ground. I cried with disappointment.

Granville yelled, "I love you, dear. I love you, Madison!" as the officers dragged him out.

I mouthed, "I wish they would've killed him."

# CHAPTER 46
## MADISON

My father held my hand.

I was on the verge of losing my mind. I'd taken more meds than usual, but the pain wouldn't go away. My husband was on a respirator because of me. Unable to breathe on his own, he'd been in the hospital for four weeks. He wasn't talking. I wasn't sure if he had nothing to say to me or if he couldn't say anything to anyone. I wanted to trade places with him.

"Daddy, all he's been is good to me," I said, crying.

"Remember what I told you. Don't cry in front of him. He can hear you. Let's step outside for a moment."

My father had come to the hospital every day with me. He didn't want Roosevelt's family harassing me. We stood in the hall. My dad wrapped me in his arms.

"Madison, I know it's hard, but it's time for you to let him go. He's never going to be the same, now that he knows you might be carrying another man's baby. They've given his job to Blue Waters. And don't forget that you still have to have surgery."

I'd put off my operation because I felt I deserved to die. Three bullets fired into the pool and Roosevelt was the only one hit, three times. "It's not fair. I can't take him off of life support. Daddy, I just can't do that."

My dad reassured me. "If you love someone, you've got to set them free. Do you think your husband wants to live this way? It's not your fault. You didn't know Granville was going to show up at the reception."

That wasn't completely true. I had an idea that he might. I should've hired security. I never should've listened to Loretta. Now she only talked to me to find out how Roosevelt was doing. She acted as if all of this was my mistake.

Loretta was so busy apologizing to Chaz and kissing his parents' ass that she was about to lose custody of her daughter. Raynell had been at Raynard's since the reception. Loretta wasn't accepting that her relationship with Chaz was over. The only reason he tolerated her was to find out what my intentions were. I hated what I'd created.

Daddy said, "Baby, sign the papers to take him off today. I'll help you make Roosevelt's funeral arrangements."

Helen walked up and stood in front of us. "Over my dead body you will."

Loretta approached me as though she had the power to make a decision. "What's going on here?"

Once I found out Madison had given up on Chicago, I stayed by his side 24/7.

"I assure you I had no idea this was going to happen," I said to Mrs. DuBois.

We sat in the room beside Chicago's bed. I wasn't sure if he could hear me, but I wanted him to hear me say that.

"I should've never stopped praying with him. Things would've been different. I'm not like Madison. She is my friend, but we're very different," I explained.

Mr. DuBois held his wife. Mrs. DuBois held Chicago's hand. Neither of them answered me. Chaz walked into the room, sat beside his mother.

I approached him, then whispered, "Can we step outside and talk?"

His lips tightened as he stood. He nodded toward the door. His parents remained quiet. Maybe they were tired of hearing my apologies. Perhaps I, too, should shut up. I tried maintaining my silence, but my conscience constantly gnawed at me.

We walked away from Chicago's room. "I know you don't like apologies, but I'm so sorry this happened to Chicago. I pray you're not mad at me."

Chaz folded his arms across his chest. Tears filled his eyes. He pressed his thumb into the corner of his eye sockets, then sniffled. I'd never seen him cry.

"If my brother dies in there, I don't know what I'll do without him. Besides my folks, Chicago is all I've got," he cried.

I blinked trying to hold back my tears but I couldn't. "Chicago is a fighter. He'll make it. It's just going to take time and prayer. And regardless what happens between you and me, I'll always be here for you. I love you, Chaz."

Opening my arms to him, he shook his head, then quietly walked away. I deserved that. But I was relieved that for the first time, I'd confessed my feeling for him, to him. I wasn't giving up on being with that man.

When the door to Chicago's room closed, two of the men I cared deeply for were inside. I stayed in the hallway and called Madison. If I could get good news from her, I could tell Chaz's family, and they'd all love me.

When Madison answered, I asked her, "Hey, what did you decide?"

"Why? So you can go back and report to Chaz and his family? Loretta, this is your fault and I'm sick of you acting like it's mine. Please stop calling me." Madison ended the call.

I called her back. "Wait. Hear me out."

"What now?"

"Granville. Are you going to testify against him?"

"Good-bye." She hung up again.

I went to the restroom. Refreshed my raspberry lip gloss. When I returned to the room, Madison was there.

"Madison, we need to talk. You need to sit down, respect Chicago's mother, and listen to what she has to say. We can't change Chicago's situation, but we can come together to decide what's in his best interest." I was the only sensible one trying to make peace.

Madison still looked amazing. If Chicago died in this hospital, Madison would have ring number ten before he was buried. The way Blue Waters had been seen out with her made me wonder if Madison had set Chicago up.

Mrs. DuBois said, "You're not going to

take my son off of the respirator. That's final."

"It would be final if you had the right to make that decision. Like it or not, I'm Mrs. Roosevelt DuBois. Not you."

Helen stood and grabbed Madison's throat. "You listen to me, little girl. You go against my wishes, and I'll make you wish you were dead."

She let go and Madison shoved Helen in her seat. "You just made my decision easier."

# CHAPTER 48
# MADISON

"I'm taking him off of life support."

I stood outside Roosevelt's hospital room and talked with Papa. I'd made up my mind, but was I doing this out of spite or had I made the right decision? My husband had made it through surgery, but he hadn't breathed on his own. The doctor would arrive any minute with the authorization that I'd requested to take Roosevelt off the respirator.

America's eagle eyes were soaring over my head. The entire football league, staff, coaches, players, and fans held me accountable for my husband's condition. The press was outside, hovering like vultures. No matter what was in my heart, newscasters from every major station waited to report a breaking story. I'd become a known face to millions on the day I'd married a person many considered one of the greatest men on earth.

"Papa, I don't want to deal with this

today, tomorrow, not ever. Can't we just give Roosevelt time and wait and see what happens?"

"Yes, if you want us to lose our company. Now that you're financially secure, you're just going to forget about whether or not we eat? Think about it this way. You didn't pull the trigger. Things happen for a reason. Soon as you sign the papers, I'll have my private jet waiting to take you away for a year. Your mother is going with you. You can have the baby and your breast cancer surgery. You don't really know that guy who shot your husband."

I heard a familiar voice say, "That's not true." Loretta stood next to my dad. "Mr. Tyler, she does know him. I know him too. And what's this about breast cancer surgery?"

What was her damn problem? Loretta wasn't going to be satisfied until we were both behind bars. I hated that she'd overheard about my condition. I bet before I got on the plane, everyone would know that too.

"Loretta, don't let your mouth get your ass in trouble. Stay out of this. This has nothing to do with you." Papa gave me a legal-size document, about ten pages long. "I need you to sign this power of attorney.

451

In case anything happens to Chicago —
and, heaven forbid, you too — I can take
over your affairs."

Loretta kept quiet, but she didn't leave.
An oversized bag was in her hand, a large
purse on her shoulder. Her hair was in a
ponytail, which I wanted to wrap around
my fist. This was a time when I desired to
kick her, or anyone else's butt to release my
frustrations.

I wished Mama were here. She'd side with
me. Papa made her stay home and wait for
the limo to take her to the airport. I signed
the power of attorney. If he could take it all
over today, I'd let him.

The doctor walked up, then said, "I have
your papers. This is a decision you'll have
to make very carefully, Mrs. DuBois. Please
don't be hasty in your response. Your husband is in there, fighting for his life."

I did have an obligation. And that was to
do what was in Roosevelt's best interest.

Loretta reached for the document. Her
voice escalated. "Mrs. DuBois won't be
needing that."

The doctor blocked her hand.

Roosevelt's mother stepped outside the
room. "Did I hear someone call my name?"
She looked at Loretta and her face lit up.
"I'm so glad you made it, honey. Is that my

care package?"

"Yes, it is."

"At least one of you has dignity," Roosevelt's mom said, giving Loretta a hug.

The doctor said, "I was actually speaking with the other Mrs. DuBois."

"If it's about my son, tell me," Roosevelt's mom insisted.

The doctor explained to all of us, "Your son has a fifty-fifty chance of surviving. If he makes it, we're not sure of his quality of life. He might be physically and/or mentally incapacitated or he could have a good recovery, but it's too soon to tell. We've done all we can. If you sign this, the rest is up to him."

"Well, we'll just have to wait and see," Helen said.

The doctor continued his explanation. "I was asking Mrs. DuBois what she wanted to do. The decision is hers. She can leave him on support or take him off."

"Over my dead body! The hell it is *her* decision. That's my baby in there. All she wants is his money. I'll be making the decisions here."

I stared at her. I didn't have to wrap my hand around her throat to make her choke. I had more power than Helen and she hated me for it. She looked away in defeat. She wasn't so bad now.

My dad had remained quiet for some time. I looked to him, wanting to agree with Roosevelt's mom. If my husband survived, would he want me if my baby wasn't his? What about when he found out that I have breast cancer? What if he lives, then in a few months he's the one who has to decide if I should live? Right now, I wanted to trade places with him. This was the most challenging moment of my life.

"Should I tear up the papers to take Roosevelt DuBois off of life support?" the doctor asked.

Loretta and Helen replied in unison, "Yes."

I looked to my dad once more. He stared back. His eyelids didn't blink. His entire body froze. His lips were drawn in, head tilted.

I asked the doctor, "Can I speak with you in private?"

"Of course. Follow me. The rest of you wait here."

We got on an elevator, went two floors up. We entered a freezing cold room. My body trembled with fear.

"Have a seat," the doctor said.

He didn't sit behind the desk. He sat in the chair next to me. Covering my face, I hid my tears.

The doctor held my hand. "Madison, if you're going to do it, don't worry about it. If you're going to worry about it, don't do it."

I held the pen in my hand.

The doctor continued, "I've seen families take loved ones off, and the second the patients take their last breaths, the family members are devastated. Then there are the ones who are relieved because they feel the person is better off not suffering. Then there is also the possibility that he may live. Do you really want to sign this?"

Silently, I stared at the paper, then I signed it.

. . . . ▪

. . . To Be
Continued

▪ . . . ▪

# DISCUSSION QUESTIONS

1. In the prologue, how many signs of domestic/relationship abuse can you identify?
2. In chapter one, Madison and Loretta have been friends since kindergarten. Based on their actions, do you believe they've outgrown their friendship? Or are they like most girlfriends who confront, yet accept one another for who they are? Do you have a longtime friend that you feel you will love forever? Is there anything that this friend can do to break the bond?
3. In chapter two, is Loretta realistic for holding on to her desire to have Raynard in her life and for them to become a family with their daughter?
4. In chapter three, what do you feel is the real reason Roosevelt, aka Chicago, wants to marry Madison? Does he truly love Madison?
5. In chapter five, do you think Madison

should be okay with Chicago's level of concern for Loretta? What would you do if you found out that your fiancé befriended your best friend?

6. In chapter five, have you performed anal stimulation with your mouth on someone? Have you had it done to you? If so, did you or the other person have an orgasm as a result?

7. Do any of the characters have low self-esteem? If so, who? What are the signs?

8. What is your most memorable moment when you didn't feel confident?

9. Did Madison win the bet? Why or why not? Could you have made the same bet with a friend under similar circumstances?

10. Have you ever met a man you liked in the beginning, but you soon realized he was not mentally stable? Would you label Granville as abusive?

11. Outside of his determination to save his company, do you believe Johnny Tyler has Madison's best interest at hand? What's the real reason he wants to send her away?

12. Is Loretta really a Christian? Would a Christian woman say one thing and do another? Why didn't Loretta use her gun? Would a Christian kill a person?

13. Who does Loretta love and why? Is it Raynard? Chaz? Or Chicago?

# BREAST CANCER AWARENESS

When I wrote the synopsis for *If I Can't Have You,* Madison didn't have breast cancer. You may or may not understand my character's choices to delay treatment, but those were hers to make.

In my world, when my sister's best friend was diagnosed and I listened to Andrea tell me how rapidly Marion's health deteriorated, I was deeply saddened. Shortly after Marion passed, my sister's other best friend was diagnosed with stomach cancer.

Then my sister-in-law Angela told me her best friend was diagnosed with breast cancer at the age of forty-eight. Myrenia shares her journey with us later in the book. Through Angela, I've known Myrenia for over twenty years. We partied at the same clubs in our midtwenties and early thirties. Renie maintained a healthy diet, exercised regularly, and I've never seen her over a size five.

Recently breast cancer hit closer to home. I shouldn't fear getting breast or any type of cancer, because my father would say, "The things you fear the most will come upon you."

In March 2010, I had a mammogram. They noticed a lump and asked me to have a biopsy the same day. That's when I started asking questions.

"Worst-case scenario, Doctor, let's say it is cancer. When you perform a biopsy, will that cause the cancer to spread?"

The doctor said, "I don't know."

I declined the biopsy for two reasons. One, she wasn't sure. Two, I was not mentally prepared to have a biopsy done. I went in for a mammogram, not a biopsy.

I then asked, "What are my other options? What noninvasive procedures can you do?"

I was advised that I could have an ultrasound. If I hadn't asked, I wouldn't have known. The ultrasound results did not indicate the lump was cancerous. I followed up with an OB-GYN appointment. The doctor did not believe it was cancerous.

I occasionally have pain in the area where my lump is. I was told pain was a good thing because cancer does not have pain associated with it. This is not always true; so if you have any discomfort in your breast, please have a professional exam.

After my sister was diagnosed, I made an appointment with my OB-GYN on February 2, 2012, to get another breast exam. I was told there was nothing of concern. But because I was uncomfortable, my doctor ordered another mammogram. The results were clear. This gave me a level of comfort. Because I have a family history of breast cancer, I get mammograms once a year.

My dad passed from stomach cancer. His two brothers, my uncles, died from cancer, and his only sister, my aunt, lost her battle with breast cancer in 2011. Both my maternal and paternal grandmothers passed from breast cancer.

When I was a little girl, and well before I understood the magnitude, my maternal grandmother had a double mastectomy. I remember seeing her scars and watching her put breast cups in her bra. I saw her stitches where her breasts once were. I'm not sure when she was diagnosed, but she lived to be eighty-seven. What I remember most about Granny was that she was happy. She drank beer (almost every day), dipped snuff under her bottom lip all the time, had a boyfriend down the hall, and she lived her life to the fullest.

Thinking of her inspires me. One day

we're all going to make our transition. While we're here, let's live it up. Play hard and work harder. Don't wait to travel, or start your business. Do it now. Whatever it is you want to do . . . do it now.

Writing this novel made me educate myself on breast cancer. Learn all that you can about breast exams, the warning signs of breast cancer, and the various types and stages.

Here's a great place to start: *www.beyond theshock.com.*

# BREAST CANCER AWARENESS

## THE IMPORTANCE OF DOING YOUR BREAST EXAMS BY MARGIE RICKERSON

I was diagnosed on January 9, 2012, with ductal carcinoma in situ (DCIS) and had surgery (lumpectomy) on January 25, 2012. I am thankful that my pathology report from surgery showed the same findings as my initial biopsy results of DCIS.

You may wonder why I am thankful. I am because DCIS is early (stage 0) breast cancer. I am thankful because I was able to have the choice of having a lumpectomy or a mastectomy and not the opposite — mastectomy as my only option.

I still have a way to go in this process. I have to have another surgery because a portion of the margin of the tissue that was removed was not clear. I also still have to undergo radiation therapy five days a week for five to seven weeks total. But once this is done, I feel that I will be a breast cancer survivor.

Please be sure to do your breast exams on

a regular basis. Young women, this includes you too. Young women can also be diagnosed with breast cancer. I found a lump when I was thirty years old. I did see a physician and had a mammogram and ultrasound done. This did not show anything at that time for me. However, you will not know if you do not do your exams if you have a lump that could be breast cancer. Also, get your mammograms done as recommended. This is how I came to be diagnosed. The results from my mammogram showed suspicious calcifications, so a biopsy was recommended.

No one wants to be diagnosed with breast cancer; but if you are, you want to try to catch it in the earliest stage possible. Doing your routine exams and mammograms may help with catching breast cancer while it is still in an early stage.

# BREAST CANCER AWARENESS

## MY UNEXPECTED LIFE'S JOURNEY
## WITH BREAST CANCER BY MYRENIA

I'm an African-American professional female, forty-eight years old. I consider myself kind, giving, loving, and God-fearing. I've always been healthy: no signs of high blood pressure; no history of breast cancer in my family; no diabetes, HIV, or heart disease; and I seldom have a common cold or flu.

I am not overweight. My diet consists of mainly chicken breast and fish. I restrict my red meat intake, but I love a good cheeseburger (lean beef, please)! Occasionally I frequent the gym, and I'm a devoted Christian. Still a diagnosis of breast cancer was in my future, and there was nothing I could do to stop it.

It all began one day in July 2011 with a throbbing ache and pain within my right breast. I thought this unusual ache might have been associated with my menstrual cycle, but I recognized it was much different than the normal soreness of my breast

467

associated with PMS.

The ache and pain continued for a two-week period. Each day, multiple times throughout the day, I felt discomfort and the evidence of what was lurking within. I was never one who conducted monthly breast exams; however, now was the time to conduct one.

Upon my exam I discovered a lump and I immediately called my physician (OB-GYN) for an appointment. During my visit my physician examined my breast and diagnosed the lump as a cyst. He then proceeded to drain it; no fluid, it was a solid mass. I was then requested to schedule an appointment, without delay, to have a mammogram and biopsy. After both tests occurred, and after speaking with the medical professionals, I felt I had cancer — it was intuition.

After the prognosis was given, my journey called breast cancer (stage 1), treatment, and recovery began! The entire process took seven months (July 2011 to February 2012). It consisted of two surgeries, chemo, radio, and hormone therapy. The processes were exhausting and challenged every breath that was within me.

There were multiple tests and X-rays before the initial surgery. I had to prepare myself mentally for surgery, not knowing if a mastectomy would be done in place of my elected lumpectomy (lump removal only). I was then informed a second surgery must occur to ensure cancer tissues had not spread beyond the original circumference.

Chemotherapy immediately followed. I decided to refer to the chemicals used during chemo as "poison," but this poison would ultimately work to save my life. After each dosage of chemotherapy, I felt horrible.

I gradually lost all body hair, except my eyelashes. The beds of my finger/toe nails turned black and developed ridges or grooves across them. I experienced nausea, constipation, loss of taste buds, and aches and pains throughout my body. I could barely walk or climb stairs; there was extreme fatigue and exhaustion like nothing I've ever experienced. I slept for hours on end and never felt rested; I had rapid heartbeat, muscle and joint stiffness, and insomnia.

This was my new reality, my life, my struggle, my journey! While trying to maintain some sort of normalcy, I experienced abandonment, attempted manipulation, hurtful words, loneliness; kindness, thoughtfulness, generosity, acceptance, love — all from family and friends.

After chemotherapy was radiotherapy (radiation). Radiation is a walk in the park compared to chemo. I refer to radiation as "being zapped." Being zapped is when radiation is administered into the area where the cancer originated in order to kill any remaining cancer cells. The area that receives the radiation will turn very dark, like a deep suntan. Next came hormone therapy.

Through my journey, there were lessons learned. When I felt alone, I would encourage myself, I wasn't afraid. Some people were manipulative in my weakest hour, wished me well and departed, never to see or hear from them again; I said farewell.

Make sure you have excellent and caring physicians. Cherish and live life to the fullest, you never know when it may be taken from you; don't take anything for granted. When you experience something traumatic in life, that's when you'll see clearly who will stand by you and who won't. Those suffering from illnesses may be afraid and need love and support — never be too selfish to lend a hand.

I encourage you, women, to self-conduct breast exams monthly and have mammograms; it could help save your life. If you or someone you know has cancer, treat them and yourself with care. Be supportive and kind; offer assistance and encouragement; hugs are good. Be careful what you say, words hurt. If someone speaks unfavorably of you or your situation, always believe the best. Smile, laugh, and love. Never truly succumb to believing death is your fate, and say to yourself and everyone else, "I will live." Most of all, pray and believe.

As for me, I kept the faith, trusting in God for healing throughout the entire ordeal. I didn't shed a tear when diagnosed or during treatment. Faith kept me strong and I knew I could endure the worst, to come out a champion at the end of the finish line. In spite of feeling alone or hurt at times, I smiled, laughed, joked, and encouraged others, while enduring my own unbelievable state. I finally cried the day I realized I was cancer free, that God had shown me favor! It was a happy day!

Life is full of surprises! Love yourself, do good and great things. Be thankful and rejoice, for you are alive! I wish you a healthy and prosperous future!

To God, thank you for life. To Mary Morrison, thanks for allowing me to enlighten others of my journey called breast cancer; Angela Lewis-Morrison, for always being there; Mom, your prayers; Wanda and Jeff, your support; Gwen, Jerome, Ron, and Deborah, for calling every week to check on me; David, for transportation from the hospital; Farley, for caring; and everyone who supported me and/or bore some burden to not let me fall, I made it and I love you.

This journey has ended, and the life afterward begins!

# PROTECTIVE/
# RESTRAINING ORDERS

If you need one, get one.

Every situation does not warrant having an order in place. However, when you feel threatened by an individual who appears to be mentally unstable, trust your gut instincts. Don't be afraid to do the right thing for yourself and the ones who love you. Here are some common types of abuse that you can get a protective or restraining order for:

- Physical
- Mental
- Sexual
- Financial
- Stalking
- Texting
- E-mailing
- Social networking

If a person proves he/she is a threat in

writing, you can use those forms of communication to present your case. I received a five-year restraining order against a man based on his text messages alone. Five months after the order was in place, he contacted me via a Facebook message. I consulted my police officer friend and was advised to respond firmly. I was asked to let the person know if he contacted me again, I'd file a police report, and a warrant would be issued for his arrest. That's exactly what I did.

Why not block him? When you block someone on Facebook, all your communications with that person are deleted, thereby making it impossible to present as evidence. I did unfriend him, but that does not prevent the person from sending messages.

Don't ignore domestic violence. Early detection can save your life. You must also know the warning signs of an abuser. Here are some:

No matter how much you love the person, if they don't respect you, you should leave them. Now I'm not suggesting you pack your bags after a disagreement or argument. No situation is perfect. Revisiting the conversation at a later time is a good idea. You might continue to disagree, but try to find a healthy solution.

Don't wait until abuse becomes physical; but if it does, report it immediately. Do not give the person a second chance to strike. After the first occurrence, if you stay, your attitude and personality will change to either fear or revenge.

Each time the person raises his/her voice, you will feel afraid that the person will beat you. When an abuser knows he or she has control over you, he or she will continue to assault you to maintain the dominance. If you fight back in self-defense, you could possibly kill that person. Not necessarily with intention, but the fear of being battered, can cause you to act out of character.

Getting a protective or restraining order should be taken seriously. If the order is granted, if you violate it and allow the person to come back into your life, your order may be terminated. Abusers are extremely apologetic. Stay strong. In many cases the violent person knows the law better than you. Their getting you to communicate with them may be their way of having your order terminated. Once that happens, the judge may not grant you another one.

Yes, couples break up and then make up all the time. It's especially challenging if you have children in common. But if you are genuinely afraid of the abuser, your relationship will never work.

Remember, you got the order for a reason.

# ABOUT THE AUTHOR

*New York Times* bestselling author **Mary B. Morrison** believes that women should shape their own destiny. Born in Aurora, IL, and raised in New Orleans, LA, she took a chance and quit her near six-figure government job to self-publish her first book, *Soulmates Dissipate,* in 2000 and begin her literary career. Mary's books have appeared on numerous bestseller lists, and she's a frequent contributor to *The Michael Boisden Show.* Mary is also actively involved in a variety of philanthropic endeavors, and in 2006 she sponsored the publication of an anthology written by 33 sixth-graders. In 2010, Mary produced a play based on her novel, *Single Husbands,* which she wrote under her pseudonym, HoneyB. In addition to her novels and play, Mary has a multi-film development deal with Codeblack Entertainment for her Soulmates Dissipate series. Mary currently resides in Oakland,

CA, with her wonderful son, Jesse Byrd, Jr., who is following in his mother's creative footsteps and pursuing a career in TV/film and writing. Visit Mary online at www .marymorrison.com.